THE SECRET SEVEN

Emily Slate Mystery Thriller
Book 7

ALEX SIGMORE

Dark Woods Press

THE SECRET SEVEN: EMILY SLATE MYSTERY THRILLER BOOK 7

1st Edition

ebook ISBN 978-1-957536-26-2

Print ISBN 978-1-957536-27-9

Prologue

WHERE *WAS* IT? JAEDEN PETERS PULLED BACK THE COVERS OF
his bed and tossed them to the floor of his bedroom, desper-
ately hoping he'd accidentally lost it in his bed somewhere.
But there was nothing on the bedspread other than a random
sock and a couple of crumbs.

Where could it be?

"Jae! You're going to be late!" his mother called from
downstairs.

"I know! I'm coming!" he replied, frantically searching the
rest of his room.

This was going to be the biggest night of his life and he
couldn't leave without it. He bundled up the comforter and
threw it back on the bed, then searched underneath the bed
itself. He pulled out his cellphone and shone the flashlight
under but to no avail. It wasn't anywhere.

"Jaeden," his mother's impatient voice said from the doorway. "Come on, now."

"Just a second. I can't find my totem."

"Your what?" his mother asked.

Mentally he rolled his eyes. She never understood. "The
pendant. With the dragon holding the ruby."

She let out an exasperated sigh. "That's not a ruby, it's just a piece of costume jewelry. And I don't know why you want that thing anyway. Is that what you're wearing?"

"Oh, my God, Mom, you gotta stop." He got back up and went over to his desk, searching all the drawers. Where could he have put it? He wore it every day and only took it off to sleep and shower. He happened to catch part of his reflection in the blank screen of his iMac. He thought he looked pretty good. All he needed was the totem to complete the look. If he was going to pull this off, he needed to be at the top of his game.

"Why can't you put on a button-down shirt, like a respectable young man?" his mother asked. "I know your date would appreciate that a lot more than whatever band you have on that t-shirt."

He went over to his shelves, even though there was absolutely no reason for his totem to be there, searching in front and on top of all the books anyway. "Yeah, that's a great idea, Mom, I definitely won't get ridiculed for that."

"I thought you two were going bowling. Don't bowlers wear button-down shirts?"

"No, I told you, we're supposed to play mini golf. Where *is it?*"

His mother shook her head and let out another sigh. He'd come to hate the sound of that sigh; it was her way of telling him she didn't approve, or thought he wasn't trying hard enough. And it had been all he'd been hearing from her lately.

She left the doorway only to return a moment later, the dragon holding the ruby dangling from a chain in her hand. "Here. I'd rather you be on time, I suppose."

"You stole it?" Jaeden snatched it from her hand.

"I...borrowed it," she said, framing his face with her hands. "Just for tonight. I thought...you're such a handsome young man, you don't need to wear all these dark things all the time. If you'd just cut your hair a little and let people see your face—"

He pushed past her and headed down the stairs. He was already cutting it close. As he reached the bottom stair he draped the chain around his neck, the dragon sitting comfortably below his collar.

"Good luck on your date, son," his father said from the living room, though he didn't turn away from his laptop.

Jaeden grunted in response as he headed out the front door. When he got back he needed to get a lock for his room. What else was his mom doing in there? What else was she going through? It wasn't like he was trying to hide anything. But just because his style didn't match what she thought was "appropriate" she thought she had the right to come in and do whatever she wanted. He was almost out of high school. He deserved some privacy.

Jaeden reached for the door of the Jeep Wagoneer that had been his birthday present from his parents last year. The driver's side door hadn't closed properly since he'd gotten into a minor fender bender a few months back. His dad said it wasn't a big enough problem to fix, and thus it opened with barely a squeeze of the handle.

Jaeden slid in and started the engine. Sure, it wasn't as flashy as some of the other cars like the Mercedes or the BMWs that showed up at school, but it was a heavy-duty vehicle. His dad said if he was ever in a real wreck, it would be like the other person had run into a tank. The vehicle was all metal and could take a pounding. Much better than those newer, lighter vehicles.

Jaeden didn't care. A car was a car. He needed to get over to Carrie Haines' house by seven p.m. or show up to school tomorrow as a pariah forever. This was his one chance to impress her; he still couldn't believe she actually agreed to a date after he'd worked up the courage to ask. Part of him had thought it just wasn't in the cards. But she had, and he wanted to show her the best time he could.

He pushed the speed limit a little, and arrived at her house at two minutes after seven. He checked his reflection in the rear-view one last time before getting out of the car and heading for the driveway. But before he could reach the side-walk to the door, it opened and there she was. For a second he thought she was going to blow him off for being two minutes late. Or maybe she just changed her mind. But then she smiled and closed the door behind her and trotted down the steps and front walk to greet him.

"Hey," she said. "Right on time."

"Yeah," he replied. It was like his mind had gone numb. He'd practiced things to talk about, so why couldn't he even start a conversation? She would never give him another chance for sure after she saw what an idiot he really was. Why did he think he could pull this off?

"I've always liked that." She pointed to his totem. "Is it real?"

He looked down at the pewter dragon with its tail curled around the fake stone. "Nah, it's just a piece of glass or something."

"Still," she said. "It's pretty." Jaeden smiled. Maybe this would be easier than he thought.

"Wow, you *suck* at mini golf." Carrie laughed as they returned their clubs.

Jaeden looked down at the scorecard. She'd beaten him by over twenty strokes. "Yeah, I guess I need practice," he said, handing her the scorecard.

"Haven't you ever played before?" He could tell she was teasing him, and was she flirting too? She actually batted her eyelashes.

"Maybe once or twice," he said. "Never really had the chance." He followed her to the exit.

"There aren't a lot of them around here, that's for sure," she replied.

"How did you get so good?"

She turned, a sly smile on her face. "I cheat."

"What? How, I didn't—"

"I know all the tricks," she said. "Like on hole three. You had to hit your ball *in* the water and a hidden compartment shoots it out closer to the hole. Didn't you notice? I was trying to show you."

He hadn't been paying much attention to the game itself, instead most of his attention was on her. Even though it was early October, she'd worn a dress that only went to the middle of her thighs and had a jacket covering her top. But he'd been distracted by her legs the entire evening. Part of him still couldn't believe this was real. "Oh…right. That makes sense. You've played here before?"

She shook her head, her blonde curls swishing as she did. "A lot of these places use the same tricks. It's easy if you know what to look for. When I was little my parents used to take us down to Myrtle Beach every year for vacation. They have, like, a million of these things down there. My dad was adamant about making me learn how to putt properly." She laughed again. "He was such a hardass about it. Like it was a skill I'd need in college or something."

"I guess he just wanted to make sure you could beat all your dates," he replied.

"Yeah, maybe," A smile played on her lips. She pulled out her phone. "Shit, I didn't realize it was so late already. I have to get back otherwise my parents are going to freak."

"Right, yeah, sorry," he said. "I lost track of time."

"Me too. Hang on a second." She came over beside him and opened her camera for a selfie, pulling Jaeden close and got both of them in the frame with the sign for the mini golf place in the background. She snapped at least ten. "Want me to send it to you?"

"Definitely," he said. His heart was pumping. He hadn't been that close to her all night and caught a whiff of her perfume. The smell was a bouquet he couldn't hope to decipher. All he knew was he liked it.

"Cool," she replied. He wasn't sure, but it seemed like she might be a little nervous too. All of a sudden, he wanted nothing more than to do anything he could for her. Maybe his mom was right, maybe he should have dressed better. But she said she'd liked his totem, so maybe this was the kind of style that she was after. He had no idea. All he knew was this was going really well—better than he could have ever hoped.

"Hey, um," he said as they reached his car. She stopped for a second and Jaeden rounded the car to open the door for her. "Sorry, the doors are wonky sometimes."

"Why, thank you, sir." She giggled, getting in. Her dress ruffled a little as she did, and Jaeden felt like he'd been hit by a bolt of lightning. He swallowed, then closed the door for her just as thunder rumbled in the distance. He ran to the other side of the car and got in, though it took him two tries to get his door closed. "I see what you mean."

"Yeah, it's an old car," he replied, turning the engine over.

"I like it. It fits you, not like some of these other guys who think all that matters is how much money you have or how much you can buy."

"Yeah?" He pulled out of the parking lot and headed back to her house.

"You can't be surprised," she said. "Obviously, the guys with the most money are going to be the biggest jerks. It doesn't take long to figure out."

"No, I guess that doesn't surprise me," he said.

"Most guys don't even know how to open the door for a lady anymore." Jaeden looked over just as Carrie reached across the armrest and put her hand on his leg. Immediately his entire body stiffened. His *entire* body. But she didn't move it, she just held her hand there until they got back to her house. Droplets of rain hit the windshield just as he pulled up.

"Shut off the lights for a minute," she said. "I don't want them to know I'm out here yet."

Jaeden did as he was told, his heart hammering. Already this night had been more than he could have ever imagined. He wasn't sure what was about to happen next, but he felt like his entire life had been building to this moment. He killed the engine too and for a moment they sat there, listening to the rain peppering the metal roof of the Jeep.

"I had a really good time," Carrie whispered, scooting a little closer to him, though they were still separated by the armrest. Her hand inched its way down his leg. Jaeden couldn't take it anymore, on an urge that came from deep within, he leaned over and pressed his lips to hers. He felt her smile as she returned the kiss, her lips then parting to allow her tongue to explore his mouth. It was the hottest thing he'd ever experienced, because at the same time her hand went to his crotch, rubbing him up and down. His entire body was like a firecracker, ready to explode.

A second later she pulled away from him, her eyes sparkling in the darkness and a smile across her lips. "Think of me tonight. See you tomorrow?"

"Y-yeah," he barely got out. "See you tomorrow."

She winked at him and opened the door to head out into the rain.

"Wait, Carrie?" She stopped and turned back to look at him. He held out his totem for her. "Think of me tonight too."

She took it in one of her delicate hands, then draped it around her neck. "I'll wear it and nothing else when I do," she whispered, then leaned in for another quick kiss. Before he could respond she was out of the car and running for the door, getting drenched in the rain.

Jaeden watched until she was in the house, then sat back, feeling faint. Had that really just happened? That was the hottest thing he'd ever experienced, and it was with a girl he really liked. He couldn't believe it. It took him a minute to catch his breath, but he didn't want to linger outside too long otherwise she might think he was a stalker or something. He started the car and pulled away, heading back out of her neighborhood.

The entire time he drove he couldn't help but think about what had just happened. He played it over and over in his head. The tender touch of her lips on his, the feeling of her hand rubbing and squeezing him. No girl had ever done that to him before, and he hadn't realized just how different it was than all the times he'd done it himself.

As he drove the rain came down harder forcing him to slow to a bare twenty miles per hour if he wanted to see. He hadn't realized just how hard it would be raining. As he came to the small bridge that would normally take him over the greenway, he realized it had already flooded. Man, it was really coming down. He'd have to take the long way around. He backed up and turned down the next side street that ran parallel to the greenway until he could get across. But he didn't care, he'd just tell his parents he didn't want to speed home in this weather.

Jaeden was still lost in his thoughts about Carrie when he realized there was something in the road ahead of him. He slowed again, coming to a stop when it came into view. From here it looked like a man in a trench coat, but he couldn't tell for sure. Why would someone be standing out here in the rain? It had let up a little, but not enough that the guy wasn't getting absolutely drenched. He thought for a moment maybe he should offer some help, but then realized just how stupid that would be. Whatever was going on with this guy, Jaeden was better to leave him to it. Maybe he should call 911 and let them know someone was out here, just standing in the middle of the road. From here Jaeden couldn't tell if he was facing toward or away from him, and he didn't care. He just wanted to get home.

But just as he began to pull forward again, someone yanked his door open and grabbed him by his arm, pulling him out of the car. He tried to fight, but the man who'd grabbed him was strong, and had Jaeden's seatbelt off before he even knew what was happening.

Jaeden hit the wet pavement with a smack, as his car began to inch forward without his foot on the brake. Strangely, he was more concerned for his car than he was for himself, before he realized the man who'd pulled him from the car wore the same trench coat as the man further on in the middle of the street. Was he being robbed, mugged? What was going on?

"What do you want?" he yelled over the rain, shielding his face from the pounding water that had already soaked him to the skin.

A second man in a trench coat appeared over him, it must be the man who had been in the middle of the road. His car was still inching away from them, the driver's side door still open. His phone was in there, in the cup-holder. If he could just get to it—

Jaeden tried to push himself up, only for a large boot to push his chest back down. He winced at the pain, then realized the boot was still pressing. He grabbed the foot, trying to wrench it off, but it was too strong. It was like an elephant was standing on him, and he was beginning to panic.

"What—" he managed to get out before he heard the first of his ribs crack, followed by another.

Adrenaline flooding his system, Jaeden did everything he

could to get out from under the boot, twisting, squirming, and screaming as loud as he could, only for it to press harder and harder, cutting off his ability to breathe. As he felt his entire chest caving in was when he saw the glint of the knife in the second man's hand.

Jaeden screamed like he'd never screamed before.

Chapter One

FIND HIS FATHER, AND YOU'LL FIND THE TRUTH ABOUT YOUR husband. Those were a dying woman's last words to me, and they came from the most unexpected source.

The woman I came to know as Camille, the same woman who killed my husband. She stalked me for over two months, breaking into my home, setting up surveillance on me, and then saved my life twice, whispered those words in my ear only seconds before she died from massive trauma and blood loss. A gunshot wound courtesy of my sister-in-law.

In the eight weeks since then, the FBI has learned her birth name was Galina Kiefer and was at one point a U.K. citizen. Ever since she's been on a few international watch-lists, though she abandoned her original identity and adopted a host of others. She had been working as an assassin-for-hire for almost a decade by the time she came into my life.

After her true identity was discovered by other members of my team and the news reached the international community, it caused a stir as she was wanted in multiple countries for a range of suspected crimes. My guess is that none of those will ever be definitively attributed to her once it's all said and done, not unless the governments are just looking for a scape-goat. But I'll leave that up to the CIA.

Still, I can't deny the impact that woman had on my life. When she killed Matt, she turned my world upside down. But even though she may have been the one to strike the final blow, she wasn't the only one involved. She was just the last cog in a long line of people who made the ultimate decision, people Matt worked for the entire time I knew him, and yet I never had any idea he was anything other than a psychiatrist at a local college. Camille was the instrument of this organiza-tion, and my husband was targeted by his own people.

"Dammit," I say, shoving the box of papers aside. Despite my best efforts, I haven't been able to find very much about Matt's father since Camille whispered those words into my ear. My best friend and fellow agent, Zara Foley, says I have an obsession, but I don't think wanting to find the motives behind my husband's actions are too much to ask. Especially when he belonged to an organization that not only kidnapped children, but until very recently subjected them to horrendous and vile acts all because powerful people think they can do whatever they want.

It seems that whatever this organization is, it was a family affair. Not only was my husband involved, but so was his brother, and his brother's wife, the aforementioned sister-in-law. A woman I once trusted with my life, not to mention she had been taking care of my dog Timber for me. We had recently reconnected, but it was a ruse to lull me into a false sense of security so she and my brother-in-law could take over where the assassin failed.

And yet, Dani's body was found six weeks ago, face down in the Potomac. A single gunshot wound to her head. When I first heard the news, I was upset not because she was my last remaining family member, but because I wanted answers. She could have told me everything I needed to know about Matt. I didn't even bother going to the funeral, for her or for Chris. Neither one of them deserved having me there for them.

But now I'm faced with a new conundrum. Not only were Matt, Chris, and Dani all involved with this organization, it seems like Matt and Chris's father was as well. I was the only one outside the loop. What I can't figure out is what their father could have to do with anything. When we were married, Matt's father was already dead. It was one of the things that attracted us to each other; both of us no longer had parents who were still alive.

But what's so infuriating is now that I've begun trying to find out more about the man, I can't seem to find *anything*.

I still have all of Matt's old things, and I've spent more time over the past few weeks than I'd care to admit going through every piece of paper and photograph in all his childhood things and I can't even find a clear picture of the man who was supposedly such a big part of my husband's life.

I get up off the floor of my apartment. Timber wakes and stands up, giving me a long stretch with a look of derision. He's been the one constant by my side this entire time, helping me research. And by helping I mean he's been asleep and snoring.

"Don't give me that look," I tell him. "I know we're late for your walk. But I needed to get through this box before work—" I glance up, realizing that it's already past eight. "Shit. Guess I'm not making it in on time today either." I shrug and grab his leash. Timber happily trots to the door, waiting for me to connect the leash before he begins pulling me down the steps of my apartment toward the nearby park. "I know, bud, just hang on, we're going."

I barely had time to grab my jacket. Summer has finally come and gone, and a nice chill has settled over D.C. in the past few weeks. Leaves crunch under my feet as we make a beeline for the park. As soon as we reach it, Timber is off his leash, playing with the other dogs in the fenced-in area. I take a minute to check my phone.

I should have known better.

I've seven missed calls. Four from Zara, two from my supposed boyfriend Liam Coll, and one from my new boss. As I look at the timestamps, I realize not all of these came in this morning. Some came in last night when I was going through a completely different box. I just shove the phone in my back jeans pocket and lean over the fence, watching Timber play.

"Good to see you out of the house again, Emily."

I look over and see my eighty-year-old neighbor Mr. Windemere sitting on a nearby bench, holding on to his cane. "Good morning, Mr. Windemere," I say.

He waves me off. "How many times do I have to tell you to call me Tom? I'd think with that fancy education you'd be able to remember something as simple as a name."

"Right, Tom," I say. "Sorry." I don't know what it is, but I've never felt calling the elderly by anything other than their most formal title was appropriate. It's like by the time you've reached that age, shouldn't you deserve a little respect? "Are you watching someone's dog for them?"

He shakes his head with a smile. "I'm afraid not. Doubt I could keep up unless it was a decrepit as I am. I just like sitting here and enjoying my mornings. But you're usually gone by the time I'm up."

"I'm going in late today," I say, turning my attention back to Timber. What I don't say is that this is probably the fifth time in the past two weeks when I've been late. Six months ago that would have been unfathomable to me. Now it almost seems normal.

"Good. I'm glad you're giving yourself some time off. You've been working extra hard. Not to mention all those times your colleagues have been around inspecting things. Did they ever catch them?"

"Who?" I ask, watching Timber chase a golden retriever

around before the golden turns back and starts chasing Timber instead.

"The prowler. The one who broke into your apartment."

I turn back to him. None of my neighbors know the person who broke in was an international assassin. And if it's up to me, it will stay that way. No need to cause a panic. "Oh. Yes, they finally caught them."

"It's funny," he says, causing me to regard him a little closer. "You don't seem very relieved."

"Oh, no, it's not that." I'm thrown off guard. Mr. Windemere—Tom—is shrewder than I would have given him credit for. Then again, he's lived next to me ever since I moved here following Matt's death. He's seen everything that I've brought to this place. Maybe Camille was watching him too, as a possible access point to my apartment, considering we share a wall. I realize now I severely underestimated that woman. "I'm just...I have a lot going on right now."

"Looks like it," he says. "Where's that nice boyfriend of yours? I haven't seen him around much lately."

"No, I've been...he's still around," I say, thinking back to the two messages that are already on my voicemail. I know one of them is Liam asking me where I was yesterday morning. We were supposed to have brunch. At some point he's going to get sick of me blowing him off and give up, and I won't blame him in the slightest. I'm kinda surprised he hasn't done it already.

"Well," Tom says, standing up. "I hope things improve soon."

"Me too," I say. He gives me a wistful smile and heads back to our apartment row while I stand there and watch Timber continue to chase the other dogs. At least today none of the other owners are running in fear because a pit bull is in there. I've already had to diffuse two separate incidents where people wanted to call the police on Timber, despite the fact he wasn't doing anything to anyone. He just wanted to play in the park with the other dogs, but the way the owners talked, it was like I had brought a Bengal tiger instead of a four-year-old pittie. Both times I had to show my badge to get people to calm down. But I can't help but wonder what would happen if I didn't have it?

That makes me think back to my in-laws, who were keeping him for me, while I was out of town on different assignments.

I close my eyes and rub my temples, not willing to go back down that rabbit hole again. It's over and done with, and I don't want to spend any more time thinking about either of them again.

I watch Timber a few more minutes before finally admitting if I don't start getting ready and head into the office soon, Wallace is going to end up firing me. I can only push my new CO so far. Somewhere, in the back of my head, the old Emily is screaming at me to get my shit together and to start acting like an FBI agent again.

But another part of me wonders what the point is anymore.

I whistle at Timber, and he comes over, wagging his butt. I hate to cut his playtime short, but I should have been out here a lot earlier. "Sorry, bud, we'll come back after I get off work." His little tail drops but he complies, and we make the short trek back across the street to the apartments.

Once we're back inside I put on some coffee as I get ready. I'm probably only averaging about five hours of sleep per night, but the strange thing is I don't really feel tired all day. Though I do feel a bit of that fog in my mind. I know I need to be getting more sleep, but every time I close my eyes all I see is the life leaving Chris's eyes, or Camille's, or even Matt's dead stare when I came home to find him lying on the kitchen floor. For a while there I thought I was getting over it, but I know that's impossible until I find out what my husband was doing with this organization and why they decided to kill him.

I don't think even Camille knew. Because she was a hired hand, she wasn't privy to the inner workings of the organization. In fact, she even tried to recruit me to help her take it down. But doing things her way meant killing all of them. While that might seem appealing, I want these people in jail.

But unfortunately we're not off to a great start. I just hope the backup I called in comes through for me, because if things don't change soon, I'm going to drive myself crazy.

Chapter Two

"Special Agent Slate," the man says, glaring at my badge through the driver's side window of my car. I'm sitting at the entrance to the J. Edgar Hoover Building's underground parking lot, waiting for clearance from a man I've never met before. Ever since the fiasco two months ago with a double agent in the ranks, things have been a lot more tense lately.

"Clear to proceed," he says after a minute of checking the computer in the small gatehouse that's been erected at the underground entrance. It's been a different guy every day for the past two weeks. I don't know how that's supposed to instill any kind of confidence or camaraderie, but it's what the higher-ups have decreed, so that's what's done.

Another three men, all armed with automatic rifles and wearing tactical gear stand to the side, guarding the entrance. Two of them just performed a cursory inspection of my vehicle, including the trunk, while the third stood by ominously, staring at me. It seems even though I already passed Internal Affairs' tests with flying colors, no one is above suspicion anymore. It's made working here a lot harder. But that's not the reason I'm late. Not by a long shot.

I pull through, waiting for the metal gate to raise and allow me in before closing back behind me again.

After taking my usual parking spot, I show my badge again to the officer near the door to the elevators and he nods, opening the door for me. Until all of this had happened, I hadn't realized how familiar and comfortable I'd become at the Bureau. I think a lot of people felt that way, that because we were in the middle of D.C. and the largest home office of the entire FBI, that we were somehow insulated from anyone breaching our security. Obviously, we'd become too complacent and someone like DuBois managed to subvert our security and work his way in. Though, given his level of espionage, I'm not sure conventional methods would have caught him anyway. Looking at his background, there had been nothing to indicate his true motives. He'd been a stellar student at Quantico, graduating with top recommendations, and had been an essential part of our team for years. To think that he'd been secretly hiding his true motives that entire time is something of a miracle.

Of course, every op he ever worked on or was consulted for is under investigation again. There's no telling what he might have let slip or what sensitive matters he could have passed on to his superiors.

To say it's been a shit show would be an understatement.

The elevator doors open, and I step out onto my floor and head for my department. I catch a few familiar faces along the way; agents that used to be in my division that have since requested a new assignment or been moved for other reasons. Less than thirty percent of the people I used to work with are still in my office, and we've had a huge influx of new agents, many of them from counterpart divisions across the country. Deputy Director Cochran is not screwing around. He wants to make sure this doesn't happen again. I was afraid I would be taking the brunt of the punishment seeing as I was the one

DuBois was trying to kill and given the fact I left the scene of the crime when Camille fatally shot him.

But unfortunately, I wasn't the one they went after.

I set my crossbody bag with my laptop on my desk and take off my blazer, hanging it on the chair. Zara's desk, which sits directly opposite mine now, is empty. I'm sure she got started early this morning and is out chasing down some leads. Thankfully this shakeup hasn't affected her at all, unless you count that she's doing really well. Her caseload is increasing— I'm sure thanks to her reputation—and she's becoming quite the rising star in our department, despite her close association with me.

Out of the corner of my eye I see some of the other agents taking furtive glances at me when they think I can't see them. Despite everything, I now have a reputation around here. Only mine has labeled me as an unreliable agent. Someone who bends the rules too often. And given my family association with the organization that managed to infiltrate this place, I'm not high on anyone's trust list at the moment.

Ignoring them, I open my laptop and connect to the secure server, downloading everything that came in for me overnight. As expected, it's nothing urgent. A bunch of requisition requests, some non-essential emails that I probably won't even respond to, and maybe a dozen data dives. Nothing but busy work. I know what they're doing; I even know why they're doing it, but that doesn't mean I have to like it.

Before I can even get started my desk phone rings. "Slate."

"Get in my office, now." He hangs up before I can even reply. I guess I should haven't been surprised that my new boss was keeping an eye out for me. He's not exactly what I would call someone who is fit for upper management, since he seems to enjoy watching over my shoulder every chance he gets.

I sigh and stand, heading for the office that used to house my last boss: Janice Simmons. But she's been put on paid leave ever since the DuBois fiasco, given there is an even larger investigation by Internal Affairs that still hasn't wrapped up yet. Since Janice was the one who brought DuBois in, she's the one who had to take responsibility for him.

Anyone who knows Janice knows she's not part of this organization, nor did she have any nefarious plans when she hired DuBois. It was just bad luck on her part. I'm not sure any amount of due diligence would have revealed his true motives, but there needs to be a scapegoat.

"Yes, sir?" I say, sticking my head into his office.

The man on the other side of the desk doesn't look up. "Close the door." He's in his mid-forties, fit, with flecks of gray in his hair. He also wears horn-rimmed glasses that you would think would be out of style but somehow he manages to pull them off. His suit is always immaculate, and today is no exception. From what I know of him, he's had a stellar career. He got his start in the Bureau early, like me. Unlike me though, he never almost botched an operation or almost accidentally shot a child because he lost his cool. In fact, he went on to have a storied career at the agency, rising up through the ranks quickly. Before here he was posted in the Manhattan office, overseeing almost all of the operations there and doing one hell of a job from what I hear.

Yep, Fletcher Wallace is the poster boy for what a stand-up FBI agent should look like. Which is, I'm sure, why Cochran chose him as Janice's replacement.

He continues writing something, leaving us both to only listen to the strokes of his pen as he scribbles on the notepad in front of him. I've learned this is just how Wallace is, he likes to make you wait, so that you know you're not there to chat or to make jokes or to do anything other than the job. I assume it's how he ran the Manhattan office too.

Finally, he finishes writing, setting the pen down and looking up at me. He makes a dramatic show of checking his watch, before settling his gaze back on mine. "Ten after ten. I think that's a new record for you."

"I lost track of time, sir," I say, knowing full well I'm in for a dressing down.

"It's strange," he says, pulling a file out from under the notepad. "In four years I can't find any instance where you were either late or didn't report in, up until about six weeks ago. And then all of a sudden you decide to start showing up to work whenever you want, as if the entire Bureau revolves around your schedule."

"Sir, that's not—"

He holds up a hand. "I don't want to hear it. This behavior is unbefitting a Special Agent with the FBI. We don't sell insurance here. People's lives are on the line. You never would have acted in such a manner with your previous SAC. Now I need to know this is the last time."

"Sir, may I speak freely?"

He pauses, letting out a slow breath. "Go ahead."

"I believe I'm being underutilized here."

His expression doesn't change. "Underutilized?"

"Yes, sir. Ever since you took over for SAC Simmons, I have been more or less chained to my desk. When was the last time I had a case that required me to leave the office?"

"Are you saying that our agents here in the office aren't necessary, Agent Slate?" He knows I'm not stupid, that I see exactly what he's doing. But the problem is I can't do a damn thing about it.

"No, sir. But I'm a field agent. That's where I've been the most effective. I don't do well with requisition requests and information searches."

He flips open the folder in front of him. "Agent Slate, when I was appointed head of this division, the first thing I did was go through the history and qualifications of every agent, which included you. Would you like to know what I saw when I looked through your file? A disrespect for the Bureau's code of conduct. You may have had a good record, but your methods to obtain those results were way outside what I consider acceptable for one of my field agents." He flips a few pages. "Take this one, for example. Breaking into a private citizen's home on a hunch that he was harboring hostages with no warrant, and no backup."

"Sir, we didn't have—"

He holds up his hand again. "Or this fiasco with DuBois. Leaving the scene of a crime. Openly admitting to conspiring with an enemy of the state. Letting said enemy go in pursuit of another suspect. Need I go on?"

"If I hadn't made a deal with Rossovich, Avery Huxley would have been raped and passed around like a deck of cards. If I had the chance to do it all again, I'd do it the exact same way. Saving that little girl was more than worth losing one old bastard."

Wallace shakes his head. "That's the trouble with you, Slate. That's not your call to make, it's your SAC's, which means now it's mine."

"Are you telling me you would have ordered me to detain Rossovich and allow the assault on Avery Huxley to happen?" I can feel my anger growing with every word that comes out of his mouth; it's like he only sees people as chess pieces, to be moved as necessary in order to obtain a win.

"I'm not the one under the microscope here, Slate. Look at this from my point of view. You had three family members who were known operatives of this organization. And you say you had no idea. You weren't aware of your husband, his brother, or his brother's wife's activities up until they were revealed to you and the world at large. I know you're not stupid, so that makes me think that you're either covering something up, or maybe you're not the agent you think you are. Now, I don't think you're a traitor. If I did, I can assure you, you wouldn't be sitting at that desk every day. But if you can miss all of this, what else have you missed while on the job? Certainly, the episode with DuBois speaks volumes."

It's as if I have something caught in my throat. I stiffen, unsure if I'll be able to respond. Like I need someone else to point out the fact that I never saw my husband's deceptions. That I was too desperate to be part of a family again that I might have overlooked something in a crucial moment when I should have had a more critical eye.

How many lives would have been saved if I'd just seen what was right in front of my face all along?

"And don't think I don't know what you've been doing these past few weeks," Wallace continues. "You may think you're fooling everyone, but I know you're desperate to find out more about this Organization. In fact, it's this obsession that gives me additional pause."

"Sir—" I manage before he silences me again.

"Slate, I've read your psychological profile. Until this organization is found and exposed, you are never going to give up searching for them. But you have to accept the possibility that your actions have already caused that. The incident with DuBois has obviously forced them to disband or cease operations until they are sure they're in the clear again. Either way, they can't be our primary focus right now. We spent two weeks using every resource this agency had and came up with nothing. Now we have other, far more urgent cases that need our attention. Something your friend, Agent Foley understands."

His mention of Zara is like a twist of the knife. "Sir, if you're suggesting that I can't handle more than one thing at a time I can assure you—"

"I've worked with agents like you in the past. And it always ends the same with you. Eventually, something will happen with the organization that will cause you to put your current cases in jeopardy. You'll think it will be a once-in-a-lifetime opportunity and someone will get hurt because your attention is not on your job. It's on revenge. And I just can't have an agent like that working in my department."

"What are you saying, sir?" I ask, using all my energy to keep from breaking into a thousand pieces in front of this man. It's as if he's stabbed me straight through the heart. He's taking everything away from me in one fell swoop, and there's nothing I can do about it.

He sighs. "I was going to wait until the end of the week to inform you of this but given our discussion today I don't see any reason to wait. I'm suggesting to Deputy Director Cochran that you be transferred out of the D.C. office."

"Sir!" It's all I can say. I knew we weren't getting along, but I had no idea he was even thinking about transferring me. "I am your best chance at tracking down the Organization. At least let me do that much."

"Not from where I sit," Wallace says. "We have no more leads on them, and I can't waste man hours on a cold case. DuBois is dead, the woman hunting you is dead, as are your two in-laws. And Rossovich has conveniently disappeared. The way I see it, until someone new pops up, we're moving the investigation to the back burner. There are actual cases out there that need our attention." He closes the file.

I want to scream and yell at the man that he's making a huge mistake; that this is how these people operate, from the shadows. "If the Bureau shelves the investigation now, it just opens up an opportunity for them to begin their operations again."

"Tell me, Agent Slate. What does this Organization actually *do*? Other than kill people, of course? What is their primary goal?"

"That's what I'm trying to find out. Or...I would like to find out," I say, correcting myself. No one else knows about what Camille told me, and I'm not about to advertise it. Which is why I can't use the Bureau's resources. Everything I searched for would be in the records and thus available for Wallace's scrutiny.

"Exactly. We don't even know anything about them, other than they seem to like to kill people of their own organization. With any luck, maybe they'll all end up killing each other and leave us to focus on what's important." He stands, straightening his tie and smoothing out his jacket. "You'll have a week to get your affairs in order. The Bureau will assist in relocating you, as well with any additional expenses you have."

I can't believe this. I can't leave D.C.; my whole life is here. What about Zara? What about Liam?

Wallace takes a look at me and his features soften, but only slightly. "Look, Slate. I know you're a good agent. You have a stellar record. But I was brought in to make sure nothing like DuBois ever happens again. And I can't do that if I don't have complete faith in all of my agents. It's nothing personal, some people just don't mesh. I hope you'll find better success in your next assignment." He holds out his hand.

I want to smack it away and scream in his face. He doesn't have any idea of what I've been through these past six months. A couple of pages in a file can't begin to explain it but removing me from D.C. is the wrong move. I might be the only one who can track down this organization and bring them to justice. But I can't do that if I'm in Chicago, or Houston or Los Angeles. Or...God forbid...Alaska. Not that I have anything against the place, but I can't live somewhere where it snows all year round. I need seasons.

I give his hand a brief shake before I storm back out of his office, flinging the door open and leaving it in my wake. If I'm being transferred, I'm definitely not doing any requisition requests today. I grab my stuff and leave; afraid I might say or do something that will put me in an even worse position if I don't.

Chapter Three

"So you just left?"

I'm looking at Zara from across the rim of a whiskey sour, but my vision has blurred from staring at one spot too long, and I'm lost deep in thought about what moving is really going to mean for me.

"I was afraid if I didn't, I might punch one of those smug new agents whispering behind my back," I reply and take a sip on my drink without focusing. My gaze is locked on something fuzzy; it's like I'm half zoned out, and I kind of like it here.

SNAP!

"Hey, I'm trying to talk to you," Zara says, her fingers snapping right in my vision, which brings me out of it. I blink a few times.

"Sorry. It's been a day."

"I bet he timed it so I wouldn't be there too," Zara says. "He knows how close we are."

"Not to mention the fact you're the division's new golden girl," I say, taking a long sip from my glass.

"Don't call me that, it makes me sound like a grandma. And no, I'm not," she says, her short, platinum hair swishing back and forth. "I've only been back in action for two weeks.

When they see what I'm really about I'm sure I'll be shipped off to Denver along with you."

I perk up. "Denver? Wait, do you know something?"

She waves me off. "Of course not, I'm just saying, Denver wouldn't be a bad place to end up. Lots of skiing. Lots of skiing instructors." She winks at me.

"You're incorrigible." I finish off the whiskey sour and place the glass next to the table for another one.

"Slow down there, hoss, it's only a Tuesday." Zara takes a sip of her wine. "Tell me again exactly what he said."

I let out of a huff of a breath and lay my head down on the table. "He said I was too much of a liability for the department and he was recommending to Cochran a transfer was necessary. He also said it wasn't personal." The last word comes out with more vitriol than I'd intended.

"Okay, so that's good. That means it's just a suggestion to Cochran. He still has the final say. You could go to him first thing in the morning and plead your case."

"He doesn't like me either." I say, my hair covers my entire face. I must look like Cousin It from Zara's perspective.

"Emily," Zara says. I don't reply. "*Emily Slate.*"

"What?"

"Look at me."

I shake my head, but all I end up doing is thumping my forehead on the table. "Ow." I lift my head up and pull my hair back out of my face.

"You are not the kind of person who gives up."

I scoff. "Yeah. Wallace made that *abundantly* clear this morning."

"So what? You're going to let him beat you? You're just going to lie down and let this man who knows nothing about what's been going on in our department for the past eight months make a life-changing decision for you? Who knows where you could end up?"

I smile. "Maybe they'll send me to the Honolulu office."

She takes another sip from her drink, giving me the eye. "Don't count on it."

I pull my hair all the way back and wrap a hair tie around it. "I dunno, Z. It isn't like Cochran is on my side. I have a sneaking suspicion he was the only reason I was in that interrogation room after the whole DuBois debacle."

She pinches her features. It's something she does when she gets angry, though it has the effect of making her look like a pissed-off faerie. "I still can't believe they gave you shit for that. What were you supposed to do, let that man do whatever he wanted to that little girl?"

"That's what I said!" I say, looking around for the waitress. "Where is she? I need a refill."

"What has Liam said about it?" Zara asks.

I don't turn back, instead I pretend like I'm looking harder for the waitress. "Um…nothing much."

"Emily Rachel Slate," she snaps, and I sit back down, staring at her. "You haven't told your boyfriend that you're being transferred? Don't you think that's information he would want to know?"

I wince. "I don't know if I'd go so far as to say 'boyfriend' per se, more like adult friend with sexual benefits."

She glares at me. "Would *he* call it that? Or appreciate you telling other people that?"

I slump in my seat. "No. I guess not."

"When was the last time you saw him?"

"Last week," I say. "We were supposed to meet up this weekend, but I…I was busy with stuff."

"What stuff?" Zara demands. "And you can't blame it on work this time. I know better. Which brings up a good point. I called you like five times this weekend and you never picked up. I figured you were with him. What the hell have you been doing?"

I avert my gaze again.

Zara reaches across the table, her hand open. When I

don't take it, she flexes it a few times. "C'mon." I sigh and reach across, placing my hand in hers. "Listen to me. I know it's important that you find them. I know you feel like it's your responsibility. But it's not—not alone anyway. And you can't put off the rest of your life while you hunt down people who have made not being found their primary goal."

"I'll find them, eventually," I say.

"You know who you sound like? Camille." I glance up in surprise and she's nodding. "That's right. Somehow, her vendetta has become yours now. I don't want you to end up like her, using every spare minute tracking these people down and ignoring everything else. Tell me this, if you hadn't gotten this news today, would I have heard from you?"

I'm too ashamed to respond.

"Emily, you know you can't keep going like this. You need to take a break."

"So you agree with Wallace," I say, trying to pull my hand away, but Zara holds tight.

"No. Wallace is trying to punish you for something you haven't done. I'm trying to help you through it."

I nod, giving her hand a squeeze back before letting go. "Thank you."

"Ya'll ready for another round?"

I look over to see the waitress in a cowboy hat and flannel shirt with half the buttons undone standing before us. "Yes, immediately," I say.

Zara holds her hand over my empty glass. "Actually, she has to go see her boyfriend. She's done for the night. But I'll take another."

"Comin' right up," the girl says before heading back off.

"What'd you do that for?" I ask.

"For your own good," she says. "Now get the hell out of here and go get horizontal with your man. It will do you both some good. Get your mind off all this mess." She waves an empty hand in the air.

I let out a grumble and push out of the booth, stepping on broken peanut shells from past patrons. "I was looking forward to a perfectly good steak."

"Then pick one up on the way over," she says. "Or better yet, order one to meet you when you get there. Though you could do with some sexy cooking time."

I roll my eyes as I head for the doors.

"And I expect a full report on my desk first thing in the morning!" she calls after me, like *she's* my supervisor, garnering the attention of all the other patrons. As I exit the restaurant, I can't help but grin.

Thirty minutes later I'm jogging up the stairs to Liam's apartment, a bag of groceries in one hand and a bottle of wine in the other. I stopped off by the pasta provisions place that sells fresh-made ingredients for making your own pasta dish and picked up a couple of options.

I feel like such a heel for blowing him off for so long, but I'm not good at this relationship stuff. Matt knew that, and yet he stuck around anyway. But now I see that all might have been just for convenience if nothing else. If you're working for a top-secret organization that requires your absence for a lot of the time, who better to marry than a workaholic who doesn't know the first thing about building a long-lasting relationship?

I take a deep breath, trying to remember not to be too hard on myself. The door rattles under my "police knock" as Zara likes to call it. I've decided to stop fighting her on it and just accept that any time I come to a door, it's going to sound like there's a bear trying to tear it down from the other side. There are worse habits.

A few seconds later the door opens to reveal Liam, his hair partially disheveled and a can of beans with a spoon in them in his hand. My heart absolutely falls. Look at what I've reduced him to. Wow, Emily, you are just a terrible, terrible person.

"Em," he says, his eyes wide. "Did we...were we planning on doing something tonight?"

"No," I say, stepping over the threshold. "And I'm sorry I didn't call. I thought...I guess I thought you might be too mad to answer. Or that you might tell me not to come. Zara says I've been being an ass toward you, and you know how Zara is, she's not wrong. Usually."

"No, she's not," he replies, closing the door behind me and setting his can of beans on the kitchen counter. "What's all this?"

"A proper meal," I say. "I can just leave it...if you don't feel like company. It looks like you don't have much in the way of food." My eyes drift to the can.

He shrugs. "Sometimes it's just easier not to try."

"Liam, I'm really sorry," I say. "I've been distracted, and Zara's right. I have been an ass. I haven't been giving this—us my full attention."

"I figured it was me," he says. "There's no harm in admitting it if that's the case. If you're not attracted to me or if it's something about the way I chew, or maybe the way I say futbol—"

I grab him and pull him into a kiss, pressing my lips on his. "It's none of those things," I whisper when we pull away. "I'm plenty attracted to you. I'm just not great at...relationships."

He takes a breath; I suspect I surprised him again. "They can be complicated. And the more you ignore them, the harder they are to keep going."

"If you'll let me, I'll make it up to you. I'm not a great cook, but I think I can handle some pasta alfredo."

He shakes his head. "Can't do it. White sauce bloats me."

I smack him on the arm as he pulls me in for another kiss. We end up leaving the groceries in the bag.

Chapter Four

THE NICE THING ABOUT LIAM'S PLACE IS THAT HE ALWAYS keeps everything so neat and tidy. I don't know if that's something from his heritage or just a personal quirk, but his bed was made, and the entire room smelled like one of those plug ins when we dragged each other into the room. By the time we're done, the bed is completely disheveled and we're both covered in sweat, but somehow it still smells really nice.

"I'd say that halfway makes up for ditching me this weekend," he says.

I glance over at him. "Halfway?"

"I'll need at least one more session before I can be sure," he says, cracking a smile. I shove him over and extricate myself from the sheets, heading for the bathroom. My hair is wet and stuck to the sides of my head, so I figure I might as well step in for a quick shower. I turn on faucet and hear him call my name from the other room. As I poke my head out the door I see him smiling seductively from the bed, his arm draped on his knee like he's the subject of a renaissance painting.

"Just wanted to let you enjoy the view," he says, though,

watching his face, I think he really just wanted to get one more look *at me* before I got dressed again.

"You are such a bad liar," I tell him and head back into the bathroom. As soon as I'm in the shower I sense him come in the room as well. "Don't even think about getting in here. I'm starving and if I have to wait another half hour to eat, I might just tear right through you."

"That doesn't sound so bad," he says, laughing. "I just figured I'd keep you company. Also I have to try and get my hair under control. After I started growing it longer it's decided to do whatever it wants."

"When's the last time you had hair longer than half an inch?" I ask, running the water through my own hair.

"Teenage years. You would have loved it. Had hair down past my shoulders. I even put it up in a ponytail sometimes."

I stick my head out of the shower. "Was that an Irish thing?"

He grins. "No, it was a school thing. They had a mandate which said guys couldn't have our hair past our collars. But the rulebook didn't say anything about guys having a high pony."

"You did not," I say.

"Swear to God. I'll have to find a picture for you sometime."

I laugh and finish rinsing off. "You sound about as stubborn as me when I was a kid."

"Yeah?" he asks, handing me a towel over the curtain.

"Oh, yeah. I was terrible as a kid. The more I couldn't do something, the harder I kept trying, sometimes to my detriment." I towel off as a second towel appears over the curtain, which I wrap around my hair.

"I hope you're not going to spare me the details."

"Okay, baseball camp. You know how baseball works, right? You know, seeing as you're a foreign national and all."

"Very funny," he replies.

"It was the first time I'd ever gone up to bat in an actual game, and this was when I was still little, so we used those tee-ball things to hit the ball."

"Tee-ball thing?"

I dry off my ears, then begin toweling down my hair. "Yeah. It's this rubber mount that holds the ball at your height so you can hit it without someone pitching it to you. Cause pitching to six-year-olds never ends well, from everyone's perspective. So on this rubber tee I missed all three times. But did that matter? Nope, I just kept on swinging."

"But it's three strikes, right? Three chances to hit the ball?"

"Yep. But little Emily didn't care one bit. She swung probably twenty times, and no one could get near me because I was swinging the bat so hard."

"So what happened?"

"I finally hit it—clipped it really—and it just kind of rolled off and to the side. But by then I was so frustrated I threw the bat farther than the ball rolled."

"Jeez," he says. "Glad I was never one of your opponents."

I laugh. "You mean you're glad you never went up against the girl who couldn't take a hint? I think I even kicked the umpire's shins when he told me I had to stop, that it was over." I step out of the shower and dammit if he doesn't have a fuzzy robe waiting for me. I smile and allow him to wrap the robe around me, letting the lower towel fall to the floor. I cinch the robe tight, and it has to be the thickest, most comfortable robe I've ever worn. Perfect for a fall evening.

Liam bends down and picks up the other towel, throwing it back over the shower curtain. He's also managed to find his boxers and put them back on.

"You know, I might not be very good at this flirting thing either," he says. "But when you look at me like that I kind of think you were lying about being hungry."

"Nope," I say and shove past him, headed for the kitchen. "Not lying at all. Give me just a minute, most of this stuff is already fresh and prepped."

He follows me in, pulling on a pair of sweatpants and an old t-shirt with some rugby team emblazoned across the front. "What can I do?"

I point to the bottle sitting next to his half-eaten can of beans. "Wine. Now."

"Yes ma'am," he says. For the first time in a long time, I start to feel myself relax. Is this what Zara was talking about? I'm not sure I even ever felt this with Matt. I mean, I thought we were in love, obviously, and we loved being around each other. But when I look back on those times now, I can't help but see them with an eye of suspicion. I can't help wondering if he was being his real self, or the person the organization raised.

I shake my head, not wanting thoughts of that to ruin the mood.

"What was that?" Liam asks.

"What?"

"You shook your head."

"Oh," I say. "It's just something I do sometimes, when I'm trying to stop myself from thinking about something unpleasant."

"Ah," he says, popping the cork on the wine. "Well, I don't think there's any reason to think about unpleasant things right now, do you?"

"Not at all," I say, taking a glass as he pours me a sample from the ruby liquid. I take a sip and relish the hints of blackberries and nectar. The meal itself is simple enough to make, the pasta itself being the only thing that needs to be "fixed". Fifteen minutes and a boiling pot of water later, I combine all the ingredients to make a decent pasta dish, and even have enough to make a side salad with croutons. It's no steak dinner, but it gets the job done.

Liam sets the only table in his apartment, which is about the size of a breakfast table and sits beside one of the apartment windows. Outside is nothing but a view of a parking lot and woods beyond, and I catch a rumble of thunder in the distance.

"I didn't know it was supposed to rain tonight," I say.

He shakes his head, taking the seat opposite me. "Neither did I. Thanks for this, it looks delicious."

"Better than a can of beans?"

"We'll see," he teases, picking up his fork. I have to admit I'm hungrier than I thought, and I start to devour the meal before really tasting it. When I catch Liam staring at me I blush and almost drop my fork and the food out of my mouth. I finish chewing and wipe away the sauce.

"Sorry, I think I worked up an appetite."

"No, no, please. Don't stop on my account. It's like watching a lioness go through a gazelle."

"Uh huh," I say then return to eating. Something in my brain decides to take a snapshot of this moment, and I feel myself getting lost in it. I haven't had something like this in a long time, maybe ever. I always thought the "normal" life wasn't for me; that it was better left for people whose lives weren't on the line every day. But maybe I was wrong. Maybe people like us can have this too.

But then I remember that I might not even be here next week, and all of this could disappear. Part of me wants to just shove it back in my head again and forget all about it. But I have to tell him. Zara was right; he deserves to know.

"You look like you're about to shake your head again," Liam says.

I put my fork down and take another sip of wine.

"Uh oh, must be serious."

"I spoke to Wallace today," I say. "He's having me transferred."

"To another department?" Liam asks, confusion in his voice.

"To another field office. And from his demeanor I feel like it's not going to be close."

He puts his fork down. "Wait, they're transferring you out of D.C.? When?"

"Next few days, I think. He said he'd already submitted it to Cochran, and he said I'd have a week to get my affairs in order."

His features are pinched, like he really wants to say something, but he stays calm. "And you don't know where?"

I shake my head. "It could be anywhere. Field office, satellite office. If he really wanted to be vindictive, he could stick me in a town that's never had an FBI office before, and make me run my own one-person operation."

Liam sits back, wiping his mouth. "So I'll put in for a transfer too."

I shake my head. "I can't let you do that. You're just starting your career here, and you're making good progress. Both you and Zara managed to avoid whatever grudge Wallace has against me, despite everything. I can't ask you to uproot everything you have going for yourself here. You can make a real difference working out of D.C. A much bigger difference than you could make in Gallup, New Mexico or Portland, Maine. You come from a small town; do you really want to go back to that?"

"I don't want to lose this, we're just getting started," he says.

"Neither do I."

"Then what do we do?"

Suddenly I don't have an appetite anymore; I feel like I've spoiled the evening. But judging from the look on Liam's face, I feel like I've crushed what little spark was brewing between us. "I wish I knew."

Chapter Five

"Special Agent Slate."

I look up at the man through my sunglasses, half expecting him to tell me I've already had my security clearance revoked.

The new guard, another whom I've never met, heads back over to the guard house and types something in on the pad while the other three carrying assault rifles eye my car.

"You're clear to proceed," he finally says, and I breathe a sigh of relief. Zara said she'd meet me in the office today and we'd start to strategize on how to handle this situation, but only if I gave her a full rundown of last night.

While things with Liam started off good, I completely killed the mood with my news. We ended up not finishing the rest of the meal and instead vegged out on the couch for a while, neither of us really watching the TV until I figured it was better I went home and slept in my own bed. If I do have to break things off with Liam, it's only going to get harder the longer I prolong it. I shouldn't have told him, or at least waited. That way the night wouldn't have been ruined and I wouldn't have soured a perfectly good memory of us together. I'm sure he'll be in this morning as well, and I don't want things to be awkward. Maybe I can get in to see Cochran before I see Liam, at least figure out where all this is headed.

As soon as I get up to the office, I catch sight of Zara at her desk, her knees pulled in tight as she hammers away on her keyboard. It reminds me of her days back when all she did was data analysis and would practically sleep in the Bureau. I'm exceptionally proud of how far she's come in such a short time, and I know even without me here she's going to do amazing. She's become one badass field agent over these past few months. Not to mention she shrugged off her first on-the-job injury like it was nothing. I mean, she was in rehab for weeks after getting hit with that buckshot, but she bounced back harder and faster than most anyone I've ever seen. Even as I walk toward her now, I feel myself growing wistful. I'm really going to miss her too.

"Hey," she says, perking up when she sees me. "Ready to get started?"

"Sure," I say, hanging my blazer on the back of my chair. Again, I wasn't sure Wallace was even going to let me back in the building after I stormed out yesterday, but it seems like he doesn't want to "waste man hours" on someone else packing up my desk. I might as well do it anyway, what else do I have?

"Have you checked Cochran's schedule yet?" I ask.

Zara nods. "I spoke with his secretary about ten minutes ago. He's got an opening right after lunch."

"Perfect," I say as I catch SAC Wallace heading into his office. He spots me at the same time.

"Slate! In my office."

"Shiiiit," I growl.

"You want me to come in there with you?" Zara asks.

I shake my head. "No one else is risking their career for me. I might not make that lunch appointment after all."

Zara grabs her phone. "I'll see if we can't move it up. Maybe he's got a quick opening somewhere."

I place my hand on hers, returning the receiver to the

handle. "We have to know when to call it. I think it's over. Just make sure no one steals any of my stuff." Not that there's much on my desk as it is. I've always kept things sparse, given I never spent a lot of time here. Most of my time was out interviewing witnesses or visiting crime scenes. In fact, the only time I ever did spend at my desk before Wallace took over was to fill out and file my action reports.

I trudge my way over to his office and step inside, while doing my best to maintain my dignity. I have no idea what he's going to chew me out for today, seeing as I'm actually on time. But it'll probably be for me leaving in such a huff yesterday. I fully expect this to be my last day in this office. I better soak it in while I can.

"Close the door," he says, unbuttoning his top jacket button and sitting behind his desk. A small pile of files sits to his right, and he grabs the top one, placing it directly in front of him.

I do as he asks and step forward, my hands on the back of one of his chairs. I don't expect this to take very long.

"Have a seat," he says. He's not coming across as angry or upset, but I know this man can hide his emotions with the best of them. I'm not sure I've ever seen him even raise his voice, but he sure knows how to intimidate people when he wants to. It's amazing what some people can do with just a look.

I round the chair and sit, unsure what to do with my hands, so I just fold them in my lap.

Wallace picks up the folder in front of him and passes it to me. "What do you make of this?"

Confused, I open the file to see it's a murder report, and an open case. "Male teenager, killed, mutilated and left out in the open," I say, reading from the report. "But the body is too disfigured to make a positive identification?"

He nods. "It just came in this morning, happened during that rainstorm overnight. Couple of joggers found him along one of the running trails. Bethesda thought this one needed an expert in these matters, so they reached out for our help."

I furrow my brow and take another look at the file, reading through all the details from the initial report which is only a few hours old at best. I then pull the pictures out and have to keep myself from gasping at the carnage.

"That was my impression as well," he says. "Not every day you see a human being flayed open like that."

"God," I say, once I've gotten over the shock. The kid has been completely eviscerated, his body cut open to expose all of his internal organs, though it looks like a few might be missing. His face is a complete mess, most of the skin has been torn away. I can only hope he was already dead when this happened to him. But this is no ordinary murder. My brain kicks into detective mode and I start analyzing everything from the images. Looking past all the blood I check for any patterns, or any indication of exactly what happened to him. "It looks like a ritual killing. The way he's been displayed like this. And there has been a lot of care given to how the body was positioned. Someone didn't just do this and leave him here. This was planned."

"Despite the lack of any other symbology close to the body?" Wallace asks.

"It's not always present, especially in certain situations. The body itself *is* the symbol." Wallace nods as I close the folder. "What's this all about? Why did you want me to look at this?"

The man works his jaw for a second, like he's trying to decide whether to tell me something or not. Finally, one side of him wins over and he resets himself, folding his hands together and leaning forward.

"Remember yesterday when I said I had read every agent's full file before taking this job?" I nod. "Yours happens to tell me you're the agent in this office with the most experience regarding specialized killings like this. I consulted with

Deputy Director Cochran this morning before you came in—
nice to see you were on time for once, by the way—and he
and I agreed that you're the agent most qualified to assist in
this case."

"But yesterday you said—"

"You'll still be transferred." He holds up a hand. "But we
can postpone it until after you've finished giving this case a
once-over. If you can't make any headway on it after a week,
we'll get you packed up then. But if you can help out the
locals on this one, you'd be doing the Bureau a solid."

"Enough of a solid to let me stay where I am?" I ask.

He gives me a grim smile. "This wasn't my first choice. I
believe you to be more of a distraction than an asset to this
office. However, I can't deny your level of expertise. You're the
only agent in this department who has racked up more first-
hand experiences with stuff like this, and I can't overlook that,
no matter how much I want to." He pauses, then stands and
buttons his blazer again before clasping his hands behind his
back. "I wish this had come in yesterday. At least then I could
have justified postponing informing you about your transfer. If
it's going to be too much—"

"No, sir," I say, standing to match him. "I'll be happy to
assist Bethesda on this one."

"Good," he says, nodding. "Your liaison will be Detective
Rodriguez, with Montgomery County. Her contact info
should be in there."

I don't know whether to thank him or not. It feels like
I've been dealt a backhanded compliment. "I'll get right
on it."

"From what I understand, the crime scene is still active.
You might want to head that way before they get too deep in
the investigation." I nod, then make my way for the door.
"And Slate." I turn, looking at the man who holds the fate of
my career in his hand. "Good luck."

Normally I'd be jumping with joy over receiving a case like

this, but I know this is little more than a stop gap before
Wallace kicks me out of here for good.

As I make my way over to my desk, Zara must sense something's off because she leaves her desk and puts an arm
around my shoulder. "What happened?"

I hold up the file folder. "Stay of execution."

"What?" she asks, letting go.

"Wallace just handed me a case. Body mutilation outside
of the city. Bethesda is taking a look at it; they wanted an
expert."

She puts her hands on her hips. "Well. You can't say he
isn't fair. You *are* the best person for the job."

"I guess. It just feels like I'm delaying the inevitable," I say.

"How long did he give you?"

"A week. Give or take."

She smiles. "Then I guess it's time for you to pull off
another one of those patented Emily Slate miracles."

I grab my jacket and my laptop and make sure I have
everything I need before heading out. "Wish you could come
along."

"Me too," she says. "I would if I didn't already have a
mountain of work myself. Who knows? Maybe you'll do such
a good job that Wallace will be forced to keep you here."

"I wouldn't count on it," I say, and her face drops. I give
her one last smile before heading for the door. If I only have
one more assignment here, I better make damn sure I don't
cut any more corners. I'm not about to leave this place with
one more black mark on my record.

If I'm going to go out, at least I'm going to do it the
right way.

Chapter Six

IT'S ABOUT A THIRTY-MINUTE DRIVE OUT TO THE CRIME SCENE. My head is swirling with thoughts of what I'm going to do when Wallace finally forces me to leave. I could quit the FBI, maybe start working for one of the local D.C. departments, but I know in my heart of hearts it isn't what I want to do. I'd see it as a step down when realistically it's probably just a step to the side. It isn't like the police departments around D.C. don't have a fair number of crimes to deal with, it's just that their influence is limited.

As an FBI agent, I have the opportunity to work on bringing down criminal organizations that span the continent or put away criminals who have built entire empires. If I were to go to a local PD, I feel like I'd just be handling domestic disputes and drug murders. Not that those jobs aren't important, it just isn't what I've spent my entire life planning for. It isn't why I spent all those years in school, working to get into the early acceptance program and then into the training program at Quantico. I couldn't have done any of that if I'd been focused on becoming a local beat cop, or even a detective. Ever since I lost mom, I felt like the FBI was my only way to rebalance the scales, so to say. The police perform a vital function, but they can't affect the kind of structural change I'm hoping to build a career around.

At least, that was always the plan. And even though she was a hardass, Janice always had my back. I was never worried about losing my job because of a judgement call that might not have been strictly by-the-book but worked anyway. I didn't realize what a shield she had become. And now I find myself all alone out here, with the very real possibility everything I've worked for is about to go down the drain.

I'm still lost in thought when I see the lights from the police cruisers in the parking lot.

The area is a greenway entrance: a parking lot where runners, bikers, and the like can leave their cars while they run along the trail that parallels the river. The parking lot has been cleared of any civilian cars and a fire truck is the only other vehicle that is taking up any space in the lot. The whole area has been taped off with yellow caution tape and I catch sight of two news vans parked off to the side. I pull up to the cruisers and show my badge before they can tell me no civilians. I'm able to maneuver my car past the cruisers and pull it just inside the parking lot, making sure I don't block the fire truck.

When I step out, I take note of how wet everything still is from the storm last night. It blew through quick, but the rain at Liam's apartment pounded on the windows for at least twenty minutes straight. It's overcast still this morning, so the sun hasn't had a chance to dry everything out yet. I don't know if that's going to be a problem or not. Not until I see the body.

"Which way?" I ask one of the officers standing by the cruiser. He points left down the greenway and I give him a quick nod as I head down the path. It's wide enough to fit a full-sized vehicle down here and it's paved, but the large wooden posts at the parking lot prevent any vehicles larger than a motorcycle from passing. Which makes me wonder if the victim was killed where he was found, or if he was brought here.

As I turn the bend, I see the flurry of activity just off the main path, on the other side of the river that runs alongside the greenway. Half a dozen people surround the site, three of them dressed head-to-toe in white coroner outfits. It looks like everyone is gathering evidence. A stretcher with a black bag on it sits on the pavement, but as far as I can tell they haven't moved the body yet. Good.

As I approach, a middle-aged woman of probably forty with short, dark hair approaches. She's got a detective's shield pinned to her blazer. That along with the fact she's the only one here who isn't in uniform tells me this is probably Detective Mariel Rodriguez, my liaison.

"You must be Slate," she says, holding out a hand.

I take it and give it a good shake. "Detective Rodriguez, I presume."

"In the flesh. I heard about that job a few months back where you found those missing girls. Nice work on that one. Always thought it was pretty ballsy you went after one of your own contractors."

I shrug. "Just because they work for the FBI doesn't mean they're saints. Trust me, the Bureau makes its fair share of mistakes."

She gives me a knowing smile. "Glad to have your help on this one. This is outside my area of expertise, but if you wouldn't mind, I'd like to stay with you on it. Who knows, I might learn something."

"Whatever you want," I say. "This is your show, I'm just here to assist."

She pauses, evaluating me as if I'm some sort of specimen in the zoo. "I have to admit, you're not what I expected from a Fed."

"What, because I don't want to railroad you into doing things my way?"

She pulls her mouth into a frown. "Frankly, yes. Whenever we've had to work with the Bureau in the past, we usually get shuffled to the back and told not to speak when the adults are talking."

I chuckle. "Let me guess. You've never worked with a female agent before?" The look on her face tells me I'm right. "Don't worry, I'm not one of those good ol' boys."

"I can tell. Let me show you what we're working with." She motions for me to follow her over to the site.

"I read the preliminary report you submitted to the Bureau," I say. "But I know those—" I stop when I see the body. Somehow, as gruesome as the pictures were, they still didn't manage to convey the level of carnage done to this young man's body.

"—usually don't tell the whole story," I manage to finish.

"Hell of a thing, isn't it?" Rodriguez asks. A couple of site techs are going over the body, swabbing it for any prints and doing their best not to disturb him. Given the amount of blood that's come out of the body and seeped into the ground, and the amount of rain we had last night, I'm not expecting them to get a whole lot.

I make a cursory survey of the rest of the scene. He's been placed off of the trail, but not far enough to hide the body. In fact, it's almost like he's been placed on display. "Joggers found him, correct?" I ask.

"Right, at about seven-thirty this morning," she says.

Seven-thirty. That's late for early-morning joggers. Some of these people get out here at four-thirty and five a.m. They have to, because they have to be at work by eight. So if no one saw him before seven-thirty, then that would mean someone had him hidden somewhere close, or they brought him to this location to be found at a specific time. But that would have been very risky. Why not just set him up overnight to be found first thing in the morning? Why risk it?

I turn and jog down the path a bit, then turn and come

back up, seeing what the joggers must have seen this morning. There was no way they could have missed it. He's splayed out like the Vitruvian man, partially leaning up against a rock that's near to the path.

When I come back to the scene, Rodriguez is holding out a pair of booties and gloves for me.

"Thanks," I say, slipping them both on before stepping into the scene itself. Everyone else pauses and takes a step back, allowing me to get a good look at the whole scene, which I appreciate.

I take it all in. There's a sickly smell in the air. Even though we're out in the open, the body is putrefying, and the wetness and humidity isn't helping things any. He's missing all his clothes, and his body has been completely cut from his sternum down to his groin, then flayed open, exposing his lower internal organs. There's also a clean cut just under his chin, where the lower half of his face was removed as well. But the skin around his eyes was kept intact, and his eyes are wide open, as if they're stuck in a last moment of terror.

All of this seems somewhat familiar to me, but I can't make the connection, not while I'm trying to keep my stomach settled and do a thorough investigation.

I circle the body, bending down so I can get a good look into the body cavity itself. "Liver is missing."

"That's right," one of the techs says, stepping forward. "There's nothing left of it, it's like they carved it right out of his body."

"This is Bjorn Jameson," Rodriguez says. "Our resident Medical Examiner. He handles most of the cases for us."

I give him a nod, noting his gloves are covered in blood from his examination. "We met a couple of years ago. Emily Slate, FBI," I say.

"Agent Slate, I remember you," he says. "One of the youngest to be assigned to the head office, weren't you?"

"I wouldn't go that far," I say. "What can you tell me about this one?"

"As you noted, the liver is completely gone," he says. "Lower half of the skin on his face is missing, expertly removed, I might add. And of course, there is the massive incision down the middle of his body. More than likely he was already dead when all of this occurred. At least, there was some pooling of blood in the body when they opened him up, which suggests his death was recent. Probably between eleven and three this morning."

"What's the cause of death?" I ask.

"Undetermined at this point. I want to get him back for a full autopsy. We'll know more once we can move him and get him into some better light."

I turn to Rodriguez. "Still no ID on him?"

She shakes her head. "We're checking with local missing persons' reports, but given this just happened, his family might not even know he's missing yet."

I turn back to Jameson. "Is there any way we can do a facial reconstruction? At least get an idea of what this kid looked like?"

"Possibly. Can you put me in touch with your people at the Bureau? As I'm sure you know, they get all the best toys first."

"Sure," I tell him, then step over the tape and back out of the scene. "My initial thought is the crime didn't occur here. It looks like he was brought here, or at least moved to somewhere more visible."

Rodriguez nods. "I've got a couple officers on a perimeter search to see if we can find anything else. I'll update that to include looking for the original murder site."

"Need some help?" I ask.

She seems taken aback. "You want to trudge through the woods, looking for a needle in a haystack?"

"Not really, but I will if it helps speed things up. If there's one thing I know about cases like this, it's that they rarely stop with one person. Someone went to *a lot* of trouble to send a message here. And if we don't figure out what that message is, and who it's for, we may end up with even more bodies like this."

Rodriguez looks away, rubbing the back of her neck. "Christ. The last thing we need is another one of these."

I check my watch. "You're going to want to get every available man you have out here to look. We need to know who this boy was, exactly how he was killed, and where. Only then can we hope to find any clues to catching this guy."

"I can help with that some," Jameson says. "I should be able to tell you the exact cause of death once I have him in the morgue."

"Great, that's one down," I say, turning back to Rodriguez. "Show me your search grid. Let's get to it."

Chapter Seven

I SPENT FOUR HOURS WITH RODRIGUEZ AND HER MEN GOING over every inch of those woods, but unfortunately, we came up with nothing, even after they brought out the K9 units. But at least it tells me one thing: our victim wasn't killed anywhere near those woods. Which means his killer or killers brought him there from somewhere else. But I still can't figure out why. What's the point of displaying him up like that in the middle of what would be "rush hour" on the greenway? And how did they do it without anyone seeing them?

Before I left, I took the opportunity to interview the two joggers who found him. They said the greenway wasn't as crowded as normal, so they were the only ones on the path at the time. When they first spotted him, they thought someone had disposed of a mannequin, but called 911 as soon as they realized what they were really seeing. Fortunately, Bethesda PD managed to arrive before anyone else witnessed the carnage.

I wonder if our unsub had stashed the victim somewhere, but then became frustrated that no one was finding him. Perhaps because of the weather, they figured they needed to do something more dramatic to get people's attention. But that only begs the question, what do they want? What are they trying to say? It's like something out of a ritualist's handbook, which is why after I left Rodriguez I came straight back to the Bureau to dive into some research.

Rodriguez is focusing on identifying the young man while I try to figure out why this case feels familiar to me. Given the FBI's resources, I have a better chance of figuring it out and since she knows all the locals, she has a better chance of identifying the kid before I could.

My initial impression of Rodriguez is she's smart and capable. And it doesn't look like she's been too jaded by the job, at least not yet. That's always a bonus. But honestly, I'm glad cases like this are few and far between. I don't think I could take it if I had to witness this kind of brutality every day.

As I sit at my desk, scrolling through case after case, I feel the presence of someone come up behind me. For a moment I think it's Wallace, watching over my shoulder again, but when a cup of hot coffee appears beside me, I breathe a sigh of relief.

"Thank you," I say, turning to Liam who is holding his own cup. "It's more than I deserve."

"That's not true," he says. "But I did go to a lot of trouble. It cost me a dollar fifty and I had to wait like thirty seconds for the machine to make it."

"Absolute torture," I reply, a smile on my lips. "Listen, about last night—"

He shakes his head. "That wasn't your fault. I was being a sourpuss, feeling sorry for myself because here I was, just getting into this great new relationship with this girl, and she'd had something really unfair done to her and all I could think about was how it would impact me."

I take the mug of coffee. "Well, that's kinda how you're supposed to think about it, right? Aren't we all selfish at heart?"

"I guess," Liam says. "But my selfishness tells me it's in my best interests to do what's best for you. And if that means going to the director himself, then that's what we should do. You have had a stellar career here over the past six months. I know because I followed all your cases while I was in training. There were cadets in my class who were in awe of the fact I even knew you."

"Okay, come on, that's laying it on a little thick, don't you think?" I ask.

"I'm serious," he says, taking the empty seat next to mine. "Wallace can't just drum you out of here because he doesn't like you."

I shake my head. "It's not that. Well, it's probably partially that. But he thinks I'm too obsessed with the Organization, that I'll let it affect my performance on my other cases." I take another sip of the coffee and it's glorious. "But then, he turned around and gave me a case first thing this morning."

"What?" Liam asks.

I give him the short explanation of everything to do with the murder, along with why I'm not packing up my desk just yet.

"That's great news," he says, a little too emphatically. "I mean, it's terrible for the victim and his family. Is this like some sort of final test?"

I shake my head. "He was adamant that I'm going one way or another, but he needed my help on this last case before I left. I could have chosen not to take it, but then I heard Zara in my head telling me I needed to do everything I could to make it look like I was a team player."

"Did she actually say that?" he asks.

"No, but I can imagine her saying it. And she would have been right. I can't let my ego get in the way of my job. If I do, I'm no better than any of those other guys. And I need to be better."

"There's that stubbornness again." Liam takes a sip of his

own coffee with a smile before screwing up his face and setting the cup aside. "I need to start bringing in my own tea. Have you talked to Janice about it?"

I look behind me at Wallace's door. It's closed, and I can see him working through the large floor-to-ceiling office windows. I lean in closer to Liam. "Why would I call Janice? She's on temporary leave."

"She must still have some influence here, she's been SAC of this department for what, six years?"

"Seven. Before I got here, anyway. But I can't do that to her. She's dealing with enough as it is. I don't want to come to her with my hands out, looking for her to save me again. She's done more than enough for my career. I need to fix this myself."

"Fair enough." He nods to my laptop. "So what are you looking for?"

I turn back to my screen. "Something about the scene seems familiar, but I'm not sure why," I say, resuming my search.

"I'd think if you had a case like that in the past you'd probably remember. That's not something you forget. Like...ever."

"No, I don't think it was one of mine," I add. "But I know I've seen someone laid out like that before, I just can't remember where. I'm really hoping it wasn't in a movie."

"That would be Rye all over again," he says.

I turn and give him a smirk. "Man, you really were following all my cases. Stalker."

He raises his glass to me. "What can I say? I'm one creepy dude."

I laugh. "Get the hell out of here already and let me work. Don't you have something you need to be doing?"

"Sure," he says, standing. "But could I bring you lunch? As an apology for going all silent on you last night?"

"Sure," I say. "Thanks."

"You got it." He heads off and I watch him go for a moment before turning back to my work. Leaving him is going to be harder than I thought. I really need to start breaking things off now, rather than continuing to engage him. But if I'm honest with myself, I don't want to, otherwise I would have done it already and spared myself the pain. I think I want this to hurt, and that way I'll know that it's real, and hasn't been just a little fling. I'm very thankful for my relationship with Liam; I don't think I'd be where I am, mentally, were it not for him.

Still, breaking things off won't be easy. Not by a long shot.

It only takes me a few minutes to get my concentration back as I pour through a bunch of old FBI cases. Something is stuck in my craw about this case and until I figure out where I've seen something like that before it's going to drive me crazy. It's like the phantom of a memory I just can't seem to grasp, just there, beyond the cusp of recognition. Hell, it might not even be a memory, it might have been from a dream or something I completely made up. God knows I've seen more than enough to concoct something like that in my nightmares.

But then I remember what Wallace said, that it seemed ritualistic. He's right about that part, given how the body was staged and the careful way in which it was opened up. The liver removal is very interesting. If I recall correctly, more than a few different cults used to do something similar, with the belief being that the liver held the key to immortality or everlasting life in the hereafter.

I narrow my search down to cults and similar organizations, which helps cut through a lot of the minutiae. Cults have always been a special kind of evil in my opinion. Preying on the desperate in order to exploit them. That's what it always comes down to. And if you're depressed or cut off from any real friends or family, then you're a prime candidate to be sucked up into one of these organizations that promises support, friendship and even love. They can be insidious, and no matter how many we seem to disband, there are always more popping up.

While the list isn't extensive, it is long, and it takes me some time to go through it. Liam returns with a couple of sandwiches and leaves one on my desk without a word, though he does shoot me a quick wink before heading off to whatever he has on his plate for the day.

As I eat the sandwich, I continue scanning through all the cult cases the FBI has investigated over the past twenty years. I didn't even bother filtering by location because I'm not sure where to begin. But as I run through the details of each case, I'm able to eliminate any that have been discovered or shut down within the past five years.

Just as I'm about to finish my sandwich, my eyes land on a case that's almost a decade old. *The Arrow of Guiding Light*. It was a cult based out of rural Pennsylvania that was accused of abducting people and forcing them to participate in brutal acts against other humans they felt weren't worthy to walk this Earth. They used the principle of the Guiding Light to justify any and all their actions, and an FBI raid on their compound in the Appalachian Mountains finally put an end to their carnage. Unfortunately, only two members remained alive once everything was all said and done, all the others having sacrificed themselves in the shootout, or having committed suicide before they could be arrested.

But it's not the particulars of the arrest that interest me, it's the accusations and evidence found at the scene. Bodies, strewn out and displayed in the exact same manner as our victim, the lower half of their faces removed, and their bodies opened from neck to groin. It's the exact same M.O.

My heart racing, I take the last bite and grab my jacket. I've just hit pay dirt.

Chapter Eight

"EVER FLOWN IN A TURBOPROP BEFORE?" THE MAN IN THE aviator glasses yells at me as the airplane dips down below a cloud bank. I've never had a problem with flying, but I've never been on an airplane this small before. It's a Cessna Caravan, which means it's just got the one prop engine at the front and that's it. Behind us are eight empty seats, all with cuffs attached to the floor with chains. As the pilot dips the plane again, they all rattle and slide along the floor of the plane.

"Not like this," I yell back.

"You're in luck," he says. "Thankfully we didn't have any prisoner transports today. So we didn't need the additional security."

"Great," I say, taking a deep breath and doing my best to settle my stomach as he pulls us back up to level. A verdant green mountain range passes slowly below us. There is nothing out here but wilderness.

After my discovery yesterday, I booked the first flight I could to Kentucky and flew out of Dulles this morning. Given our victim's positioning and mutilation match the bodies found at *The Arrow of Guiding Light's* compound in rural Pennsylvania, I decided the best way to get to the bottom of this was to speak to the only two surviving members of the cult. Unfortunately, they're both in different prisons, neither of them close enough to drive. At least, not unless I wanted to spend twenty hours in a car. And something tells me we don't have that much time.

I landed in Charleston, West Virginia just after nine a.m., but I had to charter a smaller plane to get out to the first prison; affectionately called Big Sandy. Located on a former mountaintop mining site, the area was converted into a maximum-security prison back in the early 2000s. I've never been here personally, but it's so desolate that you either spend two hours driving from the nearest town, or you take a private plane into the tiny airport. Judging by the shackles on the seats behind me, I'm assuming this is how they transport most of the prisoners there.

Just as I'm sure I'm not going to make the bumpy flight without throwing up my breakfast, the pilot says something into his radio, and I look up. Ahead of us is what looks like a concrete castle situated on the top of a mountain in the middle of nowhere. "Big Sandy?"

The pilot nods. "Kinda strange lookin', isn't it?"

I have to admit, it isn't what I'd pictured. But given this is a maximum-security prison, I'm not surprised to see there isn't a lot of outdoor space. Big Sandy houses some of the most famous criminals and killers in the country; people no one wants getting out. So it's no surprise they built it on top of a mountain in the middle of nowhere. Even if someone does escape, where the hell are they going to go? There's nothing around for miles.

"This is Filo two-six-seven requesting landing," the pilot says into his headset. I watch out the window as he turns the plane and begins approaching the small airport that's just south of the prison. I see now why I couldn't have flown a commercial flight here; the airport itself is tiny and the runway isn't that long. I'm not sure it could accommodate even the smaller commercial planes.

"We're clear to land, hang on one second, this should be pretty smooth," the pilot says. I grab the "oh-shit" handle though it turns out to be unnecessary. The pilot manages to land us and I barely feel a thing. And unlike the big commercial jets, the deceleration isn't nearly as bad.

He taxis us down the short runway and over to the "terminal" which isn't much more than a house that seems to have been repurposed into an airplane terminal. A small hangar sits off to the side, holding another plane almost identical to the one I'm in.

As the pilot pulls us to a stop and shuts off the engine, a black SUV appears from around the hangar and pulls up close to the airplane. I take a minute to undo my seatbelt as a man in a prison guard uniform gets out of the SUV and comes up to my side of the plane, opening my door.

"Agent Slate?"

"You must be Officer Gillespie," I say offering my hand.

He shakes it, then offers to help me down, but I wave him off, and pull myself out of the plane.

"Smooth ride?"

"Not bad," I say, looking over at the pilot who is checking the main engine.

"Yeah, Dusty is one of our better pilots, doesn't take any shit from the prisoners when they start acting up, isn't that right, Dusty?"

The pilot throws Gillespie the finger but there's a smile on his face.

"How long do you expect this to take?" Gillespie asks.

"Why, are the prisoners going somewhere?" I ask, following him to the SUV after mouthing a "thank you" to Dusty.

"Nah, just need to know if you're planning on staying or not. Cause if you are, I'll send Dusty back to Charleston. We like to keep a plane at the airport just in case someone needs to be transported unexpectedly."

"This shouldn't take too long," I tell him. "Depends on how cooperative he is in there."

Gillespie waves at Dusty. "Prep her for refuel, she'll be heading back with you."

Dusty gives the man a thumbs up and Gillespie tries to open the passenger door for me, but I beat him to it. Gillespie smiles, then heads around and gets in the driver's seat. "Do you roll out the red carpet like this for all your guests?" I ask.

"Just the Feds," he replies. "Everyone else gets thrown in the back of the turnip truck. We're only about five minutes away from the actual prison, so sit tight."

He pulls away from the taxiway and around the hangar, then takes a left down a windy road that pulls away from the airport. "If you want a snack for the flight back, give our *Cloud 9 Café* a try before strapping in. Got a whole host of goodies you might like."

"Where was that?" I ask. "I didn't see a restaurant."

"The house back there," Gillespie says. "Converted it into a restaurant a few years back. You'd be surprised how many people come and go from here on a daily basis. The airport doesn't just service the prison. Got a bunch of local folks coming in and out of here every day. You came in on a slow day."

"How many of your prisoners do you transport using the planes?"

"I'd say about sixty percent. Beats driving them all the way up here. Course, we have a bus that'll come in from Lexington now and again."

The road winds around a small hill, then we start climbing in the direction of Big Sandy itself. On the way we pass a group of buildings marked *Rest Haven Ministries*, then another couple of commercial manufacturing buildings. Finally, we come upon the prison itself, which is a slow climb up the winding hill to the parking lot which sits just below the prison.

Tall guard stations sit at each of the corners of the compound, connected by high, triple-wide fences, all with barbed wire strung across. Even if someone was willing to climb the twelve-foot fence and get over the barbed wire, they'd have to do it two more times before the guards in the towers shot them. Unlikely.

"We'll park here, and I'll take you through," Gillespie says. "We're getting the prisoner ready so you shouldn't have to wait very long once you're in there."

"I appreciate that," I say as he pulls the SUV to a stop. We get out and he leads me past the first set of guards, waving to them until we get to the front gate.

"Gillespie, escorting Slate, FBI," he calls out. The front gate buzzes and he pushes through, which just leads us into an open antechamber on the other side. Two armed guards stand off to the side, while another inside what looks like a small control room writes something on a pad.

"Firearm," one of the guards says and I pull my weapon out from under my jacket, eject the clip and pull back the slider to eject the round in the chamber. I place all three of them in the bin the guard holds out for me. "Please step through," he says, indicating a metal detector. I remove my shield and anything else that has metal on it, placing it in a separate container before walking through. A guard on the far side runs a wand up and down my sides and under my arms before allowing me to take all my items except for my gun back.

"Your firearm will be here waiting for you when you're done," Gillespie says, having bypassed the whole ordeal. He hands me a pass that says VISITOR, which I affix to my right lapel. "I'm taking you to a private room where you can talk with him, we won't go to the common area."

I nod, and follow Gillespie down a short hallway until we

come to another barrier, this one a solid metal door. He leans over and raps on it twice before it buzzes open.

Through the door we're back outside, though we're in the prison proper now. We cross a short pathway where a golf cart looking vehicle approaches from the north, two men, both with assault rifles sitting in the front seat. I look up to the two guard towers I can see from here that aren't blocked by the main building, and both have individuals stationed up high. From here I can see at least two in each tower. One with a rifle and the other with binoculars.

"It certainly is maximum-security," I say.

"We do all right," Gillespie says. "Haven't had as many incidents lately. The problem is finding people who want to come all the way out here every day to work. You've noticed we're not close to a town or city, so it's a drive for a lot of folks. You didn't see, but one of the businesses here manufactures mobile homes for temporary housing. They'll set them up in groups a few miles down Route Three and sometimes we'll rotate people through for about six months at a time before transferring them out to another prison."

"Is that really necessary?" I ask.

We reach another metal door, and he knocks a few times, then waves up at the camera pointing down on us. The door buzzes and Gillespie pushes through. "Back when the prison was first built, most of the staff was permanent. But the problem was we didn't realize how much being this isolated affected our guards. Had a lot of incidents those first few years. Mostly stabbings."

"From inmates?" I ask.

He nods. "All it takes is a second of letting your guard down, pun intended," he says, smiling. "But ever since we started these guard rotations, things have been going a lot more smoothly."

"Is that what you are? Temporary?"

He shakes his head. "No ma'am. I live about five miles

away on a small plot of land with more animals than I know what to do with and a wife who scares me more than any of these monsters. Nope, I'm here for the long haul." He leads us through a few different corridors, passing more guards as we go. I have to admit, it's good to see that the prison is so well controlled.

We climb a set of stairs, then turn right where he leads me to a series of rooms and opens the door to the first one. The room itself is split in two, divided by what looks like a piece of glass and a room-long steel table that goes all the way to the ground. But I know that's not ordinary glass, it's more than likely three-inch thick plexiglass that's anchored into the table itself so no one can actually get through to the other side. On the far side of the room sits another door. But on my side there are a couple of chairs already set up, facing the divider.

"He should be in here in just a minute. Want anything? Coffee? Water?" Gillespie asks.

"No thanks, you've been more than gracious."

"Just trying to make sure we do everything we can to keep our funding coming in," he says, winking. "I expect an unfavorable report from the FBI probably wouldn't look too good on our quarterly review."

"I'll make sure to give you a glowing recommendation."

He nods, tipping his cap. "'Preciate that. Holler if you need anything, I'll be right on the other side of the door." He steps back through and closes it behind him. I take a deep breath, and look out the window which is covered in a metal cage, blocking most of my view of the large yard that sits in the middle of the compound. It's all quiet out there now, I wonder when they start letting the inmates out for their daily exercise.

A buzzer sounds and the door on the other side of the plexiglass opens, revealing the silhouette of a large man, his shoulders as broad as two of me. He's bald, with dark purple circles under his eyes as if he hasn't slept in a year. He's wearing an orange jumpsuit and black shoes, and is cuffed at both his hands and his feet. A guard behind him escorts him into the room and sits him down in the chair on the other side of the divider before locking his ankles and wrists to a chain on the other side.

The guard looks at me and I nod, and he turns and closes the door, leaving the two of us alone.

In front of me sits one of the most dangerous men alive. Now all I have to do is get him to talk.

Chapter Nine

"Rasmussen 'Papa' Ewing," I say, sitting down across from him, the barrier the only thing between me and three hundred pounds of muscle. Ewing is in his early sixties, but he looks more like a freight train than a frail old man. His glare is stuck on me, though from his blank expression he doesn't seem to be in a talking mood. His lips are slightly parted, and I can see just the barest hint of drool at the edge of his mouth. I glare right back at him, though it has little effect. Not that I would expect it to.

"You were the leader of a group known as *The Arrow of Guiding Light*," I say. "A group which you started in your late twenties after being 'rejected' by society, which really meant you couldn't get a job, isn't that right?" The man doesn't respond, doesn't even blink. Now that I'm in his presence, I hadn't anticipated feeling so unnerved.

"You subsequently built that group from the ground up, gaining more and more followers of what you called 'The Divine Aura', in which you sought to purge the evil from every man, woman and child by any means necessary. And while these may have started with simple blessings and exorcisms early in your career, by the time we caught up with you they'd turned into something much more extreme, isn't that right?"

Still no response.

"When everything was said and done you were charged with twelve counts of first-degree murder, kidnapping, extortion, armed battery, attempted murder on six more counts, rape, incest, and about thirteen other charges that when totaled up, landed you with a seven consecutive life sentences. Which means your first chance for parole should be somewhere around the year 2100."

Ewing mutters something but it's too low for me to hear.

"Mr. Ewing, I'm not here to rehash the past with you. I'm more interested in your activities since you've become a resident here at Big Sandy. And while I may not be able to do anything about the length of your sentence, I am willing to offer you other benefits that might make the rest of your life a little easier. Are you willing to answer a few questions?"

He still isn't looking at me, but he mumbles something else, still too low for me to hear.

"What was that, Mr. Ewing? You have to speak up for me to hear you through the barrier."

It starts as a low growl in the back of his throat, but then it transforms into a word, delivered low and slow, like the sound of a passing train in the night. "*Whhhoooorrrreee.*"

I sit back, working my jaw.

"You are the impurity in the world, girl," he growls again. "It's your impurity that is preventing you from reaching the Divine Aura. You're dirty, just like the people you serve, just like all of humanity."

He's still clearly lost in his fantasy world. I see that a decade behind bars has done little to curb his fervor for the religion he created. "And you're nothing more than a manipulative huckster," I say. "So shall we try this again, without all the name calling? I ask you a question and you answer it."

He's finally looking at me like he's trying to stare directly into my soul, and a small grin has formed on his lips, though the drool is still there. "Go ahead then, whore. Ask your questions."

I narrow my gaze and pull out my phone, consulting the notes I made last night and on the way over here. "How many members of *The Arrow of Guiding Light* are still operating today?"

"You need purification." He leans forward, almost so his nose is touching the divider. I see his gaze flit down to my blouse. "Your soul will be damned for eternity if you don't receive it."

"That's great, and I'm sure it works on the desperate and hungry you managed to coax into your organization, but it doesn't work on those of us who know better. Now are you going to answer my questions or not?"

A droplet of drool trickles down his mouth and hangs off his unshaven chin. "A child of sin, you carry a heavy burden on your shoulders. You seek to impose justice in a world where you have no power. The people you stop will never truly change. You can't make them. Only me and my followers can truly change a person. We can cleanse them of this world. *I* can cleanse them of all impurity. Remove this barrier, let me show you. It's been so long, but I haven't forgotten…I will never forget. It's my gift to this world, to remove its evils, to purge humanity of all that has turned them away from the Divine Aura. Once you're changed, you'll understand."

He's practically pushed up against the plexiglass now, his forehead pressed up against it. His arms and legs are strained as the chains won't allow them to move any further, and yet he seems to be trying to move *through* the plexiglass to get to me. I find myself wanting to scoot back, but I'm not about to let him intimidate me.

"*Mr. Ewing,*" I say in a stern voice. "Sit down or I will sit you down."

He shakes his head, a steady stream of drool coming from

his mouth now. "No...you have no power here. Only *I* do. Let me...help you." His eyes have traveled all the way down my body now and he's practically foaming at the mouth. I'm getting nowhere here. I stand and bang on the door. Gillespie opens it and looks in, his eyes going wide. He leaves the door and a moment later, the door behind Ewing opens up and two guards come in, both with tasers and billy clubs.

"Ewing, sit your ass down, right now!" one of them yells. Gillespie appears in my doorway again as Ewing begins clawing at the plexiglass, though his arms still can't reach. But his tongue is out like a dog, and he's practically humping the table trying to get through.

"That's it, warning's over," the other guard says and hits Ewing with the taser. His whole body convulses for a moment before he hits the ground. I walk back over to the divider and watch as Ewing spasms back and forth as ten-thousand volts run through him.

"I'm sorry about that," Gillespie says. "We gave him some drugs half an hour ago to try and keep him calm. Seems like they didn't do the job."

"I'm not finished with him yet," I say as the guards hoist him back up and begin dragging him from the room. His legs drag behind him and his body convulses every few seconds feeling the aftereffects of the taser.

"Sorry, but he'll be out for a few hours at least. He's never been the most...cooperative resident."

"Damn," I say, watching as the door closes behind him on the other side. "Is he always like that?"

Gillespie nods. "Gets worse as the years wear on. Back when he first came in here he was somewhat coherent. But as time marches on he seems to grow more and more delusional. We've had psychiatrists, medical experts, even some holistic medicine experts in here to try and get him to some semblance of normalcy, but I don't think it will ever happen. He's got some strange things going on in that head of his...

medically, I mean. There's not really something he can take for it."

I shake my head. "No, that wasn't medical. Not all of it anyway. That was vitriolic, that was personal."

"Don't take it that way," Gillespie says, leading me back out of the room. "He doesn't respond particularly well to women."

"You could have warned me," I say.

"I hoped he would be more cooperative. Believe it or not, he was on two different sedatives. Things that should have knocked him out."

I follow Gillespie back the way we came. "How does he deal with the other inmates?"

"He doesn't. When he first came here, we let him in genpop. But he started trying to convert people to his psycho religion, and the crazy thing was, it started to work. We had to isolate him. Which I'm sure has only made the problem worse over the years. He only ever sees the guards, no one else. The last thing we need here is another *Arrow of Divine Light*."

"Guiding Light," I say, correcting him. "What about outside contact? Does he make any phone calls? Does anyone ever come visit him?"

Gillespie shakes his head. "In all the years I've been here, the only contact he's ever received have been letters from prison roadies. You know, people who think they know the 'person behind the criminal'?" He uses air quotes. "Most of them are people proclaiming to want to be part of his Guiding Light, or women who want to marry him. I swear, it's like crazy attracts crazy."

"Does he ever send any of these letters back?" I ask as we make our way back outside.

"You don't understand. We don't let him see them," Gillespie says. "In fact, we usually report the senders to their local police and then destroy the letters. This man is serving seven consecutive life sentences. The last thing we need is for him thinking he still has any power or influence."

While I don't condone the idea of destroying a prisoner's personal mail, I have to admit in this instance it's probably not a bad idea. "So then he has no contact with the outside world. None at all?"

Gillispie shakes his head. "Nothing. We even set up signal blockers for any cell phones that might try and find their way into the prison. I don't know if you noticed, but if you'd tried to make a call in there, you would have had zero service."

I hadn't noticed, but I'm glad to know Ewing doesn't have any way of contacting anyone on the outside. At least that helps eliminate the possibility he's orchestrating something from inside prison, or passing along instructions to a subordinate who is doing his bidding from outside the system. "Do you keep a list of everyone who tries contacting him?"

"Of course. Most come from a small pool of people who probably know we're not passing along their messages, but every now and again we get the random letter."

"Could I get that list?" I ask. "It would really help with the investigation."

"Sure," Gillespie says. "Give me a minute to get one of the guys to make a copy for you." He leaves me in the antechamber where they first took my weapon, and I went through the metal detector.

One of the other guards gives me a cursory glance. "You look pretty young to be in the FBI."

I ignore the comment and take my weapon from the tray off to my right. I replace the clip and chamber the first round, then replace it in my holster, giving him a side-eye. It's taken me a little time to get used to my new service weapon, but when Wallace came in, he said he didn't want any agents armed with revolvers, that they were too old-fashioned. And while it pained me to give up my old gun, this new one is lighter and easier to wield with less of a kick. But it also feels like it could fall apart in my hands if I squeeze it too hard. I guess there's just something about a sandalwood grip that a modern weapon can't replicate.

"Here you go," Gillespie says, handing me a small stack of papers after he emerges from a side door. "That's everyone in the past two years. If you want to go back further, just give us a call and we can email the files over."

I hold up the papers. "You've contacted the sources of every one of these?"

"When we can find them, yes," he says. "We like to give the local LEO's a heads up they might have someone dangerous in their communities. Though I expect most of 'em don't do much about it."

I fold the papers and slip them inside my blazer. "Thanks."

"Ready to head back?"

I take one more look at the place, wishing I could have gotten a better shot at Ewing. But he was so unhinged I'm not sure I could have made much headway no matter what I said. "Sure," I say. "Back to the airport."

Chapter Ten

FOR THE FLIGHT BACK, I SIT IN ONE OF THE BACK SEATS
instead of up front with Dusty. I had hoped going to see
Ewing would have given me some a lead on who might be
responsible for the kid's murder, but I'm reasonably sure he
had nothing to do with it. Though, if he had his way, I'm sure
he'd be out there, "purging" sin from every person he could
get his hands on.

And while Ewing might have been a bust, I still have one
other surviving member of the original cult. If Ewing isn't
pulling the strings, it's possible my other suspect is. He's in a
lower-security prison where they might not be so strict about
what kind of correspondence he receives. Maybe he decided
to become the "new" Ewing and start running his own cult
from his cell. In fact, I'm hoping that's the case. Because if we
have some random copycat out there who is just imitating
what they think they know, it's going to make this case immeasurably harder to solve, especially before I'm supposed to leave
for who-knows-where.

Dusty lands us back in Charleston and I have half an
hour before I need to catch my flight back to Dulles. But I
figure since I'm already out here, why not go take care of this

other inmate now? It's barely noon and I can make it over to Pennsylvania and back before the end of the workday. But when I go speak with customer service, they don't have any flights to Montoursville, seeing as it's another small, regional airport.

I sigh and head to the private booking desk, knowing Wallace is going to throw a fit for me booking two charter planes in the space of a day, but given that I'm about to be shipped off anyway, I don't see how much worse it can get.

"Can I help you?" the ticket agent asks.

"I need a flight to Montoursville, Pennsylvania. As soon as possible." I show her my badge to underscore the urgency of the matter.

"We don't have any regular flights out of there today, but there is one tomorrow," she says.

"Listen, this is of some urgency and an FBI matter," I say. "I need to get over there as soon as possible."

"Yes, of course," she replies. "We can arrange to have a private charter leave in less than an hour, if that will work."

"Perfect," I say. While she's giving me the details I can't help but think about Ewing and how completely off-the-wall bonkers he seemed. I only hope I have more luck with the only other surviving cult member, though given what I know about him, I think my chances are good. Not to mention I have the list from Big Sandy. If nothing else, that gives me another list of suspects to track down; people who are obsessed with *The Arrow of Guiding Light* and who might just be crazy enough to do something about it. As soon as I get back, I'm going to cross-reference the list with anyone who lives within a hundred miles of where the body was found.

"Here you go," the agent says. "Just take this and head down to the end of the concourse there. A man will take you down to the charter area."

I give her a nod of thanks and head in that direction. Charleston doesn't have a big airport, but at least it's larger than Big Sandy's restaurant and hangar. Though I have to admit I was tempted by that restaurant on the way out.

Once I find my way and present my credentials, another airport agent escorts me outside to a small golf cart. "What's that for?" I ask.

"The Capital Jet Area hangars are just down the road, but it's a bit of a walk. Less than two minutes on one of these. Sorry for the inconvenience."

"No problem." I hop on, not really thinking about it. My mind is preoccupied with tracking down whoever could have done this. Strangely, I realize I haven't thought much about the Organization in the past two days. It's like this case has been a welcome distraction. One that I didn't even know I needed.

"Shit," I say as soon as the driver pulls us around to the front of the hangar and get a look at the plane. Wallace is going to blow a fuse. Chartering a skimmer is one thing, but a jet is something else entirely. And before me sits a Gulfstream G400.

"Is this…right?" I ask the man as he's getting off the golf cart.

"Yes, ma'am," he says. "Just head on over there and they'll take care of you."

I head up to the airplane where I'm greeted by a young woman in a generic uniform. "Welcome Agent Slate. I understand we're taking you to Pennsylvania today," she says in an overly sweet voice.

"Um…that's right," I say.

"Any luggage?" she asks, looking at the man who escorted me over to this hangar.

"Nope, I travel light," I say. "I didn't mean…I mean, I thought it was just a quick flight. Is a jet really necessary?"

She gives me a smile. "The G400 is one of our fastest models. We'll have you to Montoursville in less than an hour."

"Wow," I say. That sure beats almost throwing up on a

little prop plane. Who knows, maybe this is one of their older planes they keep just for law enforcement or emergencies. Plus, screw Wallace. He's about to ship me off, it's not like I can get in any *more* trouble. "Sounds great."

"Please follow me," she says, leading me up to the brown and white jet sitting on the tarmac. I notice a pilot is already aboard, I can see his head in the window.

The stairs to the jet are already extended and the attendant steps aside, letting me go first. I take the first big step, then climb all the way aboard.

"Ah," I say when I get a good look at the inside. I was hoping this wasn't as bad as it was looking.

"Something wrong?" the woman behind me asks.

As I stare at the plush accommodations, I start to rethink my "screw Wallace" mentality. The inside of the plane is like the kind you see in music videos and movies. There is a couch against one side of the plane, along with two rows of very plush seats, as well as a small bar and service table.

I've gone and chartered myself millionaire's airplane. Wallace isn't just going to be furious, he's going to fire me, and probably make me pay the government back for this trip.

"No, nothing wrong," I say, finally looking down at the information the ticket agent gave me. Only now do I realize what kind of flight she booked me on. Man, I picked a terrible time to zone out.

"If you'd like to make yourself comfortable, I'll let you know when we're preparing to take off," the attendant says. "My name is Bradley. If you need something, just let me know. Would you like some champagne before we depart?"

"No, that's…how about just a water?" I ask. Though I figure at this point, the champagne is probably free. But I'm not about to go into a prison tipsy.

"Of course." She heads past me to the serving area in the back of the plane and returns with a glass and a napkin, placing them on the small table at the seat I've chosen. She then opens a bottle of Perrier and pours it for me.

The entire time I'm biting my lip, dead sure that at any second a squadron of police vehicles are going to come screaming down the tarmac and have me arrested for misappropriating government funds. Why on earth did that agent think I needed a private jet? I just needed something small and easy to get me to this tiny little town in Pennsylvania and back. I don't need the full rock star treatment.

But as I watch Bradley push a small button that retracts the stairs and locks us in, I realize it's probably too late to do anything about it. Zara is going to pitch a fit she didn't get to come along, though I think she'll be proud of me for going out with a bit of style.

Ten minutes later we're taxing down the runway and Bradley has reminded me to buckle my seatbelt until we're in the air. It feels really strange being the only passenger on a jet like this; that's not something I've ever done before. I hold on to my water as the jet rockets down the runway and lifts off. Compared to the ride with Dusty, it's already immeasurably better.

We climb at a good pitch for a few minutes before Bradley unbuckles her seatbelt and comes back over. "Wi-Fi is available if you want it," she says. "Can I get you anything else? We shouldn't be in the air long."

I shake my head. "No, thank you, this is plenty." She nods and heads to the back again. Do I tip her when we land? I have no idea what people normally expect from something like this. I never planned to be in this situation, and I probably never will be again. But for the time being, I'm here, so I might as well enjoy it. I try to relax into the seat and take in the view out the window. We're already a lot higher than I was in Dusty's plane, and this feels more normal to me. More like the flights I'm used to. It's so smooth I could probably fall asleep right here.

Instead, I pull out my phone and connect to the onboard Wi-Fi. Even though I'm landing in Montoursville, the actual prison is over the mountain in a town called Allenwood. It's about a thirty-minute drive which means I'll need to rent a car to get over there and back. Hopefully it won't take much longer than my time at Big Sandy. But then of course I'll need to catch a flight back. And given the size of the regional airport I'm flying into; I doubt I'll be able to get back to D.C. by this evening.

Unless…

"Hey, Bradley," I call. She comes up from the back. "Can you help me book a return trip?"

"Sure," she says. "I can contact the agents on the ground. We can make this a round trip if you want."

I shake my head. "How about a direct flight back to D.C.?"

"Oh sure, that's no problem," she says with a smile. "I'll go get that set up for you right now."

"Thanks," I say and settle back into my chair as she heads off. Wallace is going to absolutely tear me a new one. But given I'm already halfway to hell, I might as well go the rest of the way in style.

Chapter Eleven

By the time I reach Allenwood Medium Correctional Facility it's almost two in the afternoon. Fortunately, the weather has been cooperative, and the drive over from the airport was easy. My phone has two missed calls from Wallace, as I'm sure the requisition reports are reaching his desk already, but I'm not about to return the call until I'm done with my second suspect. Hopefully by then I'll have a little more to justify all these expenses.

It's funny, just a few days ago I was the one handling all the requisition requests for my department, and now here I am blowing more money than I have any right to in order to track down a killer.

I pull into the parking lot, noting that the security for Allenwood is already lighter than what I saw at Big Sandy. There are no guard towers at the corners of a thirteen-foot-high barbed wire fence. Instead, it looks more like an office park, just one with more security. And there is a fence, but it's not nearly as high or as imposing.

After a quick check, they allow me through into the visitor's area where I have to check my weapon again. Fortunately, my badge expedites the process and twenty minutes later I'm sitting at a table in a large room full of identical tables, waiting for my second suspect.

He comes in wearing a dark brown jumpsuit, and while he's cuffed at the hands, he doesn't have any restraints on his feet. Buster Markham is a thirty-five-year-old drug dealer from Brooklyn who fell in with *The Arrow of Guiding Light* a few months before the final FBI raid. In fact, he was instrumental in shutting down the cult, as he worked for an informant for the ATF and FBI in the final few weeks, having witnessed more carnage than he signed up for.

Unfortunately, that didn't keep him out of prison. Despite his help, he still participated in some horrific acts.

Markham regards me with suspicious eyes, though he seems more nervous than anything else. His hair is thinning to the point where it would probably benefit him to just cut it all off, and his clothes are baggy on him. Markham comes across to me as someone who doesn't thrive in prison, someone who is used by the other prisoners as a sort of currency, which can only work to my advantage.

He takes a seat across from me and pulls out a pair of glasses from his jumpsuit pocket. They're prison-issue standard glasses, and there's a tiny chip in the corner of one of the plastic lenses. When he sits, I catch him tremble before he clears his throat like he's trying to shove his nervousness away.

"Anything else?" the guard who escorted him in ask.

"No. We're good," I say without taking my eyes off Markham. The guard retreats to the far end of the room and pulls out his cell phone, oblivious. But it at least tells me they aren't in blackout procedures here. Markham could get and receive messages if he wanted to.

I stare at the man across the table for a minute. This is really no different than any other interrogation, except for the fact this man has already confessed to a crime. But to get him to open up about *The Arrow* or any of his recent activities will prove difficult unless I can make it worth his while. Then again, from the way he's shying away from the table all I might need to give him is an end to this interview.

"My name is Special Agent Emily Slate, with the FBI," I say. "Do you know why we're here?"

He shakes his head, not taking his eyes off me.

"The Arrow of Guiding Light," I say.

He winces. "Man can't get a break."

"What was that?" I ask.

"I said, a man can't get no break! How long are ya'll gonna hound me 'bout them people? That was over ten years ago. I was only in there for a few months. Worst decision of my life."

I nod. "Considering it landed you with a seventeen-year prison sentence, I'd have to agree."

"Can't ya'll just leave me alone and let me serve my time?" he says, an undercurrent of disgust in his voice.

"Is that what you really want? Because from where I sit, it doesn't look like you're doing too well in here. Are you getting enough to eat?"

He turns away from me, staring at the wall.

"Or are they stealing your food when the guards aren't looking? Let me guess, they're taking your commissary credits too."

He wets his lips. "I...I like helpin' people out."

"Sure you do," I say. "Maybe I can help *you* out. Make sure your credits stay with you. And your meals."

He turns to me. "You wanna help me, get me outta here. I already dropped a decade. Ain't that enough?"

"The state of Pennsylvania didn't think so," I tell him.

He pushes back from the table, somewhat agitated. "Three months! I was with them people for three months! And you think it's fair I gotta spend seventeen *years* in the lock-up? How does that work out?"

"Well," I say, folding my hands together. "You not only witnessed but participated in the brutal murders of two innocent people, not to mention you helped dispose of the bodies. You also participated in the kidnapping of a young man who, had you not come forward when you did, probably would be dead today."

"See, that's what I'm talkin' about! I turned. I saved that kid. I saved all the rest of them kids. You're with the FBI, you know that." He stares at me a minute. "Wait a second, *are* you with the FBI? You can't be much older than what, twenty-three?"

I sigh and pull out my badge to show him. "Mr. Markham, it was because of your assistance to our organization and your cooperation during the trial of Rasmussen Ewing that you didn't receive a life sentence. Given the circumstances, I think you got off lightly."

"That's easy for you to say," he says, leaning closer, barely even looking at my badge, instead his focus is on me. "You don't know what it's like in here. These people, they can eat you up, man. I need to get outta here."

"You're eligible for parole in two years," I tell him. "Now, I can either help make these next two years easier, or I can walk out that door and you go right back into the situation you came out of. Which will it be?"

Markham brings his hand to his mouth and chews on his thumbnail, looking back at the guard then at me again. "What do you want?"

Since it won't do to have me come right out and accuse him, I need to finesse this situation some. But the fact remains Buster Markham is familiar with how his cult killed people, helped display the bodies once it was over, and was an integral part to the process. If anyone would have the means to start the killing again, it's him. Though I'm not sure about his motive.

"What can you tell me about how *The Arrow* would make its sacrifices?"

He winces again, pulling away from the table. "Aw, man,

really? Don't you have all that info already? What, you gotta make me re-traumatize myself by reliving it? Like I don't already see it every night when I close my eyes. 'course that's before Large Randy decides to start talkin' in his sleep. Boy don't know when to shut up."

"Just the basics, Mr. Markham. You can keep it brief," I say, though now I have a picture in my head of Large Randy and it's not particularly flattering.

He lets out a long breath. "Fine. Ewing would call a meeting. Tell us all we were sinners. Said we needed to purge the sin from the world. He'd tell us to go out and find out the sinneriest sinner of them all. We'd go on our treks, looking for pretty much anybody. You could buy a pack of gum and Ewing would say it was a crime against the Divine Light. Whatever. All I knew was they were giving me shelter and food and so yeah, sometimes I had to go out and find someone. But I'll be honest with you, Agent. I was high ninety percent of the time I was there." He leans back. "But Ewing never said a thing. Prolly 'cause he knew I'd do his bidding for him and go find him someone to 'purify'."

He takes a breath. "So we all come back with candidates, and those who aren't selected are put to work in the camp, and the one who is selected would be set up for the ceremony. They'd often be sayin' they just wanted to go home, and it was my job to try and calm 'em down and lie to them, tellin' 'em it would be okay, and they'd be goin' home soon."

"Must have been tough," I say, trying to picture this man calming anyone down. He's a bundle of nerves now, I can't imagine what he was like ten years ago.

"Why d'ya think I was high all the time?" he asks, throwing his arms up. "Can't nobody look another person in the eye and tell 'em they'll be alright when you know damn well they won't be without some kind of substance in the system.

"Anyway, then Ewing would come out, we'd lay the...

chosen person down on the block in the center of the camp, and Ewing would get to work. Then, once it was all over, me and a couple of the others would take the body and display it for everyone to see."

I nod, listening intently. The more Markham speaks, the more worked up he's becoming, like the memories are ramping up his anxiety. "What exactly would Ewing do to the bodies?"

Markham lets out a low, guttural sound. "You really gonna make me go through it?" The look on my face tells him to continue. "He'd start by cuttin' 'em down the middle, startin' at just below the neck, all the way down to they privates. 'course they was screamin' and cryin' the whole time; it was the most awful thing to listen to, believe me. But he wouldn't let any of us cover our ears, said it was the punishment for being a sinner, and we had to experience what it was like for sin to leave the body. I swore if he tried doin' that to me, I'd slit my throat rather than go through that torture."

"Continue," I say, though not without difficulty. I'm finding this harder than I anticipated.

Markham swallows, hard. "Then he'd start cuttin' out the liver. Usually sometime between the initial cut and this point, the person thankfully died. And I only witnessed it twice. But one of the others told me about this guy they had one time, made it all the way until his liver was all the way out before he passed. They say he watched Ewing remove it from his body. Personally, I think it was nothin' but a tall tale. But who knows. You got a cigarette?"

I shake my head. Though the more I hear from Markham, the less I'm thinking my victim is one of his. He's becoming more and more anxious the more he talks about this; unlike Ewing who leaned into it. I'm not even sure Markham has the constitution to order more killings on the outside. Not to mention I still don't have a motive.

His leg is bouncing like crazy under the table. But he

continues. "Once he had the liver in this scale-like thing he built—something about measuring a person's acts in life, I dunno—then he'd start in on the face, cutting the bottom half of the facial skin off, up to just below the eyes. He said the eyes were the purest parts of us, that they shouldn't be disturbed, but it was the mouth that caused all our woes. The mouth needed to be removed in order for the soul to reach the Divine Light, as that was the only way to salvation. To see, but not be heard. Always sounded like a bunch of bullshit to me."

Markham is rubbing both his arms at the same time and clearly shaking. I motion to the guard, who puts his phone away and comes over. "Can you get him a cigarette?"

"Sure," he says and pulls a pack out, handing one to Markham who takes it in between his shaking fingers. The guard lights it for him and Markham takes a long pull on it before blowing the smoke out and up.

"Thank you," I say, and he nods, retreating back to the wall again.

"Jesus, you'd think I'd be over this by now," Markham says after taking another pull. Already I see the cigarette is having a calming effect on him. He's not shaking as much and his leg has stopped bouncing.

"It's a trauma," I say. "Was that it?"

"For the most part. A few of the others showed me how we were supposed to display the bodies. Arms out to the sides, legs spread, and with the body cavity open as well as the eyes, always looking to the sky."

I perk up. "Wait, what about the sky?"

He takes another drag. "Ewing was adamant they be looking at the sky when we displayed them. Said it was the only way they could 'traverse the distance'. Always seemed creepy to me. At least let the dead rest, y'know?"

"Does that mean they have to be flat on their backs?" I ask.

"Yeah, why?"

"What about if they were leaned up against something, or if they were laying say on some rocks, at an angle?"

He shakes his head. "Nah, that's not how you do it. They gotta be lookin' straight up, see? I don't pretend to understand that man's thinkin', I just know what I was told."

Our victim was laid out more at an angle, not looking straight up. Which means whoever displayed the body didn't know *everything* about the rituals. Which also means Markham is probably not involved. I can't see a man like this running some kind of cult on the outside, risking being found out and only adding to his sentence. He's got nothing to gain by it, unless he's doing it as some kind of trauma response.

"Okay," I say, shifting in my seat. When I came here I didn't expect Markham to come across as so...pitiful. "Let's change gears. Tell me about your friends, family."

He barks out a laugh and I notice the cigarette has already burned halfway down. "Whadya mean? Like, people on the outside?"

"Sure," I say. "Who comes to visit you these days?"

"Well," he says, squaring his shoulders. "Usually there's a small group outside the gates on visitation day, every now and again there's a *Guiding Light* nut among them. Want to see me hanged for turning on Ewing."

"Any of them try to contact you directly?" I ask.

"If you count the three death threats I receive per month as contact, then yea," he replies.

I have to wonder if any of the people that show up here are the same people who are trying to get in contact with Ewing. If I can find a common denominator between the two...

"Do you happen to know who sends you those threats? Or save them?"

He shakes his head. "They never have any names on 'em. Cowards. And I sure as hell ain't respondin'. I just give 'em back to the guards and they throw 'em away for me."

"What about people that come to see you, personally."

He takes a long drag on his cigarette before answering. "Agent Slate, don't nobody show up here for me. Any family I got's too ashamed to show they faces and anyone else either wants to record a podcast or bash my head in." He shakes his head again. "You're the first person who's wanted somethin' to do with me in a long time."

"So then you're not in constant contact with anyone on the outside," I say, just to make sure I have a straight answer.

"No ma'am."

I take a deep breath. It's looking like neither Markham nor Ewing had anything to do with this killing. Which means we're looking at a copycat, and apparently not a good one. If they don't even know all the "rules", I have to wonder how they got their information. Most wasn't released to the public for this very reason.

"Mr. Markham, do you know of anyone who might want to start up the cult again? Anyone in particular?"

"Just those nuts waving the signs I see sometimes. But they don't show up a lot no more. Back when I first got in here, they were out there every weekend. But it tapered off after a few months. Every now and again I'll see one, but it's rare these days."

"Is it the same one each time?" I ask.

"Yeah, I believe it is," he replies.

"Can you describe them for me?" I pull out my phone and open my notes app.

"Now wait a second. You said you was gonna help me in here. I can't be goin' and givin' away my ace in the hole without some sort of promise." He finishes the cigarette and puts it out on the metal table.

"Don't worry, Mr. Markham. I'm not about to go back on my word. I'm not the kind of person who does that. You've already helped me out a lot today. I'll make sure those other prisoners won't mess with you anymore."

"No, don't do that, it'll just make things worse," he says, his voice hushed. "But if you increase my commissary limit, at least somethin'll be left over when they done with it. I don't want to make no more waves in here, it's hard enough as it is."

"Very well," I say. "I'll have them double your limit, will that work?"

He nods. "Very fine, thank you. And you're sure you can't do nothin' about my sentence?"

I lean forward. "I'll tell you what. If your intel leads to the capture of a current fugitive, then I will go to the state board myself on your behalf. Try to get some time shaved off your sentence."

"Really?" he asks.

"But to do that, I'll need a description."

His eyes seem wide with excitement. "You got it," he says. "I'll be as accurate as I can."

Chapter Twelve

AFTER PROVIDING ME WITH A DESCRIPTION OF THE MAN HE'S seen outside the prison, the guard escorted Buster Markham back to his cell and I took a moment to speak with the prison's quartermaster. Unfortunately, I don't expect his description to go very far. It's generic, as the man he saw doesn't have a lot of distinguishing features and is often in a hat or glasses. That will make a positive ID hard. Not to mention I don't like the idea of relying on a convicted criminal to ID yet another killer.

But Markham did give me some valuable information regarding this case. I now know that our killer probably wasn't part of the original cult at any time and has since only discovered information about it either online or possibly through the black market. I'm convinced now that neither Ewing nor Markham had anything to do with our victim. Ewing because he doesn't have the means and Markham because he doesn't have the motive. I do feel bad for the guy, he fell into the wrong group at the wrong time. But my sympathies end there. While he might not have killed anyone himself, he was still a part of it for a time before finally reporting the group to the authorities.

As I get back on the jet, I pull out the list of names I got from Big Sandy. Once I'm back at headquarters I want to cross-reference this list with the description of the guy Markham gave me. Maybe I'll get lucky and get a lead. Hopefully Rodriguez is having better luck identifying our victim. I consider giving her a call from the air, but instead I sit back and let the low rumble of the jet engines put me to sleep as we take off. It's been a hell of a day and I'm beat.

But just as I feel myself sinking into the seat and beginning to nod off, I feel a presence beside me.

"Excuse me, Agent Slate?" I look up to see Bradley standing there with a phone in her hand. It looks like it came from the receiver in the back of the plane. "This is for you," she whispers, holding it out for me.

I take the phone, confused as who even knows I'm on this plane. "Hello?"

"Slate."

Adrenaline floods my system and immediately I'm sitting straight up like someone has shocked me with a taser. "SAC Wallace."

"Is your cell phone dead?" he asks.

"No, sir. But I didn't want to call you back until I had something solid."

I can *feel* his anger, even through the phone. "Just what in the hell do you think you're doing on that plane?"

"It couldn't be helped," I say, determined not to let him rattle me. "I had to get in to see both inmates today and neither is close to a commercial—"

"Have you ever heard of this magical thing called a car?" he fumes. "They can get you from one place to another without costing a year's salary."

"Sir, it would have been a seven hour drive out to Big Sandy, and then another eight hours to LSCI Allenwood. I thought in the interest of time and with a potential killer out there—"

"Slate, listen to me very carefully," he says, cutting in. "There is a procedure for these kinds of expenses. I know you know this. I also know you purposely took off without final approval from me because you knew I would never approve such a large expenditure."

"Sir, in my defense, I didn't mean to book a private jet," I say. "It was all they had."

"I don't care," he replies. "I could have you fired for this. Not only have you disregarded procedure *again*, but you've cost this department financially. Private jets are not in the budget. And from now on, you leaving Washington D.C. on anything other than a bicycle goes through me personally. You can bet I will find a way for you to repay the Bureau for this expense. Even if I have to go see Senator Marshall himself."

I roll my eyes. Senator Marshall is the head of the Senate Finance Committee. And while not directly responsible for the FBI's budget, he has a lot of pull with the various committees that are. The last thing I want to do is get embroiled in another situation with some Senators or House Representatives. I had enough of that with Jack Hirst and Adam Huxley.

"I'm on my way back to D.C. right now," I say. "We should be landing in…" I look over to Bradley, who holds up five fingers. "…about fifty minutes."

"If you weren't already in the air, I'd have put you on a Greyhound," he says. "And if I'm not being clear enough by my tone, you are *not* to charter any more flights out of the city."

"Yes, sir." Though he's angry, he's not as angry as I figured he'd be. I thought he might fire me right on the spot or have me arrested when we land. But something is wrong; he's acting like he's going to let me keep working on this case. Why? If I'm such a liability, why doesn't he just get someone else to handle it?

"Did you at least find anything useful? And I swear, Slate, if you tell me you didn't get anything out of this trip, I'll make sure your reassignment is dead center in the middle of the Nevada desert."

"I was able to determine that the two surviving members of *The Arrow of Guiding Light* don't have anything to do with our victim," I say. "I also have a new list of suspects, people who have tried contacting both of them over the years. Kind of like a fan club."

"A fan club?" he says with palpable disgust.

"Yes, sir. It seems Mr. Ewing continues to influence people, even from prison. Thankfully they're not allowing anyone to contact him, and they're keeping a record of everyone that does. If someone is out there copying Ewing's methods, they could have been trying to get in touch with him for years."

"What, as in they're looking for approval?"

"Maybe," I say. "Or maybe this killing is a way of getting his attention. Even if the messages don't get through, I'd bet news of the killing will, through other prisoners. Especially when the media gets wind of it."

"We're doing everything we can to keep that from happening," he says. "As much as I hate to say it, sounds like the trip was productive. As soon as you're back, I want you on it asap."

"Yes, sir."

"And come see me tomorrow about this expenditure. We're going to get this worked out, one way or another."

"Understood." I don't quite know what he can legally do to me, given that I didn't explicitly break any laws or regulations, it was just a matter of timing. But knowing Wallace, I wouldn't put it past him to figure something out.

He hangs up without another word and I hand the phone back to Bradley, who returns with it to the back. Despite how long the day has been and the sky outside the plane already beginning to grow dark, I'm completely awake now. As Bradley comes back down the aisle, I hold my hand out to stop her.

"I think I'll finally take you up on that drink."

Two hours later I manage to get through the door of my apartment and am welcomed by Timber who nearly knocks me down. I give his ears a good scratch and rub his face before depositing all my things in the tray beside the front door. I pull my blazer off and hang it on the back of one of my kitchen chairs as I grab the small pink note on the counter.

Welcome home, Emily!
Timber did great today, we
took a walk, had some
playtimes, and watched a
movie. See you tomorrow!

- *Tess*

I smile and look down at Timber, who is grinning and wagging his tail. "Did you have fun with the babysitter today?" He licks his lips and gives me a bark. "Yeah? You guys had some fun? Good boy. Let's take you out for a minute."

I grab his leash and take him out the front to do his business. I should have hired a dog sitter months ago. Rather than let Timber stay with my in-laws, it just would have made more sense. At least, that's how I feel now. But back then I was still worried about the assassin and had no idea my in-laws were plotting my demise.

Still, Tessa has been great. She's a local college student who only has night classes, so she doesn't mind watching Timber during the day for a little extra cash. It keeps him happy, he's home when I get here, and I don't have to worry about anything happening to him.

And to be honest, I sleep a lot better with him, even though he takes up a good seventy percent of the bed, always pushing himself up against me during the night. If things between me and Liam get any more serious, I'll need to switch out my queen for a king.

Then I remember: I won't even be here in a few weeks. And I guess Timber won't either. I'll need to find a dog-friendly apartment wherever it is I'm going cause I'm sure as hell not leaving him behind again.

Once we're back inside I find I'm almost too tired to do anything other than eat and go to bed. But I don't feel like cooking anything.

"How about we get a pizza, huh bud?" I ask as Timber digs into his own food. "Yeah, sounds good to me too."

I take a second to order the food on my phone, then head into my bedroom to change into something less restrictive, taking off my weapon and placing it on the bedside table like I always do. At least I've gotten to the point where I'm not carrying it to the front door all the time anymore. But a few months of living under constant threat will do that to a person.

As soon as I'm dressed and heading back out into the living room, I catch sight of all my research on the Organization. I know I shouldn't, but I take a minute to parse through it all for a few minutes, reminding myself of everything I've found so far, which isn't much. All of my efforts have been focused on Matt's father, and I'm still waiting on a couple of sources to get back to me, not to mention I've already put a few other balls into motion. But it's funny, with this new case I haven't been thinking nearly as much about this whole mess, but as I stand here and go over all the details again, I can't help but become engulfed in it once more.

Before I know it, the doorbell sounds and Timber pads his way into my room to figure out why I haven't made it to the door already.

"Right, right, I know," I tell him, getting back up off the floor and leaving my research for later.

But even after I've retrieved the pizza I find myself distracted with all the same old questions. I take a few minutes to eat, giving Timber small bites of the crust, which he gladly accepts. I hate that this still plagues me, that I can't let any of it go, even when facing a sadistic killer. It's like my mind just won't give up on Matt and everything he was involved with. I should just let it all go, but I know I won't. Wallace is right, I *am* obsessed.

Maybe a transfer wouldn't be the worst thing in the world. At least I could get some distance from all my memories here, and from everything that's happened over the last ten months. I sure wouldn't say no to a fresh start somewhere new.

I only end up finishing half the pizza before shoving the rest in my empty fridge and heading to bed. Timber, disappointed we didn't eat the whole thing in one go, sits by the fridge until I call him to bed. And just as I'm about to shut off the light, I glance at my pile of research one more time, hoping tonight my dreams will be a little better.

Chapter Thirteen

"THAT LOOKED ROUGH," ZARA SAYS AS I COME OUT OF Wallace's office the following morning. He spent the better part of an hour extolling the virtues of "proper procedure", all without actually punishing me. I'd expected the hammer and all I got was a slap on the wrist.

"Wasn't as bad as it seemed," I tell her. "How's your stuff going?"

"Great. We're tracking an international terrorist who landed here last night. I'm about to head out to one of his known contact points, see if we can't pick up his trail." She gives me a wink. "Speaking of flights, I heard you had a good one yourself."

"Christ, news moves fast," I say. "Who told you?"

"Caruthers," she says with a grin. "He got a look at the expense report."

"Is there anything that man *doesn't* stick his nose in?" I ask.

She immediately breaks into song. *"So you wanna be a Rap Superstar? And live large. A big house. Five—"*

"Stop," I say before she can recite any more.

She can barely contain herself and bursts out laughing. "I

just wish you would've taken a girl along, is all. You're back at fieldwork one day and all of a sudden you're flying private?"

"It was just a mistake. I…wasn't paying attention."

"Now that doesn't sound like you," she says, eyeing me.

"It was nothing," I say as my phone buzzes. I look down and see it's a call from Rodriguez. "I gotta take this."

"Kay," she says, waving as she heads off. "Good luck!"

"You too," I yell back, then tap my phone. "Slate."

"Morning," Rodriguez says. "I would have called yesterday, but I didn't have any new information. But I just got this in. We might have an ID on our victim." Her voice is tense; she sounds like she's been up all night.

"Really?" I say, grabbing my blazer and heading for the door. "Who is it?"

"Jaeden Peters. At least that's what we believe for the moment. His parents reported him missing yesterday afternoon, he was out on a date Tuesday night and never came home. It just came across my desk twenty minutes ago."

I push through the double doors, heading for the elevator. "So it's not a positive ID?"

"Not yet, because of the facial mutilation. We're waiting to hear back on the dental and fingerprints. I want to make absolutely sure. But I figured you'd want to know."

"Do you have pictures of the boy to compare?" If his family reported him missing, they probably provided recent pictures for comparison.

"We do, they're here if you want to take a look."

"I'm already on my way."

Rodriguez meets me in the lobby of the Bethesda Police Department and escorts me back through the station to her desk, which sits among half a dozen others in an open bullpen. The space is large, open and welcoming, not one of those stations where everyone is shoved into the smallest spaces possible. Of course, Bethesda isn't lacking in funds like some of the inner-city departments.

There's a large whiteboard at the head of the pen where details from three different cases have been sketched out and a couple other cops mill about. The place is relatively calm, though, which is good. Not a ton of large-scale crime up here.

"Did you have any luck yesterday?" Rodriguez asks as we get to her desk.

"Some." I fill her in on what I found from both previous members of *The Arrow.* "I was going to cross-reference this list with anyone who might have shown up at Buster Markham's prison, but I was in a…meeting all morning. I haven't had a chance to take a look yet."

"I'd be happy to split the list with you, make the work go faster," she says.

"Sure," I say. "Though we'll probably have better luck at the Bureau, seeing as we have a wider database. If you don't mind working with a bunch of feds."

"Hasn't been too awful so far," she says with a grin. "Here are the pictures the family pointed us to." She pulls out a couple of printed images that have obviously been copied off a social media website. They all show pictures of a young man, though in most he's not smiling and trying very hard to pretend he doesn't care about having his picture taken. A couple are obviously with his family, but most of the others are with friends. He seems about as normal of a kid as I've seen. Nothing that makes him stand out. You never can tell what's going to make a killer choose their victims, sometimes it can be something as simple as the way a person's nose is shaped, or how tall they are. And sometimes it has nothing to do with that at all.

"Hair color is right," I say. "As is the body type. I think this might be our vic."

"I thought so too," Rodriguez says. "We can always get the family down here to make sure."

I shake my head. "They don't need to see him like that. Maybe if it was a gunshot wound or a stabbing, we could at least position him in a way where they couldn't see it. But seeing as the bottom half of his face is missing…"

"They'd never be able to forget it," Rodriguez says.

She's right. Having the family do the identification is always iffy. Emotions are high and as much as people think they're ready to see their loved ones like that, they never are. I always opt for other types of ID if we possibly can.

"Let's just hope they plan to have him cremated," I say, going back over the pictures. Even if his family were to come down here, I'm not sure they *could* make a positive ID. Not unless they happen to know about a birthmark or other unique feature the boy might have.

I take the rest of the file and go over what preliminary information Rodriguez has on Jaeden Peters. Last year of high school, been a resident of Bethesda ever since he was born, one sister, parents are still married. Though his school performance leaves something to be desired. It doesn't look like Jaeden was planning on college, not like it matters now. Social activities are limited, almost non-existent. From the preliminary information, it doesn't look like Jaeden made much of a dent to a lot of people. It wasn't as if he was the star football player or head cheerleader. He seems like one of those kids who fades into the background of his school, happy to not be the focus of anyone's attention. But he found himself on someone's radar.

"Shame," I finally say. "Where is your man on the fingerprints?"

"He should be working on them now," she says. "Initial autopsy report was done last night, but he hasn't called yet so —" She looks down at her pocket and takes out her phone. "Well, speak of the devil. Rodriguez." She looks at me and nods. "Yep, we'll be right there." She snaps the phone closed. "Autopsy report is ready."

Chapter Fourteen

GIVEN THAT THE CORONER'S OFFICE PROVIDES SERVICES FOR most of the departments in the greater D.C. area, it's a bit of a drive from the Bethesda office. Rodriguez offers to drive us over there and I don't argue. I didn't sleep great last night and already feel like I need another cup of coffee.

"Hell of a case," Rodriguez says as we approach the beltway. "You ever seen anything like it?"

I make a noncommittal motion. "Not exactly, no. Studied a lot of similar cases though. It's how I knew about *The Arrow*. It just took me a minute to remember."

"They were back in the what, late 2000's?"

I nod. "Yep. FBI broke up the cult in 2009, back before I joined." I don't mention I was still in high school myself then. Rodriguez has at least ten years on me, and I don't need her thinking I'm still a rookie.

"So if this isn't the remaining cult members, what are we thinking? Copycat?"

"That's my assumption for the time being," I say. "As soon as we're done with Jameson's report I want to get started on this list. See if any of Ewing's 'fans' have decided to try and make a name for themselves." I rub my temples, doing everything I can to keep this headache at bay.

"You okay?" Rodriguez asks, looking over.

"Yeah, just tired. It was a long day yesterday. Flights always wear me out."

"Not me," she says. "I love flying. Wish I got to do it more often. Guess that's a perk of being a fed."

I scoff. "Actually, my boss wasn't too happy. He would have rather I drove. Of course, it would have taken two full days to visit both prisons and I'd be operating on even less sleep than I am right now. The FBI isn't as loose with its funds as you might think."

"No?"

"Every case I've worked on I've been forced to drive." I chuckle. "And stay in the shittiest, most rundown hotel rooms you've ever seen in your life."

She grins. "You serious?"

"Oh yeah. We in the Bureau don't believe in extra *frills*. If it's good enough for the cockroaches, it's good enough for us."

She laughs aloud. "Wow, and here I was thinking you guys were on easy street over there. Damn. I might need to reconsider."

"Are you looking to join the Bureau?" I ask.

She gives me a shrug. "I've thought about it a few times. What cop hasn't? I love my job and everything, but sometimes I feel like I can do more."

I have to remember I'm not talking to Zara, or Liam. I need to be a better representative of the organization I work for. The organization that I dreamed about working for when I *was* still in high school. "Sorry, I'm making it sound worse than it is. They do treat us well, and the accommodations aren't *that* bad. It's just my boss *really* wasn't happy about me flying yesterday. Especially since it hasn't led to any actionable intel."

"Yet."

"Right, yet," I say.

"I don't mean to be nosy," she says. "But I kind of can't help it. Maybe that's why I do the job I do. But you seem more than just jetlagged."

I can't exactly tell her while I'm dealing with this case, I'm also trying to find information and hunt down the organization who both employed and killed my husband. Nor can I tell her that its members are potentially in some powerful positions across the country, unknown to anyone but themselves.

Or can I?

For some reason, I feel like I can trust this woman. And unlike Zara and Liam, she has no stake in the game. I've looked at Rodriguez's record; she's well-respected in her department and has a few impressive commendations under her belt.

"Actually, there is something else," I tell her. She doesn't prod for me for more, only sits there quietly, waiting me to become comfortable enough to continue. It's a tactic I recognize, one we use all the time with informants.

Without giving myself any more time to back out, I start with Camille, and the fact that she killed Matt, then hunted me for months, before finally turning to me for help. I tell her about the Organization and Zara hunting down Matt's boss, before we found him dead. I tell her about the rest of my family, who had been working for the Organization the entire time, and who were plotting to kill me themselves, seeing as I'd learned too much. I also tell her that the official story around House Representative Kirby's death was a fabrication, made up in order to keep the public from panicking.

When I'm done, she doesn't say a word, only continues to look straight ahead, navigating the mid-morning traffic. Maybe I shouldn't have said anything. I'm not sure why it all came spilling out like that; I'm not usually one to go airing my personal business all over the place. Maybe it's because the only person I've had in my life lately who is older than me and can offer some advice was Janice. And I'm not even sure she's coming back.

"That's...a lot," Rodriguez finally says. She still hasn't looked over, nor has she changed her body posture in any way. I wonder if she thinks I'm full of shit, or if she's just taking the time to process it all.

"A secret organization, with members in government, business, and who knows what else."

"I know," I say. "It sounds crazy. Even me saying it out loud sounds crazy."

"Doesn't sound crazy to me. Have you seen how things operate out there? You think all these people live on the streets because they want to? No, it's because people like that have taken everything away from them. If I were you, I'd be doing the exact same thing. I'd be hunting them down to my last breath."

I can tell there's something more behind what she's saying, something personal. I figure as long as we're sharing...

"Something about that strike a nerve?"

She purses her lips and I feel the car accelerate, but only slightly. "My family doesn't come from much. Grandparents came here looking for a better life, but for people who look like me, it's harder." She glances over at me, and I nod. I can't pretend to know what she or her family has gone through. But I can at least be supportive.

"I was the first kid in my family to get all the way through high school. And then into college where I got enough of a degree that when a chance for detective came along in my department, I was the most qualified. They couldn't deny it. But it was the people like this...organization as you call it, the people who hoard everything for themselves and make things harder for the rest of us...they're the real villains of this world. No wonder they don't want anyone to know who they are. They know their power is in their anonymity."

"That's true," I say. "It seems like secrecy is their biggest asset. If everyone knew who they were and what they'd done…they'd be ruined."

"Then that's the job you need to make for yourself," she says. "Find them and expose them. Show the world who they are and what they've done. Maybe they have enough power to avoid the courts, and maybe they don't. But the court of public opinion is far more powerful."

"Does that mean I can call on you for help when I find myself neck-deep in shit?" I laugh.

"You can count on it," she replies with a grin. "I'll be happy to help you take those bastards down. But I'm sure you have more than enough resources with the FBI."

"Actually," I say, knowing I'm treading on shaky ground. "We're pausing the investigation. My boss says there isn't enough to go on, that they've either disbanded or gone under-ground until the heat dies down."

"And what do you think?"

"That they wouldn't let a little thing like a few of their members being killed stop them. From what Camille told me, Matt's father was involved with these people. Which means they've been around a while. This isn't anything new. And I doubt this is the first time they've faced scrutiny."

"Then you need to double-down," Rodriguez says. "Who cares what your boss says? Was it his spouse who was killed? Or his family who came after him? Does he even understand what you're going through?"

"Unlikely," I say. "He's more of a numbers man. If the numbers work out and make sense, then he's all for it. If it's not in the budget…well…"

She *tsks*, shaking her head. "I hate guys like that. Pencil-pushers. When was the last time he was out in the field?"

"Five years ago, at least," I say.

"Then he has no idea. It's a completely different world now." Rodriguez gets off the at the next exit, slowing the car at the stoplight at the bottom of the ramp. "If it were me, I wouldn't let anything stop me. For my kids' sake at least."

I perk up. "I didn't know you had kids."

She holds up a peace sign. "One's just heading into high school and the other is in middle school."

"How do they feel about you being a cop?" I ask.

"They're proud. I'm a big hit at career day," she says, smiling. "But they know it's dangerous. It's funny. Before them, I wasn't even interested in being a cop. Trying to raise kids in today's world though, it's tough." She looks over. "You have kids?" I shake my head. "It changes everything. I figured the best way I could protect them was to become a cop, to try and make the streets as safe as they could be. But like I said, there's only so much I can do. Only so far my influence will get me. Which is why I've always had my eye on the Bureau."

I turn to her. "It makes sense. Though you might want to make sure you're ready to deal with international assassins and serial killers before you sign up."

"Tell you what," she says. "Give me a grade when this is all over, let me know how I did. And if you think I'd be a good fit, then I'll apply during the next round." She holds out one hand.

I take it, giving it a firm shake. "You got it."

"Good." She turns onto the main thoroughfare, and I see the coroner's office just at the corner of the intersection. "Now let's see if our hunch is right."

Chapter Fifteen

"Jameson," I say, nodding as Rodriguez and I walk into his office next to the morgue.

"Agent. Detective," he says, holding out two identical folders. "These are for you. But I wanted to go over the initial results personally, given the severity of the case."

We take the folders and sit in the seats he offers. He's behind a well-worn desk that sits in front of cases full of books. Jameson himself appears bright-eyed this morning, despite having spent the entire evening on the autopsy. "I received the information about the ID at the same time you did, Detective. No fingerprints on file for Jaeden Peters, but I was able to find his dentist. I'm waiting to hear back on the dental records. As soon as I do, I'll do a thorough comparison and confirm the ID."

"Does the body have any other distinguishing marks?" I ask. "Birthmarks, anything that is unique enough to identify him?"

"Not that hasn't already been cut away." Jameson motions to the folders. "From his medical records, Jaeden had a small mark on the underside of his chin from an accident involving a vehicle when he was a baby. But given the skin was completely removed and we do not have it, I can't provide a positive ID using that method. I'm afraid we're stuck with the dental records. Of course, we could always do a DNA test, but that will take some time and the parents' permission."

"Dental it is," I say, opening the folder and taking a quick look at the initial report. "Blood type is a match."

"Yes," Jameson says. "But it's Type O, the most common."

I look over at Rodriguez. "Hair color, build, skin, eyes, blood type. If this isn't Jaeden Peters, he's had a doppelganger walking around all these years."

Rodrigues nods and turns back to Jamison. "You said you wanted to deliver these in person. Why?"

Jameson hesitates a moment. "How are your stomachs? Okay with seeing some anatomy up close?"

"Not a problem for me," I say.

"Let's see it," Rodriguez says.

"Turn to page three." Jamison sits up in his chair, waiting for us to get there. When we turn to the page, it's full of close-up, graphic photographs of the body and where the cuts were made. On instinct I have the urge to look away, but I force myself to examine the information with a critical eye. I'm not about to let the fact that this was a living, teenage boy just a few days ago distract me. Not if we want to find out who did this.

"Pay attention to the particular types of cuts across the body," Jameson says. "Most notably, the incision down his middle, the largest cut."

I furrow my brow, examining the close-up images. "It looks as though the skin is shredded," I say.

"Very good, Agent," he replies. "Yes, that is what I found. Which means the cut was made with a crude weapon, like an old knife, or perhaps even a serrated blade."

"*The Arrow of Guiding Light*, Ewing in particular, never used a normal knife," I say. "His blades were always sharp as a scalpel to minimize the damage to the body." Rodriguez looks over at me with an arched eyebrow. "I figured if I was going into the lion's den, I better know everything about them. I spent a lot of time studying all the case evidence from the raid on the way up there."

"Makes sense. So our killer then isn't as meticulous as Ewing was."

I shake my head.

"There's more," Jamison says. "Turn to page five please." We do and I see more pictures, this time of the body's back and legs, which I didn't pay much attention to at the crime scene. Most of us were looking at his internal organs.

"He's covered in bruises," I say. "Are these a result of the fluids pooling in the body?"

Jamison shakes his head. "No, this damage was done prior to the boy's death. He was severely beaten, but because of the mutilation of the body, it's difficult to see at first glance."

Beaten before the "ceremony"? That doesn't sound right. "Was he dead when they cut him open?"

Jamison nods. "Almost certainly. He also has some fractures of his ribs, his skull, and his arms and wrists, possibly from fighting back." I recall what Buster Markham told me about the killings he witnessed. He said they were all still alive when Ewing began working on them.

"Is that significant?" Rodriguez asks.

"*The Arrow* would never harm their victims before the ceremonies began," I say. "Each person would be in great health, with no signs of being hurt or punished beforehand. The fact that our killer did this to him before they cut him open tells me they really know nothing about *The Arrow* as a cult at all. That information is out there and available for people to find if they wanted. A few news organizations reported on it back in the day."

"So then…what is this? Our killer leaving his own particular brand of calling card?" she asks.

I shake my head. "I don't know. Why go to all the trouble of trying to re-create a famous cult killing at all if you're going to be doing your own thing?"

"Maybe our killer is saying he's been inspired by Ewing, but wants to make his own mark," she suggests.

"Maybe," I say. "I need to work on our unsub profile, this isn't making a lot of sense." I turn back to Jamison. "Is there anything else?"

"Nothing noteworthy. The liver was removed in much the same manner; carved out rather than removed carefully."

"He was in a hurry," I say. "He didn't have time to go through all the methodical motions that would make this a true *Arrow of Guiding Light* death. It's almost like our killer just did this for shock value and has no real connection to *The Arrow*."

"Couldn't it still be one of those people on your list?" Rodriguez asks.

"Possibly," I say. "And I intend to research them all carefully. But I would think people who are that fanatical would do their due diligence before finally committing to such an act. If they were trying to impress Ewing, they have failed spectacularly." I'm sure someone will eventually get word to him, once the news breaks of this young man's death and the similarities to *The Arrow* killings. The press is going to have a field day when they get a hold of it.

"Another possibility," Rodriguez says. "We could be dealing with someone whose mental issues prevent them from being methodical. This might have been the best they could do."

It's definitely possible, but I'm not sure it tracks. Our killer had to get the body ready and display it in a relatively popular place. Someone who can't pay attention to details is either going to get caught or botch the entire operation. I believe we are working against someone who is smart but may not be as clever as they think they are.

"May we see him?" I ask Jameson.

"Of course, but I don't know why," he replies. "The report is thorough." Jameson is usually solid, though it seems as though I may have hurt his feelings. It's subtle, but the pitch of his voice has changed, and he seems somewhat defensive.

"I'm sure it is," I tell him. "This isn't an indication of your work at all. I just like to get a close look at the victims. There are some things a camera just can't capture."

"Yes, I understand," he says, though I'm not sure he does. He stands and leads us from his office down to the morgue, where there is a wall of drawers. He opens the third one from the left, pulling out a long, metal tray with our victim on it. The units are refrigerated, thankfully, otherwise we'd be dealing with one hell of a smell. Even with the cool air, I still catch a whiff of some of the chemicals Jameson used on the autopsy.

Jameson pulls the sheet back and as he does, his cell phone rings. "Excuse me for a moment, please." While he takes the call, Rodriguez and I examine the body.

"Thoughts?" I ask.

She smiles. "Is this a test or something?"

I shrug. "Just wanted to get your opinion on it."

She takes her time looking over the body. Usually, autopsied bodies have a giant Y-shaped incision in the chest to access the internal cavity. But in this case, since he was already cut open and flayed, Jameson has carefully worked around the initial incision, as not to disturb it and keep the cuts intact for inspection.

"You can see even here that the flesh wasn't cut evenly, like you said," Rodriguez says, pointing at the flesh that had been pulled apart.

"Definitely someone in a hurry," I say, taking the time to examine the boy's jawline, which is completely devoid of flesh.

The killer managed to do a serviceable job of taking the skin off without causing too much damage to the underlying muscle. Which tells me even though they were in a hurry, they have some skill. This isn't an amateur we're working with.

Jameson returns to us, folding his phone into his pocket. "I have just heard from the dental office and they've sent over the records. If you will give me just one more moment, I believe I can confirm if your victim is Jaeden Peters after all."

"If you don't mind," I tell him.

"Not at all. When you are finished, please return him to the drawer." He heads off back to his office.

"Anything else I should be looking for?" Rodriguez asks.

I spend a few more moments examining the body, thinking I'll come across something that perhaps Jameson missed. But the man is good at his job; I have no reason to believe he hasn't been completely thorough. There's just something about this case that is not lining up, and I don't like it when things don't line up.

"Nothing else I can see," I tell her. I pull back the sheet a little further to take a look at the additional damage to the abdominal cavity, and only see what I saw in the original report. "I was hoping for..." I trail off.

"You were hoping for a brand," she says.

I cock my head at her, intrigued.

"I had this rape case a few years back. Guy was snatching girls off the street, having his way, then tossing them back out like nothing had happened. But for the life of me I couldn't get any of them to talk about it, or to admit anything. Half the time I wasn't even sure I was talking to an actual victim because they'd all deny it. The only way we knew it was happening was from bystanders or other witnesses, but there was never anything solid."

"I think I remember that case," I say, screwing up my features. "Didn't the guy abduct the same girls over and over?"

She nods. "Exactly. He kept taking the same ones and we couldn't figure out why until finally one of them came forward. She told us that the first time she'd been abducted, the kidnapper hadn't just raped her, but he'd *married* her. Apparently, he was marrying them all, using a different name for each one."

"What? Why?" I ask.

She shakes her head. "Some kind of harem complex, I think. Thought he'd like having multiple wives. But the way he kept the women quiet was through the courts. He had some scummy state rep on his payroll that authorized all the marriages and made sure that if they ever talked, the husband could sue them for everything they had. And these girls were no older than twenty-two or twenty-three, they didn't know better. Come to find out, he'd been doing this a while, and we even managed to find "old" wives of his that he'd finally divorced and let go. Know how?"

I shake my head.

"He gave each of them a small tattoo, on the inside of their thigh. It wasn't large or flashy, just enough to signify they were his. And he did it to every single one. So when we finally caught the son of a bitch, we had no trouble finding enough witnesses to take him down for good. In all, he'd ended up marrying over forty women during the course of twenty years or so."

"Wow, I never realized it was that extensive," I say.

"It was a while ago," Rodriguez says. "I was still a rookie back then. But it opened my eyes to this world and sick things people will do. But yeah. You're looking for your killer's tattoo. Something that will distinguish them from Ewing and the rest of his people. Something that makes him stand out."

"It might be his signature is the speed in which he kills," I say. "Whereas Ewing took his time, our killer is quicker, and the victim doesn't suffer in the same way. That might be the only difference."

"Where do we go from here?" Rodriguez asks.

I open my mouth to respond, only to see Jameson standing in the doorway.

"I thought you would want to know," he says, his eyes downcast. "It's him."

Chapter Sixteen

"I HATE THIS PART," I SAY AS RODRIGUEZ DRIVES US TO THE Peters' home in the Quail Hollow neighborhood.

"I think I'd be a little scared if you liked it," she replies.

Jameson was able to show us the dental records that came in from Jaeden Peters' dentist and how they were an exact match to the teeth belonging to the young man in the cooler. Jaeden had apparently already had two crowns at his age, both of which were still in place when he died. And he'd also had corrective braces a few years ago, which matched his bite line with the body.

There is no doubt about it anymore, we have a positive ID. But as difficult as it was identifying our victim, what comes next is going to be even worse. But it's part of the job. We have to inform families of their tragedies because more often than not, families are our best lead to finding out who committed this crime. More often than people would think it's a family member themselves, which is why its procedure we don't inform a family alone. At least one of us needs to be watching their reactions, seeing how they take the news. While not everyone grieves in the same way, most people have similar tells when they're not being completely honest. And it's up to me to find those tells.

"Did you talk to them when they made the initial report?" I ask.

Rodriguez shakes her head. "They took it at dispatch and sent it on. I was going to get in contact with them this afternoon to let them know we were looking into it, but that's apparently no longer necessary."

I take a deep breath and pull out my phone, shooting off a text to Zara. I let her know I'd much rather be in her shoes of tracking down an international terrorist than doing this again.

A moment later her text back comes through. It's nothing but a bunch of hearts, but that's all I need it to be. I consider texting Liam too, but decide to hold off until after this is over. This is already turning into one hell of a day.

"Here it is," Rodriguez says as we pull up to the house. "Nineteen eleven Sycamore." It's a standard two-story with a clean lawn and two cars in the driveway. There's a basketball hoop at one end, but it's covered in green algae from years of not being used. From all outward appearances, it seems like a typical family home.

And now we have to go in and completely shatter it.

"If you'd prefer, I can tell them," I say to Rodriguez.

She looks at me like I just kicked her dog. "No, I can handle it," she says, but doesn't elaborate. I realize I probably just questioned her competency without realizing it. She's been a cop longer than I've been part of the FBI; surely she's handled more than one of these kinds of situations before.

"I'm sorry, I didn't mean…" I begin, then start over. "How do you normally handle these types of situations?"

Her features soften. "As straightforward as I can. I go in, don't sugarcoat it, and watch for their reactions. I lend a sympathetic shoulder when I need to."

I nod. "Then yeah, you should definitely be the one to tell them," I say. She continues to look at me when I don't elaborate. "I don't have a problem telling people the worst news of their lives—well, sometimes I do. But where I really fall short is the sympathetic shoulder part. I'm not great with people overall, and despite having done this more times than I care to admit, I still am not the best when the family becomes inconsolable."

"I can understand that. It's not wired into everyone the same way."

"I didn't mean to suggest you couldn't do it," I say. "I think I'm still just worn out from all this…"

"…drama?" she asks with a smirk.

I can't help but smile myself. "Yeah. Apparently, I'm a magnet for it." I look up at the house again. I wouldn't be surprised if they already know we're out here and are just waiting to hear what we have to say. "Ready?"

"No, but are we ever?"

I nod and we both get out of the car at the same time and head up the short driveway to the front door. I take note of the vehicles in the driveway which sparks a thought in my mind. We haven't found a vehicle yet. And the family said he was out on a date.

Rodriguez leads us up to the door and rings the bell. Less than ten seconds later it opens to reveal a woman with curly dark hair, her eyes red-rimmed. She's wearing what look like pajamas and a robe, despite it being close to noon. "Yes?" she asks.

"Ma'am, I'm Detective Rodriguez with the Bethesda Police," Rodriguez says. "May we come in?" Cleverly, Rodriguez doesn't introduce me yet. When people hear *FBI* it can muddle things, and we need to get a clear picture up front if we can.

"Is this about Jaeden?" she asks. "What's going on? Have you found him?"

"It would really be better if we could discuss this inside," Rodriguez says.

"Oh, God," she mutters and opens the door all the way for us, her entire body trembling. "Roger!" the woman calls out. "The police are here!"

"The police?" a man's voice calls from the back of the house. "Do they have him? Have they found him?" He appears around the corner. He's tall, and I notice he has the same color hair as his son, with just a little more gray speckled throughout. He stops short when he sees the two of us, then comes forward, taking his wife by the shoulder. "What's going on? Have you found Jaeden?"

"Is there somewhere we could take a seat?" Rodriguez asks.

I keep my mouth shut, watching their reactions. They take furtive glances at each other, then lead us into their living room, which is tidy, though there are a lot of blankets on the couch, like one of them might have been sleeping here last night.

Roger helps his wife down to the couch while Rodriguez takes a seat across from them and I settle in on the other side of the room. So far they haven't paid me any attention yet, all their focus is on Rodriguez. I take in the room. It seems like a typical middle-class home. There are a few pictures on the walls of Jaeden when he was younger, but the similarities are definitely there. It's him, no question. The pictures also show a girl as well, his younger sister. As I'm looking around I notice I can see the stairs from where I sit. At the top of the landing sits the girl in the pictures, her arms wrapped around her legs. She's looking directly at me and I feel that burst of adrenaline that comes with knowing she can hear everything Rodriguez is about to say.

Maybe another person in my shoes would speak up, at least let the parents know that she was there. But if I were her, I'd want to know. I don't know these people; they may try to keep the truth from her. Or they may tell her outright, in which case the outcome would be no different. I realize it's not our place to step into their family affairs, but I'm not going to betray her secret.

I look away for a moment and I can practically feel the concern of being caught waft off her.

"Please, just tell us," the wife—Shanon—says.

Rodriguez leans forward. "I'm very sorry to tell you this, but your son is dead."

The wife covers her mouth and squeezes her eyes shut, collapsing into sobs as her husband holds her shoulders. Tears are streaming down his face as well, but he's trying to remain strong for her.

I look up to the stairs and see the girl staring at me, even as her eyes shimmer and tears begin to fall.

Rodriguez and I give them all the time they need to process the news. It's never easy, and it's never quick.

"Are you sure it's him?" the father manages to ask between his own sobs. "Maybe if we came down to look—"

Rodriguez shakes her head. "We're sure. We managed to match his dental records. Again, I'm very sorry."

Every few minutes I glance from the couple up to the stairs and back, but so far I haven't seen anything that would make me think anyone in this house knows anything about this. This has come as an absolute shock to them; they were expecting him to be found alive and brought home.

"Can we get you anything? Water?" Rodriguez offers.

Shanon manages to compose herself. "No, no, we should be offering you," she says, though her voice trembles as she does it.

Rodriguez puts a hand on her shoulder. "You don't need to be doing anything right now." She stands and heads to the kitchen. The girl at the top of the stairs disappears somewhere above us, probably to her room, but Rodriguez doesn't see her. She returns a moment later with two full water glasses, handing them to the distraught parents.

The husband takes a few sips, then places the glass on the table. "What happened? Was he in an accident?"

Rodriguez's face turns grim. "I'm afraid not. It appears Jaeden was murdered."

This elicits another wail from Shanon, who drops the glass which spills all over the floor. I get up to find a towel, but the husband's stern look stops me in my place.

"Leave it," he says, then turns back to Rodriguez. "What do you mean, murdered?" His tone and body posture have changed, he's more defensive now, as if he's preparing to fend off a wild animal.

"The condition in which his body was found leaves no doubt," Rodriguez says. "I hate to ask this during such an emotional time, but do you know anyone who might have wanted to hurt Jaeden? Anyone he wasn't getting along with?"

"Yeah, I'll tell you who it was," Roger says, his voice even harder now. "It was those little shits that go to his school, always teasing him about what he's wearing and picking on him for no good reason other than the fact he doesn't happen to play a sport."

Rodriguez pulls out a notepad. "Can you tell me more about that, please?"

"Roger, don't," Shanon says, placing her hand on her husband's arm, but it seems Roger has a bone to pick, and he's not about to let anyone stop him.

"I practically had to drag it out of him," the man says. "A bunch of kids at the high school he goes to. I don't know all their names. But I know one of them is Anthony Armstrong. Him and his little posse."

"What exactly did they do to your son?" Rodriguez asks.

"Jaeden has come home with a black eye more than once," Roger says. "I called the school, but they said there was nothing they could do since there weren't any witnesses. They don't even know if it happened on school grounds. So then I called Armstrong's father. He's one of those prepper-types.

Always has a ton of guns and knives around. Thinks the world's going to end tomorrow."

Rodriguez shoots me a look. I've already made a note to look into Anthony Armstrong and his father. It's not a strong lead, but it's a lead. While I don't think high school kids did this to Jaeden—it's too clean—I'm not going to discount the possibility. Some serial killers get their start young, and there are always signs. We can't discount the possibility that these kids might have had something to do with it.

"What—what happened to him?" Shanon asks.

Rodriguez winces then looks at me. "It's probably better we don't go into detail," she says.

Both parents look at me for the first time. "Why not? What's wrong?" Roger asks.

Rodriguez takes a breath. "Mr. and Mrs. Peters, this is Special Agent Emily Slate, with the FBI. She's been handling your case along with our department to try and find the person or persons who killed your son."

"The FBI?" Roger says. "Why are you involved? What's going on here?"

I lean forward. "Mr. Peters, I'm very sorry to tell you your son was the victim of what looks like a cult killing. We don't have all the details yet, but given how his body was positioned and how it was found, it suggests that it was ritualistic in nature."

"Ritualistic?" Roger asks.

"Who would want to do something like that to Jaeden?" his mother asks.

Roger shakes his head. "It's all that demon paraphernalia he wears," Roger says, still talking about his son in the present tense. "I told him more than once to take that crap off, but I think that just made it worse."

"Can you tell me exactly what you mean?" I ask.

He holds up both his hands. "You know how kids get at this age. He's almost out of high school. I'd hoped he'd grown out of it by now. But he's always wearing these all black outfits, sometimes with eyeliner. And he's always got that damn demon necklace on. As well as those rings of his."

"Rings?" I ask.

Shanon wipes at her eyes. "They're like costume jewelry. Cheap things molded with devil faces or skulls, usually holding a fake jewel. His necklace is a pewter dragon, holding a faux ruby. He probably had it on when—" she begins sobbing again.

I don't tell them that when we found Jaeden, he was completely naked, and had no jewelry on him. The killer must have taken it all with them and disposed of it. Still, those are some specific items. We'll need to put out a BOLO on those in case they happen to show up.

"We'll need a detailed description of everything he had on him when you last saw him," Rodriguez says. "Which was Tuesday night, correct?"

Roger nods.

"Do you know where he went? Who he was going out with?"

"He had a date," his mother said. "With um—Carrie Haines. She's a girl at his school."

I write down the name, as does Rodriguez. "Do you know if he ever got to her house?"

"I don't know," his mother says. "The last we heard from him was when he left. He was upset with me because I'd tried to—tried to—" she breaks into sobs again and Roger takes her hand.

"She just tried to get him to not wear that ridiculous necklace before going out. She just wanted him to look respectable for his date."

"Would you mind if we took a look at Jaeden's room?" I ask.

"If you really think it might help," Roger says. He gets up, stepping over the wet spot and turned-over glass on the carpet and leads us to the stairs. When we reach the top, I notice one of the bedroom doors is closed, the one belonging to their daughter. Inside I can hear music that's been turned up loud. Out of all of them, she might have the hardest time with this, seeing as they looked close to each other in age. I don't know many brothers and sisters who are best friends at this age, but they often rely on each other in a way they don't realize.

At least, that's what I've been told.

Roger pauses at his daughter's room, then thinks better of whatever he was going to do and continues down the hall until we reach the last door. It's already cracked, and he pushes it open for us.

"Have you been in here since Tuesday?" I ask.

He nods. "We went through, looking for anything that might have explained why he didn't come home. But his computer is locked, and he took his phone with him. Other than that, there wasn't much."

That phone has more than likely been destroyed by now. And I doubt we'll have any luck with the computer, but we'll take it anyway, with their permission. It's possible Jaeden got in contact with someone online who decided to target him. I'll also make sure to get the phone information from the parents. I don't expect we'll be able to track it, but we'll try.

His room is what I'd call typical for a teenage boy. And it has that distinctive smell of sweat and body spray mixed together which makes for a somewhat toxic combination. On his walls are posters of bands I've never heard of, but they all seem to lean toward the heavy metal variety. There are also a few black lights, along with a bunch of stickers and a computer setup that would make even Zara jealous. It looks like Jaeden did a lot of online gaming, seeing as he has a two-monitor setup and two different towers running everything. It's also clear he's put a lot of time into caring for the setup as it's the only thing in the room that's clean. Moving this out of here might be more of a job than I thought.

"Did anything in here look out of place when you came to look?" I ask.

Roger shakes his head. "Just as messy as it always is. I couldn't tell any different." He looks behind him and down the hall, then steps into the room with us. "Tell me, how bad is it? What did they do to him?"

Rodriguez drops her voice. "I'm sorry Mr. Peters, I really don't think—"

"I am—was his father, dammit. I deserve to know," he says. His strong jaw is set and I know there's no getting beyond this until we tell him.

"We think he died before he was, displayed," I say, trying to be as tactful as I can. "But they cut him open, from throat to groin. They removed his liver and then they cut off the bottom half of his face, just below the eyes."

His hand goes to his mouth and he looks like he's going to be sick. Perspiration appears on his brow. "My *God*," he finally says. "Who would do—I mean, what's the reasoning behind something...so..."

"That's what we're trying to find out," I tell him. "I would recommend keeping your family away from seeing the body if you can help it. Have him cremated. It will be easier on everyone."

"Won't that—don't you need him for evidence?" he asks.

"We'll let you know when you can take the body," Rodriguez says. "The sooner we have a suspect in custody, the sooner you and your family can move through this process."

He nods again and takes one more look around. "I just wish...he and I, we just never could get on the same page. I guess now it's too late."

"Go be with your family, Mr. Peters," Rodriguez says. "We won't be much longer."

Still looking a little green around the gills, Peters nods and heads back down the hallway. The music coming from his daughter's room hasn't decreased in volume any.

"What do you want to do?" Rodriguez asks once he's out of earshot.

I look around the room. "I don't think we'll get much here. I'll call forensics to come retrieve the computers, maybe they can find something. It's possible he met someone online that decided to target him." I put my hands on my hips and take a deep breath. There are so many different avenues to explore, it's hard to know where to start. We need to go with our strongest lead first, but there might be a way to split this work up some.

"In the interest of time, I think we should split up. You work on this Anthony Armstrong and whatever group he's running around with. Let's see if we can't at least eliminate him. I'll find the girl he was supposed to go on a date with. She might have been the last person to see him alive."

"And the list?" Rodriguez asks.

I give her a smile as I know just what to do. "We'll outsource it."

Chapter Seventeen

AFTER LUNCH ON FRIDAY, I GET RODRIGUEZ TO DROP ME OFF at my car and then head over to Jaeden Peter's school to try and find Carrie Haines. She's probably a senior like he was, and I know how often seniors either don't have classes on Friday afternoons or just outright skip. I'm just hoping Carrie is more of the studious type as I really don't want to try and track her down at her home.

To get in the front door during school hours I have to show my badge to the security guard out front. It's a sad state that we live in that people can't come and go from schools anymore, but until something big changes, I don't see it getting any better. I find the office easily enough and inform the office assistant who I'm looking for. Thankfully, unless she's ditched, Carrie should still be in her study hall before her last class of the day. The assistant offers to call her up to the office which is a better plan than me pulling her out of her study hall myself.

Five minutes later I'm waiting out in the main hall when I hear the click of heels coming down the hallway. A girl, who barely looks any younger than me, struts my way. She's wearing honest-to-god high heels and her skirt is barely long enough to leave anything to the imagination. She has bright blonde hair that comes down past her shoulders and is carrying both a purse and a roller bag behind her. She looks more like something out of a fashion magazine than a high school student, but then again, that's how things were trending even when I was in high school.

But as I watch her make her way to the office, I can't believe this is Carrie Hines. At least, I can't believe that someone like her would go on a date with Jaeden Peters, given the *vastly* different social circles they must come from. I was expecting some goth girl with purple hair and a black tank top that says "abort the patriarchy" on it.

Then again, I've been wrong in my initial assumptions before.

"Carrie Haines?" I ask, approaching her.

She glares at me like I'm wasting her time, but stops, nonetheless. "Yes?"

I pull out my badge and show it to her. "Can I have a word with you for a moment?"

She huffs, then sets her rolling bag upright and crosses her arms. "Are you why I was called to the office?" I nod. "What does the FBI want with me?"

She's more brash than I'd expected too. Carrie comes across to me as someone who is used to getting their way. "Do you know Jaeden Peters?"

"I *knew* him," she says, her mouth turning in disgust. "But now he's dead to me."

I perk up, examining her closely. "Why do you say that?"

"Because the jerk never texted me back!" she yells, then realizes how loud she's being. She lowers her voice. "You don't just do that to someone. Not to mention he hasn't been back to school for three days. I'm done with him; he had his chance."

"When was the last time you spoke with Jaeden?"

"Tuesday night, when he dropped me off," she says, then furrows her brow. "Wait, what's this about?"

"So you did go on the date?" I ask. "He picked you up at your house in a blue Jeep Wagoneer, is that correct?" Jaeden's parents gave us all the information on the vehicle he was driving that night, which I've also put a BOLO out on.

"Yeah. We went to play mini golf. Then he took me back home and I haven't heard from him since."

"Did something happen on the date?" I ask.

She looks around, like she's afraid someone might be listening. "No, it was actually really nice. Or, at least I thought it was. I thought he felt the same way. Guess not."

"Tell me what happened." I'm keeping an even voice and doing everything I can to keep her talking. I know once I tell her what happened to him, there's a possibility she may clam up. But knowing that they actually made it out on the date is very helpful. That narrows the possibilities of when and where the murder could have taken place.

"There's nothing to tell. He picked me up around seven. We grabbed some food quick, then went and played golf. I kicked his ass on every course. Then he brought me back home. That's it."

"Nothing else happened?" I ask. "He didn't try something that made you feel uncomfortable? It's okay if he did, I'm just looking for a complete picture."

"Jaeden?" She laughs. "No. I think he was *afraid* to touch me. He's not the kind of guy who does that. Trust me, I could tell you some stories about some of the guys here. But he's not one of them."

"So what happened at the end of the date? Did he just go home?"

She uncrosses her arms. "As far as I know." She reaches into her purse and produces a small pendant on a chain. It's of a dragon holding a faux ruby. "He gave me this before he left. I thought it meant he liked me. But I already decided, as soon as I see him again, I'm giving it back. You don't just ghost someone like that."

"Did you talk to Jaeden anymore that night? Either on the phone or by text?"

"I…uh, I sent a few texts, but never heard back," she says. "I thought he'd gone to sleep. But then when I didn't hear anything by Wednesday I got pissed. I called a few times, but never left a message." She looks around and huffs again. "Can you please tell me what's going on?"

Technically she's not family, nor was she and Jaeden in any serious relationship. Telling her the truth won't do anything to further this investigation and may indeed hamper it. I can't take that risk, not right now.

"He's…missing," I tell her. "And his parents are concerned."

"Missing? Like he didn't come home?" I nod. "Have you checked all the roads? There was that big storm that night, he had to drive back in it." Her entire body posture has changed. Where she was defensive before, now she's completely morphed into concern.

"We're still working on it," I say. "Do you happen to know which direction he drove when he left your house?"

She shrugs. "I dunno, um toward the old gas station, I guess. The one that sits at the end of my neighborhood."

I'll have to look up the map for her address, as I'm not familiar with where she lives. "Did he give you any indication anything was wrong that night? Or that he was going anywhere other than home?"

"No, I'm pretty sure he was going straight back."

"What makes you say that?" I ask.

"I just…he told me, in a way," she replies.

I take a deep breath. I don't have time for these kinds of games. "Carrie. Tell me what you know."

"Okay, jeez," she says, holding up one hand. "We fooled around in the car for a minute. Trust me, I know how good I am. He was nearing his peak and ready to blow, get it? I feel like he wanted to get home as fast as possible."

"Right, got it," I say. "All right. If you think of anything else, please let me know." I hand her my card.

"I can set up search parties from here," she says as I turn to head back to the car. "Trust me, I can get a lot of people to do what I want. Whatever you need to help find him…"

"Thanks, but we have it covered," I tell her. "I'll let you know if you can help in any other way."

As I leave, she's holding herself tighter than when I first saw her. I know what she'll be thinking, which will only be confirmed as soon as Bethesda Police releases the story to the media. But I want to hold off on doing that as long as we possibly can. Someone out there is looking for attention, and until I have a better understanding of who and why, I don't want them getting the spotlight. It might encourage them to strike again.

As I head back outside, I realize I need one more piece of information before I proceed. I head back into the school and back into the office once more, noticing Carrie has already dispersed somewhere.

"Oh, Agent Slate, did you find Ms. Haines?" the office manager asks.

"I did, thank you. But I still need one piece of information. Could you please give me her home address?"

Chapter Eighteen

"You look like you've had a day," Liam says as I come through the door. My apartment smells like minced garlic and rosemary, and honestly I don't think I've ever smelled anything better.

I smile when I see his face. "When I said to make yourself at home, I didn't actually think you'd do it."

He walks around the kitchen peninsula and hands me a glass of whiskey, with a large piece of ice in it. "That's what happens when you give your boyfriend a key."

"Is it?" I ask. Before I can take a sip, Timber nearly plows into me, his butt going a million miles per hour. "Hey there, bud." I give him a few good hard pats on the side.

"He's already been out and fed," Liam says. I can't help but glare at him. "What?"

"Is this because you feel guilty about the other night?"

"There might be an element of guilt," he says, and then he gives me the deepest, most sensual kiss I've ever had. "Then again I might have just missed you."

It takes me a moment to gather my bearings as he heads back into the kitchen. I haven't even put my bag down yet.

"Just gonna do that and leave me hanging, huh?" I ask, setting my stuff down on a nearby chair and taking my blazer off.

"Yep. A cook's work is never done."

"It smells delicious," I say. "What are we having?"

"Seared flank steak with au gratin potatoes and a side salad." He looks over his shoulder at me, grinning. "And a surprise for dessert."

I honestly was not expecting this at all when I came home. After the day I've had, I figured I would probably just come home and hit the sack. But Liam being here has invigorated the evening with new life and I find myself wide awake.

"Kick your feet up, this is going to be a few minutes," he says.

"Actually, I think I'll change," I say, taking a brief sip of the drink. It's smooth. Smoother than anything I have in the house. Did he bring this with him? Who is this man?

Timber follows me into my bedroom, still vying for my attention as I begin stripping off my clothes. After everything at the school and dealing with the emotions of both Carrie Haines and the Peters family, I'm absolutely drained. I thought about heading out to try and track down Jaeden Peters vehicle, but another storm has rolled in, and I'll have better luck tomorrow morning.

The fact that Liam was here waiting for me must have meant he spoke to Zara, as I called her after everything at the school. While I'm glad her case is going well, I miss her expertise and just her in general. Even though Rodriguez is there, I feel like I'm all on my own for this one, which is both something I crave and also something I don't do great with. I know how contradictory that sounds. I know how contradictory it *feels*. I guess it's just all part of that ongoing battle inside me that never seems to end. That pull between needing only myself and needing others.

But tonight I'm glad I'm not alone.

I pull on some workout leggings and an oversized sweat-shirt, as it's started to get a little chilly outside and when that happens, no matter how warm it is inside, I start dressing for fall. It always seems like the shortest season.

I give Timber a head rub before heading back out. "You like Liam, don't you?" I ask him. He just looks at me with those big brown eyes of his, and that little round head. "Yeah, I don't want to leave either." I drop my voice to a whisper. "But we'll deal with that later, won't we?"

I head back out into the living room and again the smell of the food hits me. It's practically intoxicating. "Either I'm really hungry or that smells like the best flank steak ever."

Liam grins. I notice he has a matching glass of whiskey beside the stove. I grab mine from the counter, taking another sip. "Wanna talk about it? Your day? Looks like it was a tough one."

"Just that we had to inform the family after we got a positive ID on our victim," I tell him. "You know how that goes."

He turns to me. "It's never easy. I feel like they should have professional counselors that specialize in that. People who are experts at helping families cope."

"Especially with these cases," I say. "It's bad enough to learn your kid has been killed in something like a car accident, but to know he was targeted and murdered…especially in this way, it adds an entirely new dimension of grief. Trust me, I know."

"Any luck on a suspect?"

I shake my head. "I've got my list from the prison. And the parents pointed us to some kids who had been harassing him at school. There's also the possibility of an online predator; he was big into gaming. Honestly, the possibilities are almost endless."

"How has it been working with a local cop again?" he asks, smirking.

I point my glass at him. "A lot less of a pain in the ass than you were."

"Ouch." He takes a sip. "Maybe you can get her over here to cook you dinner."

"Nah," I say, smiling and leaning forward. "Too much trouble. Especially when I seem to already have you trained."

He leans in and we kiss again until something crackles and pops on the stove and he turns to flip the steaks.

"What about your day? Anything exciting?"

"Not really," he says. "Wallace has me working on prepping surveillance for a new operation, but I don't know a lot about it. Right now, it's just a lot of grunt work."

I shake my head. "I wish we could get Janice back. I know the whole DuBois thing happened on her watch, but c'mon. No one would have seen that coming. If they're going to suspend her, they might as well suspend all of us."

He begins plating the food. "It's all politics. Someone needs to be the scapegoat, even if it's meaningless. Do you think they'll let her keep her job with the Bureau?"

"I'd be willing to bet she gets offered a severance, though it will probably be generous enough that she doesn't raise a stink. Then again, I wouldn't want to be on Janice's bad side. That's just asking for trouble."

As we sit down, the smell of the food both makes my mouth water and puts me in a kind of trance. I'm so used to eating whatever is convenient, I forgot what a properly prepared meal smelled like. You can only eat take out for so long before you become numb to it. But this has reignited my senses and I can't wait to dig in.

"Thank you," I say. "You didn't have to do any of this."

Liam smiles. "I know. But you're so easy to bribe."

I give him a stern look. "Seriously. I really appreciate this. It's…above and beyond."

"Well, I figured we might as well go out on a bang. That's the term, right?"

"Close enough," I tell him.

"Eat up, you don't want it to get cold."

As I pick up my fork and Timber lays his head on my leg, looking up at me and hoping for a bite, I realize it's not just the food that I've become bewitched by. It's the whole experience. Coming home, having someone here again, sharing a meal together, the house filled with more than just my neuroses. I could get used to this very easily. And I have to decide if it's something worth leaving my career over. I could stay here, with Liam, but it would mean giving up everything I've ever worked for. Deep down I know I can't do that. But at the same time, it's so very tempting. My only hope is to somehow try and ingratiate myself toward Wallace and hope he has a change of heart. But I'm not the best at kowtowing to people, and as Zara likes to remind me, I often have to pull back on the abrasiveness…if I want things to go my way. Despite everything I think I've achieved; I'm still living in a world dominated by powerful men who like to use words such as "emotional" and "hysterical" when women say or do things they don't like.

I'm not sure I can do that. I'm not even sure I want to. But to keep *this* in my life, to have a sense of normalcy after all the shit I've been through…it almost might be worth it.

"Emily?" Liam asks. "Is something wrong with the food?"

I look down and realize I still haven't taken a bite. I carve a small piece and place it in my mouth only to discover an explosion of flavor and juices. This man is some kind of cooking god. And this food is like a drug. For a brief second, I almost reconsider it all.

"It's perfect," I tell him. "Absolutely perfect."

Chapter Nineteen

THE FOLLOWING MORNING, I'M UP EARLY AND REINVIGORATED. The meal and the company were just what I needed to help me process the emotional weight from yesterday. This morning I'm feeling better, clearer-headed, and more energetic than I have in weeks. I've almost completely forgotten about the Organization. Maybe this is what it takes. A stable home life, fulfilling work, and good friends are all ingredients I've been missing in some form or another ever since before Matt. Even when we were married, there must have been some subconscious part of me that knew something wasn't right. Because spending this time with Liam has shown me a brand new way I hadn't even known was possible before.

Maybe I really can let it all go.

I haven't heard from Rodriguez by the time I reach Carrie Haines' house, despite calling and leaving a message. I figure she's probably got her hands full tracking down Armstrong and his friends. While my meeting with Haines yesterday wasn't particularly illuminating, it did help me narrow down a timeline of the events of Tuesday evening. As best I can tell, Carrie probably was the last person to see Jaeden alive, other than his killer. And we now know his murder definitely took place after eleven p.m. that night.

Since I already spoke with Carrie yesterday, there's no need for me to go back in and question her again. I doubt she has much to add to her story anyway. Instead, I'm hoping to figure out what happened to Jaeden's 1998 Jeep Wagoneer that his parents said is still missing. I checked with the local junkyards as well as the surrounding police departments. No one has found an abandoned vehicle that matches the description of his car.

So then where did it go?

Now that I'm in Carrie's neighborhood, I see the gas station at the end of the block she was talking about. Which at least gives me a direction to try and follow Jaeden's path. I leave Carrie's house in the direction of the gas station, while looking at a GPS map that shows the shortest route between Carrie and Jaeden's houses. It's about a fifteen-minute drive, and there's no guarantee he took the shortest path, but still, I feel like it has to be worth investigating.

At the gas station I take a right, following along a main thoroughfare. It's busy enough out here that it's unlikely anything would have happened, even at that time of night. It's too exposed, and I don't see the vehicle anywhere as I drive. Following the GPS, I make the next left onto a side street that takes me alongside a creek bed. Today the creek is almost overflowing from all the rain last night. When I reach the bottom of the hill, there are caution placards up at the bridge, which looks like it has recently flooded. I stop the car a minute and get out, looking at the small bridge that dips down where the creek runs, then continues to the other side.

If this bridge was flooded last night and has just been cleared, then there's a good chance it was flooded Tuesday night as well. And seeing as the GPS is taking me straight over the bridge, Jaeden would have needed to find another way around. I suppose it's possible he could have risked it, and his car could have been washed away, but that wouldn't explain how he got out of the river and became the victim of some sadistic killer. Jameson didn't mention anything about any water in his lungs or any of the other markers consistent with someone drowning.

I'm forced to conclude Jaeden didn't come this way that night. I get back into the car and re-route the GPS, showing me the next-quickest way to get back to his house. If he was as "wound-up" as Carrie said he was, he wouldn't have wanted to linger. The GPS gives me a five-minute detour, which takes me through a wooded section of town—one devoid of any other houses.

The road twists and turns, and there's not even a stripe on this section, which means it doesn't get a lot of traffic. It's taking me through what looks like a neighborhood park, where all the trees have already turned their colors for fall. It's beautiful through here, all those reds and oranges, and for a second I forget why I'm out here. I follow the road over another, much higher one-lane bridge back over the same creek, and find myself in a thick set of trees that almost seem to bear down on the road itself. Driving along this at eleven o'clock in a downpour would have been difficult, to say the least. Especially for a young driver, which means he was probably forced to slow down. I slow as well, keeping a sharp eye out for anything that might be out of the ordinary.

About half a mile past the bridge, I bring the car to a stop. The thick overgrowth on one side seems to have a portion where it's been cleared. Or at least pushed to the side. I stop the car and get out again, this time examining the crushed branches and smashed overgrowth. I think if I wasn't looking for it, I never would have seen it, but something definitely smashed a lot of the foliage here away. And when I look down, I see two tread marks in the dirt, leading away from the road.

As a precaution, I pull out my weapon but keep it by my

side as I make my way into the undergrowth. The sounds of nature are all around me, oblivious to my presence. Once I'm past the initial growth at the street, it opens up a little, but not much. But the path in front of me is unmistakable. Something large pushed through here, snapping branches and crushing the underbrush. All the while I'm following the tracks in the dirt-slash-mud. My heart is racing, because somewhere deep inside I know what this is leading to. It can't be anything else. And almost before I see it, I sense the Jeep, sitting deep within the woods all by itself, completely hidden and isolated from the waking world.

Even though it's unlikely anyone is still around, I keep my weapon out as I approach the vehicle. All the doors are closed, and it doesn't seem disturbed in any way, other than the fact it's out here in the middle of nowhere. Using the flashlight on my phone, I look into the interior of the car, but nothing looks out of place. There's also no sign of Jaeden's phone on initial inspection. But maybe when we get inside the vehicle it will turn up.

Then again, I'm never that lucky.

I pull a glove out of my pocket and slip it on, after holstering my weapon. Gingerly I try the doors, but they're all locked. But when I give the driver's side door a bit of a yank, it pops open, even though the button is down. I take a whiff inside the car, but don't smell anything that would lead me to believe Jaeden was killed in here. In fact, it seems unre-markable.

I need to get my curiosity under control before I disturb something. I take care not to disturb anything else and remove the glove again before calling the FBI's forensics team.

"Slate, you always get the weirdest cases," Caruthers says as he approaches the vehicle. He's brought a three-person team with him and they're getting all their equipment set up, preparing to take any evidence from the scene.

"Yeah, my luck seems to go that way, doesn't it?"

"I can already tell you that whoever put this car in here did it by hand. Probably put it in neutral and rolled it in here before locking it up."

I look around, trying to find the answer before asking him. "No secondary tire tracks?"

"That's part of it, and also look at the treads in the mud. A vehicle under its own power would have made deeper indentations from the torque pushing the thing forward. But we happen to have all these convenient shoe patterns beside the tracks, which are deeper, and indicate someone was pushing and steering at the same time."

"So they rolled it in here to keep it from being found," I say. "And they wanted it done quietly. My question is, how did they get to Jaeden in the first place if he was driving?"

Caruthers walks over to the front door, which is still open from when I yanked on it. He bends down, inspecting it for a second. "Take a look at this. The frame around the latch is slightly bent here. It could prevent the door from securing all the way."

"So someone could have pulled him out of the car," I say. "But that means they would have to have known about this damage."

Caruthers turns to me. "Either that, or they were determined to get to him no matter what, and the door wasn't as much of an obstacle as they expected."

Right. That tracks. I should have thought of that. But this whole thing continues to confuse me. If Jaeden was targeted, how did the killers manage to track him down to this specific place? Did they know he'd be coming back from Carrie's house and have to take a longer, more secluded way home because of the storm? And if so, how could they have predicted that?

The more about this case I learn, the less of it makes sense to me. I'm not seeing a big piece of the puzzle, and it's driving me insane.

"Slate!" I look over to see Rodriguez pushing through the undergrowth. I thank Caruthers and head to meet her halfway. "Found the car? Good work."

"I had a hunch after speaking with the girlfriend yesterday," I say. "Well, not formal girlfriend. But I'm pretty sure she was the last person to see him alive other than his killer. She confirmed they had their date and he headed home after. Seems like someone caught up with him between there and his house."

"Are you thinking this is where he was killed?" she asks.

I look around. "I don't think so. I think this is where he was taken, and his car ditched. But remember Jamison mentioned all the bruising. I think he was probably beaten then taken to another location before he was killed and... displayed." I cock my head at her. "How did you find me out here?"

"Oh, I called your office, spoke with someone named Zara. She's an animated one. She told me you'd just called your forensics department out here."

"Sounds like Zara," I say. "I would have called you, but I didn't want to be the kind of person to leave a bunch of messages."

Rodriguez looks to the side. "Sorry about that. I was busy tracking down that Armstrong kid all day yesterday, then I had something of a...family emergency. All clear now, though."

"Everything okay?" I ask.

"Sure, sure. Just my oldest daughter. Teen drama. You know how it is."

I shrug. "I guess I knew how it *was*. But I don't know what it's like to try and parent that."

Rodriguez smiles. "More or less impossible. You learn to live with the failure."

I can't help but chuckle. "What did you find on Armstrong?"

"Right," she says, pulling out her notepad, like she's just remembered. "You're not going to like this. I was able to discern that Armstrong hangs out with a group of three other boys, which I believe are the same ones Mr. Peters was talking about yesterday. These four do everything together. But the bad news is all four of them have records."

"All *four*?" I ask, incredulous.

"Yep. And two of them are minors, so I can't get a look at anything. The other two, Armstrong being one of them, are no longer minors obviously, but whatever they did, they did it before they turned eighteen, so I can't get a look at that either. We'll need a judge to unseal those records, and right now we don't have nearly enough to do that. I don't even know if we can call these four suspects."

I shake my head. "Not unless we have some concrete proof they were threatening Jaeden. Let's check the FBI database before we do anything else, just to make sure we're not missing something obvious. Maybe there's something in there on one of them that will give us a clue as to what's in those records."

"Do you really think it could have led to this?" she asks.

I look over at Caruthers measuring the size of the footprints left behind. Even though it's unlikely this was done by a bunch of teens, psychopaths often get their starts young, and can also recruit others to assist, even without the others really knowing why. It's possible Armstrong or one of the others is a natural-born killer and has zero empathy for anyone, making it much easier for him to kill. The way in which the body was staged did feel very purposeful, but I don't want to jump to any conclusions. Hopefully Caruthers and his team will find something here that can help narrow our suspect pool.

"I don't know," I tell her. "I guess anything is possible."

Chapter Twenty

"I USUALLY DON'T LIKE TO ADMIT WHEN I'M AWESTRUCK, BUT in this case, I don't think I can help it," Rodriguez says as we head into the J. Edgar Hoover Building.

"Never been in here before?" I ask.

"I think I took a tour once, when I was a kid," she says. "Why else would I be here?"

I shrug as I lead her down to the elevator bank. "I just figured it wasn't your first time working with the FBI and maybe you'd wrangled yourself a trip."

She gives me a sly smile. "I'm not that pushy."

We take the elevators up to my office and push through the double doors. Being a Saturday, things are calmer than on the weekdays, but there are still a lot of agents around, all working their cases. I look over to Wallace's office and see the lights are off and the door closed. I breathe a sigh of relief; at least I won't have to deal with that today.

"This is me, right here," I say, showing Rodriguez my desk. "Have a seat right there, let's see if we can't find anything on these four."

Rodriguez takes a minute to soak it all in, then places her hands on her hips. "Yeah, I could see myself doing this job.

This is where the real work gets done." I look over and notice Zara's station is active as well, but she's not at her desk. As I'm looking, I spot her coming back from the bathrooms on the other side of the room.

"Well look who finally decided to come back and do some of all this work she saddled me with," Zara calls out for the entire office to hear.

"Yeah, how's that going by the way?" I ask with a smarmy grin, my voice just as loud.

She narrows her eyes. "Oh, I'll tell you. But you know what it'll cost you."

I groan. "Aw, c'mon. Can't you do a friend a favor without dragging her to that stupid karaoke bar again?"

"Nuh-uh, not karaoke. Not this time, sister," Zara says. "This time, it's serious. I'm taking you to this club where you can show off your best TikTok dance."

I place my head on my desk. "For the love of God, please no."

"Oh yes, you're gonna be shaking your ass for the camera all day long," she says, taking her seat across from us. I look back up and she has a wicked grin across her face. Then she seems to notice Rodriguez for the first time and stands back up, holding out her hand. "Hi, I'm Zara."

"We spoke on the phone," Rodriguez says, giving her a firm shake.

"Watch out, you're shaking hands with the devil and don't even know it," I tell her.

"Don't mind her, she's just a grade-A introvert. Do you realize how much work it takes to pull someone out of their shell?" Zara says.

Rodriguez smiles. "I can see you two have something of a rapport."

"In all seriousness," I say. "Zara was there for me when no one else was. She's a better friend than I deserve."

"Aw, Em," Zara says and comes around the desk and

wraps her arms around my neck, squeezing me tight. "Okay, no TikTok dancing. But you still owe me."

"I'll get you a really nice bottle of wine," I say as she lets go.

"And I will drink that will glee," she replies. "So what are you two doing here? I figured you'd be out looking over Caruthers' shoulder while he inspects your vehicle."

"Doing some recon on potential suspects," I tell her. "We've got four minors, well two minors and two legal adults who committed crimes as minors, but their records are sealed. We were going to check in the database, see if we could find anything, known associates, stuff like that."

"In other words, my specialty," she says, cracking her knuckles.

I shake my head. "Oh no, you're already going through one list for me. I'm not putting you on double duty." I pause when she doesn't respond. "You *are* looking through that list, aren't you?"

She chuckles, opening her drawer and tossing me a stack of stapled papers. "Of course I am. And I finished at two a.m. this morning."

"Z! I didn't mean for you to work through the entire night. It's the weekend."

She waves me off. "It's fine. Doing work helps to keep me from staring into the abyss, you know, now that you have a boyfriend and all. Speaking of which, how did that go last night?"

I can already tell my face is beet red. Normally I'm used to Zara's antics, but with Rodriguez right here, I suddenly feel like a teenager again. While I know age doesn't matter, I can't help but want Rodriguez to respect me. And my age, along with my looks makes that hard for some people. The last thing I want is for her to think I'm not a professional at my job.

"I'll let him know you said hello," I tell Zara, hoping she'll get the hint. She squints at me a moment, then seems to realize something is off. Whether she gets it completely, I'll find out later, but she clears her throat and sits up in her seat.

"Thanks. So can I help?"

"Don't you want to go home? Especially if you were up until two a.m.?"

"Home is overrated," she says. "Gimmie some names."

I exchange a look with Rodriguez. "She's really good at this stuff. And as you can see, it's hard not to let her help."

Rodriguez chuckles. "I wish people in my department were as forthcoming. It's like pulling teeth over there just to get the most basic thing done."

"Oh, it's like that here too," Zara says. "I just prescribe to a different way of life. Plus, Em and I made a pledge to each other that just because something has been done one way in the past, we weren't going to keep doing it that way if it didn't make sense. We're trying to help bring the FBI into the twenty-first."

"All on your own?" Rodriguez asks.

Zara and I share a look. "I mean, there are a few others who help. Liam."

Zara points at me. "Caruthers is one."

"I think we could get Sutton on board," I say, leaning back in my chair.

"And Holsey. Over in payroll. She's a good one." Zara turns back to Rodriguez. "But yeah, it's pretty much just us."

I figure by this point Rodriguez has probably heard enough from the both of us, but she just keeps smiling. It's a smile that reaches her eyes, and she shakes her head a little as if she can't believe any of it. "This really isn't what I was expecting from the FBI."

"Good or bad?" I ask.

"Good. A thousand times, good," she says. "Do you know what a relief it is to hear something like that from people who are already in the field? You hear it from the public all the time, but to know that there are people like you, actively trying to change a culture that has existed for…I don't know…ever since law enforcement began? Where can I sign up?" She's animated, her eyes wide and excited. It's the first time I've seen her anything but absolutely serious.

"Jeez, Em. Wallace should send you out on recruiting trips," Zara says. "First Liam and now our new friend here."

"What does she mean?" Rodriguez asks.

I shoot Zara a look. "I partnered up with another local officer a few months back. He ended up joining the Bureau and works in this office now. But it was just the one."

"Sounds like my odds are pretty good, then," Rodriguez says.

Zara holds out her hand, clamping it open and closed like a fish waiting to be fed.

I sigh. "Give her the names."

Rodriguez opens her notepad. "Armstrong, Anthony. Parkinson, Joey. Delgado, Thomas. Hawes, Richie."

"Got 'em. Give me just a few minutes," she says and goes to work on her computer.

"They're not going to believe a word of this back in my department," Rodriguez says.

I try to play it off like it's just another normal day. "We still work as hard; we just do it in different ways. At least, Zara and I do."

"Looks pretty good to me," she says. "Where's the application form?"

"Just like that, huh? What's kept you from signing up before?"

She looks away for a few minutes. "To be honest, my children. I figured a job with the Bureau would take me away too much, especially when they were little. I didn't want them growing up with a sitter as their primary caregiver. But they're a little older now. Old enough where at least one of them is sick of me being around all the time." She looks off into the distance and I imagine for the first time how this case must be hitting her. Jaeden probably wasn't much older than her own children. No wonder she was able to console both of the parents as effectively as she did.

"I'm sorry, I didn't consider what kind of impact this case must be having on you."

She gives me a quick smile and looks down. "It's no big deal. This is the job, right? We do what we're supposed to."

"Okay," Zara says, causing us both to turn our heads.

"Already?" Rodriguez says, surprise in her voice. "That was fast."

"Yep, fast and good, but not cheap," Zara replies. "So I found the sealed records, we're not going to get anything there obviously. But I did find out that Richard Hawes has an uncle who is part of a local biker gang. I don't know if there's any connection there or not and there's no way to tell if that had anything to do with this. But Richard is over eighteen, which means you could always question him about it."

"What about Armstrong?" I ask. "The father was adamant about him."

"Other than this one incident, his record is clean. Of course, he's also the star of the school's football team. I'm not saying there's a coverup going on, but I wouldn't put it past a school that is known for its football program to cover up for players."

"Is it?" I ask. "Known for its football program?"

She looks at the screen. "Franklin Pierce High School has been notable for sourcing many student athletes who go on to have illustrious college and professional careers." She looks up. "That's from their website."

I rub my hands down my face. "None of this tracks. What would a football star and his cronies want to kill Jaeden for? Is there anything on their socials? Anything threatening?"

Zara's hands fly over the keyboard again, running through various search programs as she types. "Nothing that stands out. Peters wasn't very active on social media, so there aren't a lot of posts for people to comment on. Looks like he was more of a lurker."

"That fits with what we know about him," Rodriguez says.

"Great, so now we have to go interview these guys and try to figure out if one of them is a psychopath in disguise?" I ask. "That won't be awkward at all with their parents around."

Rodriguez turns to me. "What do you think the odds of another killing are?"

"I have no way of knowing. From the initial scene I thought it was pretty good, but it's already been four days and we haven't found another body yet, so I'm thinking there's something else going on here. The longer we go, and no other body is found, the more it confounds the case. Why?"

"If there's no immediate threat, then why not wait until Monday when they're all back in school? That way we can interview them all at the same time, try to play them off each other and see if we can't get one to break."

"And that will give you time to go over that booklet I conveniently put together," Zara says, nodding at the stack of papers she handed me.

"Was there anything noteworthy in any of this?" I ask, holding up the packet.

"Hard to say. I didn't want to draw conclusions for you, you'll have to go through it and see if you think any of that is legitimate or if it's all a bunch of big talk."

"That settles it then," Rodriguez says, getting up. "We'll reconvene Monday morning at the school where we can go after these four. I'd say we should have a good idea within an hour or two if we have anything serious on our hands. In the meantime, I'll be happy to take half of that and go over it at home."

I turn to Zara, and she shrugs. I pull the packet apart and give half the reports to Rodriguez. "Nothing like embodying the new FBI spirit, right?"

"Not at all," I tell her, and put the rest of the reports in my own bag. "Thank you."

"I'm happy to do it," she says. "Can I get out with this?" She points to her visitor pass.

"Sure, you remember the way?"

"Absolutely. Though I can't promise I won't stand around and gawk longer than I probably should. See you on Monday?"

"See you then," I say. She gives us a short wave and then heads out, disappearing through the double doors.

"Well, well," Zara says. "Looks like the rest of your weekend is free."

I turn to her, immediately on alert. "No, it isn't."

"Oh, yes, it is," she says, getting up as well, eyeing me like a tiger who has spotted its prey. She comes over to my side of the desk and grabs both of my arms in an attempt to pull me up. "Dead or alive, you're coming with me."

"I knew you were lying about those dances!" I yell at her.

We continue to struggle until she finally wins out, getting me out of my seat. While ninety-nine percent of me doesn't want to go with her, I'm grateful for the distraction.

Maybe it won't be so bad. But it probably will.

Chapter Twenty-One

THE FOLLOWING MORNING, I'M SITTING IN THE J.R.'S DINER, nursing a headache the size of Mount Vesuvius. It turns out Zara's "club" was a place filled with twenty and thirty-somethings all looking for a little more than what I had in mind. It took a large quantity of alcohol before I finally began to relax and after that most of the night is fuzzy, punctuated by random memories of guys coming up to our table and us needing to shoo them away. I also feel like I may have sprained the arm of a particularly insistent individual but that could have been a dream.

I don't know why I let her drag me to places like that. I'm almost thirty and even though I'm not what anyone would call "old", it's not as easy as it used to be. Nor is it as enjoyable. Not that it ever was. Give me a quiet bar where I we can talk over a loud club blasting music and artists I've never heard of any day.

Thankfully, the black roast coffee is doing wonders for my head, which feels like someone has placed a drum inside and is beating it over and over again.

"Morning," a man's voice says. Before I can look up, he

slides into the booth across from me, a smile permeating through his thick, gray beard.

"Can I getcha' something to drink, hon?" a waitress says as she's passing our booth.

"Just a coffee, black." As soon as she's gone he glares at me. "You're looking well."

I stop myself from groaning and sit up straighter. "Morning, Mr. Parrish."

"I can always come back later," he says. "But you did say you wanted to meet this morning, correct?"

I nod. Parrish contacted me late yesterday afternoon to let me know he'd finished with his initial investigation. As I was with Zara at the time I shot him a quick text telling him to meet me here this morning. I just hadn't expected to come in here with a monster headache. "You found something?"

"Let me get some coffee in me first," he says, though I can't help but eye the manilla folder he places on the seat beside him. "Looks like you could use some carbs to soak up whatever you got into last night."

"It's been a stressful week," I say. Reginald Parrish works as a private investigator these days, though he used to be a local cop. After his stellar work on helping me find a picture of Camille back before I knew her name or anything else about her, I decided he was my best option for tracking down what little Camille gave me before she died.

The waitress returns with a cup of coffee for Parrish, and I order the basic breakfast, though I'm not sure I feel like eating. I'm sure I'll feel better once I have something solid on my stomach, but right now the thought of consuming anything is not appealing at all.

Parrish is one of those guys who seems comfortable anywhere, and he has the ability to blend into his surroundings, which is probably what makes him such a good private investigator.

"Don't make me wait," I tell him. "What did you find?"

He picks up the folder and hands it over to me. "Open that in private," he says, lowering his voice. "Given the parameters you provided, it's a miracle I found anything at all."

"You mean something actually came up on James Hunter?"

He leans closer and lowers his voice even more. "Look, I don't know what you've gotten yourself involved in, but whoever these people are, they are working very hard to keep themselves concealed."

"I think that's their number one goal," I tell him. "The man I had you investigate was my husband's father. He's the only reason I know anything about any of this."

"Is that why you didn't want to do this yourself?" Parrish asks. "Personal connection?"

"I didn't want to do this myself because every move I make at the Bureau is being scrutinized," I tell him. "I needed someone with your skillset, and who wasn't bothered by potentially bending the law a little to find out what I needed."

He chuckles. "It's a good thing you're paying me well. Had I known it was that hot, I might not have taken the job."

"I pay what you charge," I tell him, though I can tell he's joking with me. He has an easygoing manner about him. It's too bad Parrish isn't in the Bureau himself; he'd be a good ally to have. But then again, if he were, he couldn't have done any of this for me.

"Why are they scrutinizing you? Aren't you their star Agent?" he asks.

"Not anymore. Not since the change in leadership. A lot went down in my department. It's a long story."

He shrugs and leans back as the waitress brings me what I ordered. I have to admit it smells better than I'd anticipated. Two scrambled eggs, a waffle with a dollop of butter ready to be smothered in syrup, and a side of sausage links.

"Enjoy," the waitress says and heads back off.

I start cutting at the eggs, adding salt and pepper as my stomach rumbles in anticipation. "So what did you find?"

"It took me some time to track down James Hunter. At least, the one you were talking about, there are a bunch out there. But this James Hunter, who died in 2013, worked for a company called MelCor. It's a programming firm that went belly-up in the dot-com burst around 2002. *Except...*"

I look up and can tell he's leaving me hanging on purpose. He enjoys telling a good story. I make a motion with my fork for him to go on.

"...it was never real in the first place."

"What?" I ask, my mouth half-full of egg.

"The company was some kind of front. For what, I can't determine. But I do know they had nothing to do with programming or supplying customers with electronics of any kind. How do I know? Because I contacted about three dozen people in the industry who worked back then and none of them had ever had anything to do with MelCor."

"Maybe they only did overseas transactions," I suggest.

He shakes his head. "No records at any of the ports and no records of any shipments to or from MelCor. It operated here, out of D.C. for almost three decades and no one ever suspected it wasn't a real business."

"How could they do that?" I ask. "Wouldn't they have had real customers walk into the store?"

"Who said they had a store?" he asks. "This was a company on paper only. No physical location. No actual product going in or out. And as far as I can tell, no one was ever hired or fired from the company. Not that I can find, anyway."

I sit back a minute, thinking about the company Zara found where my husband's boss "worked". That place had been a front too, though it had been more intricate and detailed. They'd actually set up offices, even hired unwitting personnel as cover. Still, it had all been a cloak for the real organization beneath the surface.

It looks like Matt's dad worked in a similar environment. "You said they went out of business?"

He nods. "Shut down in 2002. The reasoning with the IRS was cash flow problems. They couldn't cover their debts."

"That's bullshit," I say. "These people are loaded. Which means they wanted to shut that division down for some reason."

"What people?" Parrish asks.

"Keep going, what else did you find?" I pour a thick layer of syrup over my waffle and begin cutting.

"I figured you'd want to know as much about James Hunter as possible, so I found out where they buried his body. Apparently he died of a heart attack." I nearly choke on my waffle, and it takes me a minute to clear my airway.

"Emily, are you all right?" he asks, getting up and coming to my side of the table. I feel his hand on my back, ready to knock any stray waffle from my throat.

"Fine," I say, then grab for the coffee, think better of it, and take the untouched glass of water on the table instead. A few gulps later and I'm back to normal. "I'm fine, just startled is all."

"You sure?"

I motion to his seat and take a sip of coffee.

"You all right hon?" the waitress asks, coming back over.

"Yeah, just went down the wrong pipe."

"I'll bring you another water," she says, and heads back to the kitchen.

I take a deep breath, letting the air fill my lungs as I try to process what Parrish has told me. A heart attack, just like with Matt. These people certainly have a signature. "Where's the body now?" I ask.

Parrish looks to the side, then back at me. "Records show it was cremated via the wishes of the family."

"Great," I say, sitting back. "So how am I supposed to follow that?"

"What do you mean?" Parrish asks.

I work my jaw as the waitress returns with another water. Once she's gone, I decide maybe if Parrish has some of the context, he can help me put the pieces together. "That woman you tracked down for me? She worked for the people that killed him," I say. "She told me if I wanted answers about my husband, that I needed to *find his father. Find his father and you'll find the truth about your husband* is what she said."

Parrish nods, then looks to the side.

"What?"

"Seeing as none of what I was seeing made much sense, I decided to dig a little deeper," he says.

"Deeper?"

"I began looking into James Hunter's history. His parents, siblings, home life. Anything I could find. Because you're right, James Hunter might not be alive today, but his past still might be able to tell us something."

I admit I'm intrigued. I didn't expect Parrish to go above and beyond. He really is worth what I'm paying him. "What else did you find?"

He takes a sip of coffee and leans forward again. "Interestingly, his father, your late husband's grandfather, also worked for a front."

So it *was* a family affair after all, just as I suspected. No wonder both Matt and Chris were involved. "What about the rest of the family, were they in it too?"

He shakes his head. "Not as far as I could tell. His mother didn't work, and his brother and sister worked for legitimate organizations, and all their descendant family members seem to be healthy, contributing members of society. It was only Hunter and his father as far as I can tell."

"And his two sons," I say. My hunch was correct, that Matt had been in this since the day he was born, whether he knew it or not. But for whatever reason, he never opened up to me about it. Perhaps knowing that I was a law enforcement official kept him from saying anything, or maybe he just didn't want me to arrest him. Whereas Chris obviously told Dani, who joined him in becoming part of the Organization. As stupid as it sounds, I feel as though I've been left out, even if what I've been deprived of was a criminal organization that goes against everything I believe in.

"Are you all right?" Parrish asks me. "You look a little sad."

"Just thinking," I say. Despite all these revelations, it still doesn't bring me any closer to Matt's motives. Did he stay in the Organization because he felt he had no choice? Or did he want to be there, to be part of this family venture and carry on the title from his father, perhaps hoping to pass it down to a son?

"Were you able to find anything else? Any clue that might help me find out more about James Hunter? Or anyone in the family, really."

He gives me a noncommittal shrug. "I suppose you could ask your husband's aunt and uncle or their subsequent families, but from what I learned they never had any part of anything nefarious. It's possible they never even knew about it."

I hadn't even known Matt had an aunt and uncle. Or cousins, I suppose. No one from his side of the family showed up to the wedding, only some of his friends and acquaintances. He'd been insistent his family was gone, like mine. Turns out that had been just another lie.

"All of what you've told me is in here?" I ask, holding up the folder.

Parrish nods. "Every bit. But I'm afraid that's all there is. Unless you find someone better than me. And I wish them good luck."

"Thank you," I say. "You always come through for me."

"I try," he says. "If you ever have any other jobs, don't be a stranger. Always happy to cash your checks."

I smile. "Might be a while before the next one," I reply. "Seeing as your rates keep going up."

"If you're good at something, never do it for free." He gives me a wink, then slips out of the booth, leaving a ten on the table for his one cup of coffee. Before he texted last night, I had almost forgotten about the Organization. At least, it wasn't in the forefront of my mind all the time. But after learning all of this, I know it's going to be hard to go back to the case with a clear head.

Still, that's what I have to do. I owe it to Jaeden Peters.

I take a few minutes to finish my breakfast, then retrieve the envelope and head back home to spend the rest of the day pulling it all apart and putting it together again.

There has to be something more there.

Chapter Twenty-Two

AFTER ANOTHER NIGHT OF RESTLESS SLEEP, I ARRIVE BACK AT the school first thing Monday morning to find Rodriguez has already beaten me there. I wanted to wait until all the kids were here before questioning the four boys, who could be potential suspects. I still feel like this is a dead end, but Rodriguez seems to think there's something here and we need to be thorough. The only problem is I didn't even glance at the list Zara prepared for me yesterday; I was too preoccupied with Parrish's findings.

"Morning," Rodriguez says, leaning on the hood of her car as I approach. "Would you like a coffee? I brought a second." She nods to the car.

"Sure, thanks," I tell her. I didn't eat much for breakfast, seeing as I spent most of the rest of yesterday nursing my hangover and going over the notes from Parrish, comparing them to what little I had found. Unfortunately, I seem to only be left with more questions than when I started, and I'm running out of places to look for answers. Hiring Parrish had been a long shot, but I knew if I wanted to stay off Wallace's radar, a PI was my best alternative. Especially one who isn't friendly with the Bureau. Still, while what Parrish found for me was helpful, it hasn't gotten me any closer to the Organization. And as a consequence, it turns out Wallace might be right after all. I'm not putting as much time on this case as I should.

"Have a good rest of your weekend?" Rodriguez asks, reaching into the car and handing me the coffee. It's still warm enough to drink.

"Not really, you?"

"Good enough. Spent some time with my daughters, which is a rare thing these days. I also took a few hours to go over all the information Agent Foley pulled on our list of suspects. Though all of mine looked like little more than loud-mouthed idiots who would be afraid to actually speak their mind in person. But for some reason, behind the anonymity of a keyboard they're the bravest people alive."

I turn away, attempting to hide my shame at the fact I didn't go over my half of the list at all, and instead spent all of my extra time working on finding the Organization connection and only ended up more frustrated than when I began. "Right," I say. "If anything pops up on the people on my list, I'll let you know, but nothing yet."

She takes a deep breath. It's cool again this morning, almost chilly, and the brisk air feels good against my lungs, so I do the same, only trying not to make it obvious. I love the fall, it usually fills me with a sense of calm, like the world is headed down for a long hibernation. But I'm not feeling any sense of calm regarding what we're about to do. Teenagers—especially older ones—are notoriously difficult to read, even in the best of situations. And the fact that all four of these *gentlemen* have sealed records doesn't make me feel any better. It's the one thing that's keeping me from calling this interview off entirely, because there is a very real chance we could have a young killer in our midst. And if we miss it, I'd never be able to forgive myself.

I just need to stay *focused*.

"Shall we head in?" Rodriguez asks.

I give her a nod and we both head to the main entrance, where the same cop from before stands guard. "Morning Mont," Rodriguez says.

"Mary," he replies, giving us both a nod. "How are those daughters of yours?"

"Wildfire and spitfire, both of them," she laughs as he opens the door for us.

"Good to hear they're keeping you on your toes." He nods to me. "Morning Agent Slate."

I'm impressed he remembers my name. "Morning," I say. "Thanks."

Rodriguez leans close to me once we're inside. "Montell and I used to work the same beat before I became detective. He's a good officer, likes the quiet life."

"Is that why he's here?"

She nods as we make our way down the main hallway. "He was the first to volunteer when the city council decided that every school always needed at least one officer on campus. Has a son in college now, I think."

"Glad to know he's on the job." We head back into the same office I visited on Friday and the same office manager looks up, surprise on her face upon seeing me again.

"Agent, I didn't expect you back. Did you need to speak with Ms. Haines again?"

I shake my head. "This is Detective Rodriguez with the Bethesda Precinct. We need to see Armstrong, Parkinson, Delgado, and Hawes. Preferably in an open room where we can talk to them all at once, then one at a time." I look over my shoulder, then turn to Rodriguez. "Do you think Officer Connelly would be willing to give us a hand?"

She smiles. "I think he'd like nothing less."

Ten minutes later we've been set up in an empty classroom, filled with about fifteen desks. Connelly stands by the door while Rodriguez is seated at the head desk. I'm leaning up against the heater that runs under the windows that span the room, my arms crossed, positioned in a way where I'll be able to see each boy as they come in. I want to try and get an initial read on them before a word even comes out of their mouths.

The first kid appears, his mane of brown hair dominating most of his head. He looks somewhat bewildered as he enters the room and sees Connelly and then us. His face is covered in stubble that looks like it's trying to conceal pock marks on his skin. Though his hair is longer, he's not unkempt at all, instead wearing a button-down shirt that's open halfway down to reveal a tank top underneath, and jeans.

"Is this…am I in the right place?" he asks, looking around.

"Name?" Rodriguez asks.

"Joey. Parkinson."

"Have a seat Joey," she says.

He takes a look at me, then sits in one of the front desks, still somewhat bewildered.

A few seconds later, another boy comes in, though he's noticeably taller, and clean-shaven. He pays no attention to Connelly, Rodriguez or me and instead looks straight at Parkinson, his blue eyes going wide. He has on a light designer jacket and expensive sneakers. Before he even opens his mouth, I know this is Armstrong, the de facto leader of this little group.

He finally seems to realize we're in the room as well and he looks to Rodriguez first. "You wanted to see me?"

"Name?" Rodriguez says in the same tone as before.

"Tony. Anthony, Armstrong," he amends.

"Take a seat, Tony," she tells him, indicating one of the desks close to the first boy. I have to give it to Rodriguez; she's not giving anything away.

A couple minutes later the final two boys enter together.

Both are laughing as they come in but stop immediately upon seeing the occupants in the room.

"Misters Delgado and Hawes," Rodriguez says.

Both the boys who had been staring at the other two already in their seats turn their attention to her. But only one of them answers. "Yeah?" He's got lighter hair, cut short, and expensive-looking sunglasses on his face.

"Remove those, please," Rodriguez says, indicating the glasses.

He shoots the boy beside him a look and takes them off with an exaggerated motion, clipping them inside the "v" of his polo shirt.

"Name?" Rodriguez asks.

"Hawes," he replies. "Dick Hawes." He says it like he's playacting as James Bond.

The other three boys snicker. His official record from the school has his nickname listed as Richie.

"Then you must be Mr. Delgado," Rodriguez says, indicating the fourth boy who seems to be the most nervous of the bunch. He's not exactly hiding behind Hawes, but he's not doing anything to make himself stand out either. He's got short, black hair that's also cut short and while I can tell he's trying to put on a brave face, I can see he's terrified.

Maybe there's something here after all.

"Take a seat, please," Rodriguez says, rising as the boys find chairs behind their compatriots. Armstrong sits with one leg out, like he couldn't care about anything less in the world while Hawes stares at me, trying to get a rise out of me as he wiggles his eyebrows. The other two boys don't seem nearly as cocky. Parkinson is looking to the others for guidance while Delgado has his eyes on the floor.

"I'm Detective Rodriguez with the Bethesda Police Department," she says. "And this is Special Agent Slate with the FBI. Do any of you have any idea what this is about?"

No one speaks up, but a couple of them shoot each other looks.

"No one? Guess we'll start with the individual interviews then." She turns to me. "Who do you want first?"

"Let's go in alphabetical order," I reply. "Mr. Armstrong, if you'll follow me."

He huffs and gets out of his chair. I make a motion to Connelly. "Make sure they don't talk to each other while we're in there with him."

"You got it, Agent," Connelly says. Armstrong follows me across the hall to another, smaller room we've procured. I motion for him to take a seat at the desk while Rodriguez shuts the door behind us.

"What is all this?" he asks. "I'm missing important study time." His tone suggests he believes anything but what he's saying.

I take a seat across from him, locking my gaze on his. "What can you tell me about Jaeden Peters?"

He scoffs, looking up at Rodriguez then back at me. "Is *that* what this is about? Boy, you guys really are on that woke train, aren't you?"

"Care to explain that?" I ask, already not liking his tone.

"What'd he do, complain to his mommy?"

"Complain about what?" I ask.

"It was nothing. It's not my fault if he's soft." I only stare at Armstrong, waiting for him to continue. He rolls his eyes. "We were just messing with him. It's not like it was a crime or anything. I don't know why the FBI would even care about a little hazing."

"Hazing," I say, not as a question.

"Yeah, just messing with him, you know? He always dresses in all that goth crap, wanting everyone to think he's some kind of badass. But when you put him to the test, he crumples."

"What kind of test?"

He sits back, pursing his lips. "Don't you already know? Isn't that why I'm here?"

I lean forward, my face like stone. "Mr. Armstrong, you're here because Jaeden Peters is dead. And you have a reputation for bullying him."

His eyes go wide and his entire body language changes. "Wait a second, dead? I didn't have anything to do with that."

"You don't seem particularly disturbed by the news," I say, though I can see he is rattled, just a little.

"What do you want me to say? Peters was a little shit. I'm sorry, but that's the truth. Always thought he was better than everyone else. You think we were picking on him? We were just getting him back for things he'd done to us."

"Such as?" I ask.

"I dunno, stuff. Nothing big."

I look down for just a moment, then I fold my hands together and lock my gaze with his once more. "Mr. Armstrong. Listen to me very carefully. Either you provide me with details of these allegations, or I will be forced to assume you are a suspect, as you plainly had motive to retaliate against Peters. Maybe things went too far, and you didn't mean for him to die. Or maybe they went exactly to plan."

He pushes back from the table, clearly spooked now. "Okay, look. Me and the guys…we spiked his water with laxatives. Nothing big. He missed a day of school, okay?"

"Did he know who did it?" I ask.

"No, he was clueless," Armstrong says.

"And this was to get back at him for…" I trail off, waiting for him to finish it for me.

"I don't know, just stuff. He's just annoying, okay?"

"So then you caused a student to miss a day of school after spiking his water in response to him being annoying." It's mostly a harmless prank, nothing to get too worked up over. But I can't tell him that. Nor can I let him think he's off the hook.

"Yeah, so, not murder. Not even close."

I narrow my gaze. "I doubt this has been the only incident." Armstrong averts his eyes again and I realize I'm seeing someone who has a pattern of negative behavior against another person. And I'm not sure he has a good reason.

"Look," Armstrong says, his face not betraying a hint of a lie. "Do I like Peters? No. Do we harass him and mess with him a lot? Yeah. But that doesn't mean I wanted him to die. I'm going to be in college next year. You really think I'd screw that up because of some little shit like Peters?"

I shoot a look at Rodriguez who seems to confirm my suspicions. Armstrong may be an asshole, but my general sense of him isn't that he's a murder, even an accidental one. He's showing none of the telltale signs of someone with that kind of mindset, even though being a brash, entitled young man isn't doing him any favors. Still, I can tell we're barking up the wrong tree.

The interviews with Delgado and Parkinson go about the same as Armstrong. Both of them recount other instances when they've harassed Peters, but none of it rises to the level where I think he was ever in any danger. If anything, some of their hazing feels almost fraternal, like what some college kids do during pledge week. I've certainly heard worse. And while bullying is no minor matter, none of what I'm hearing makes me think any of these kids even knew Jaeden was dead.

"Mr. Hawes," I say as he comes into the room as the last interviewee. He's got his sunglasses on again and almost struts his way to the chair before taking a seat. "Or is it Dick? Is that the name you'd prefer us use?"

"You can call me whatever you want," he replies. "But if you're partial to Dick, I'm happy to oblige." He gives me a shit-eating grin before leaning back in his chair again.

"Do me a favor and remove those sunglasses," I tell him.

"Why?" he asks. "So you can tell if I'm lying or not when you ask me a question?"

The kid is sharp, I'll give him that. He strikes me as one of those young men who is used to getting whatever he wants *when*ever he wants. I didn't do a lot of background research on any of them—I wanted to see what they were like first—but I'd be willing to bet he comes from money. And while Armstrong might be this group's "leader", I can already tell that Hawes is the real brains behind everything. He's smart enough to work behind the scenes.

"You guys have no sense of humor," he finally says, removing his sunglasses, then shoots both me and Rodriguez a look.

"Maybe you're not as amusing as you think you are," Rodriguez says.

Hawes only shrugs, then gives me that look again. The one that he seems to think is going to make me jump in the sack with him. It's a look I'm used to seeing and even saw on Saturday night when I was out with Zara.

"What is your relationship with Jaeden Peters?" I ask.

He considers the question for a minute. "Intimate."

"How so?" I ask.

"We jerk each other off," Hawes says with a grin. "Is that what you want to hear?"

I shoot Rodriguez another look. Yep, if any of them is our suspect, it's going to be Hawes. Already his blatant disregard for authority and his narcissism puts him in my sights. "Mr. Hawes, I need you to answer our questions truthfully."

"Why? Am I under arrest here or something?"

"No. We just want to—"

"Then I don't have to answer anything," he replies, sitting back and crossing his arms. He pushes the chair up on to its back two legs and teeters on them, glaring at me.

"Do you admit to bullying Jaeden Peters? Or causing him bodily harm in any way?"

He remains silent. I can see he thinks he's too clever to be here. That, and he believes he's got the upper hand in this situation.

"Okay, Richie," I say. "You win. You don't have to answer any of our questions. So let me just talk for a minute. See, the thing is, the FBI doesn't usually get involved unless we're dealing with a very serious case. And in this one, we've got a murder."

He doesn't flinch, or react in any way.

"Jaeden Peters was found murdered last week. Haven't you wondered why he hasn't been in school since Tuesday?"

"I don't keep up with his schedule, what am I, his daddy?" Hawes says, crossing his arms.

"Would you like to know how he was murdered?" I ask, catching a concerned glare from Rodriguez. I don't normally give out details like this, but given Hawes' lack of cooperation, I believe I can accurately assess him using this method. The only problem is it's going to hit the news feeds now. But maybe that's what we need. It's been almost a week and we don't have a solid suspect yet, not unless Hawes here is our man.

He shrugs at my suggestion, like it doesn't bother him one way or another.

"First off, he was cut open," I tell him. "From right here, below his adam's apple, all the way to his groin." Hawes squirms a little, some of his bravado faltering. "Then his body cavity was opened, and his liver was carved out, and not all at once. They left little bits of it there, inside his body and had to go back and get them all out."

Hawes' eyes have gone wide and while I can tell he's trying to maintain his composure, he's slipping. "Next, they sliced right across here, with a sharp blade," I say, making a cutting motion across my face, right above the bridge of my nose and below my eyes. "They then peeled the skin down all the way past his jawline, tearing it off."

All four legs of his chair hit the floor. He's looking away.

"Okay. Christ. Okay," he says, holding out one hand. "Is that what really happened to him or are you making that up?"

"I can show you pictures if you'd like," I say. "Our coroner documented everything thoroughly."

Hawes has gone a little green, and all traces of his bravado are gone. He's not our man either. Just as I suspected. "Where were you last Tuesday night, between ten p.m. and five a.m. the following morning?"

He looks up at me, his eyes like saucers. "You can't think I…I mean…"

"Tell us, Hawes," Rodriguez says, approaching the table. "Your friends have already admitted to bullying, hazing. Maybe you decided to take it a step further."

"No," he says. "No, this is something…that's messed up, man."

"Where were you?" I ask again, more forcefully.

"I was at home," he replies, anger in his voice. "Where else would I be on a Tuesday night?"

"Anyone there with you?"

"Yeah, my dad. My two sisters," he looks at me like I'm stupid. "They know I was home."

"No chance you could have left without anyone knowing?"

He shakes his head. "No. No way."

I nod, pretending like I accept his answer. "Tell me about your uncle."

"My uncle?" he asks.

I open my phone, making a big show of checking my notes. "William Hawes. Or Billy, as I believe he's better known."

"Wait, what does Uncle Billy have to do with anything?" he asks.

"Just a question," I say. "Did your uncle ever have any contact with Jaeden? Any opportunity where they could have interacted?"

Hawes shakes his head, confused. "I haven't even seen my uncle in ten years. He's not around."

I nod. Just as I suspected, nothing but another dead end.

"Hey," Hawes says, leaning forward. "Did that really happen to Peters?"

Now it's my turn for the silent treatment. I want to give him a taste of his own medicine for being such an ass, but I decide against it. I've found out what I needed to know; any more time spent here would be time we could be hunting down the real suspect.

"You're free to go," I tell him.

He looks at the door like it might be a trap, then gets up and heads out.

"Oh, and Richie," I say, holding up his sunglasses. "Don't forget these."

"Kinda rough, don't you think?" Rodriguez asks as we head back out to the school's parking lot.

I shake my head. "That kid is just itching for a good ass-kicking. But I doubt my boss would be very happy about that."

Rodriguez's features are turned down. "He'll talk. To the media."

"Not if we release the info first," I tell her. She stops and I stop with her. "We're running low on suspects here. I'm willing to open it up to the media if you are."

"You didn't leave me much choice back there," she says.

"Do you have a better idea?"

She lets out a long breath. "No."

"Me either. We'll need to follow up on their alibis, but I don't think any of them is our killer."

Rodriguez looks out toward the parking lot. "Damn. Sorry, I thought we might have had something here."

"You know as well as I do that ninety percent of this job is eliminating suspects and running into dead ends."

"I guess I had just hoped the FBI might have some magic power that made the whole process easier."

I head back to the car. "When you find out what that is, be sure to let me know."

Chapter Twenty-Three

"So, INVESTIGATOR TO INVESTIGATOR, WHAT IS YOUR determination?"

I glance up at Rodriguez, three French fries stuffed in my mouth. She has her own plate of food in front of her that she's barely touched. Meanwhile here I am going at my own plate like it's my last meal. "What?"

"I just mean, you must have a hunch about this case. Surely, you've seen things like this before. Isn't that what you do at the FBI? Create profiles that are supposed to predict who your suspect is?"

I finish the fries and wipe my hands on my napkin, considering her question. "Sure. I mean, we have specific agents where all they do is profile. But most of us are trained in the basics."

"So what does your training tell you about our killer?"

I sit back a minute, clearing some stray fry bits from my teeth. "That's what's been bothering me about this entire case," I say. "It doesn't line up with what we'd expect from a traditional killer. Take the method in which Peters was killed, for instance. We're obviously looking at a copycat, someone who is looking to emulate *The Arrow of Guiding Light*. And yet, despite easy access to information that would make the death seem more like those Ewing performed, our killer has missed some details. Which means he's either done it on purpose, or he was in such a hurry that he couldn't be bothered with setting the scene exactly.

"Which brings up something else. If he was in such a hurry, how did he so expertly remove the skin from Peters' face? Furthermore, we have no indication that he plans on striking again. Personally, I feel like the whole job was more clinical to him, that he's using the shock factor of how *The Arrow* killed their victims to cover up that he may not have any connection to Jaeden Peters at all."

She screws up her face. "You really think the killer what... picked him at random?"

I hold up one finger. "We know none of the kids who bullied him at school had anything to do with it. Zara's still checking on anyone in his circle online who might have targeted him, but from what she's told me about his computer setup, is it was designed more for solo play than cooperative online games. Obviously, the girlfriend and parents are out as well. I think it's much more likely some fanatic went out and grabbed Peters because he was convenient, not because he ever did anything to stand out."

"How do we find someone like that?" she asks.

I shake my head. "We have to hope something comes back on his car, because right now it's the only piece of evidence we have. There are no cameras in that area, and I doubt there were any witnesses the night of the murder. Our only other hope is someone saw the killer staging Jaeden's body the following morning, but considering no one has come forward yet, I don't have a lot of hope."

She finally picks up her sandwich. "Maybe someone will come forward once the media reports on the story."

"That's the dream," I say, stuffing a few more fries in my mouth.

We sit in silence a moment longer before she speaks up again. "So if you had to narrow down a type of person, who do you think would have done something like this? What's your read?"

I tilt my head back and forth a little. "Traditionally, killings like these are generally perpetrated by white men, ages twenty to forty. I'm relatively confident that's who we're looking for, not that it really does much to narrow the field down. But if we assume this was random, and that the killer was looking more to send a message than hurt a particular person, it means we're dealing with a true psychopath. Someone who either has no empathy in them or can turn it off at a whim. They're someone who blends into society easily, who doesn't make waves and doesn't stand out, but they still have something to say. They could be a follower of *The Arrow*, or they could just be using them as a way of gaining attention and not care about Ewing or his insane ideology one bit."

"But if that was the case, wouldn't they have just come up with their own way of killing Jaeden?" Rodriguez asks.

I point at her with one of my fries. "That's what's sticking in my craw. I can't figure out why the killer would want to use *The Arrow* if they don't care anything for it. Logic tells me there has to be a connection somewhere, but from what we've seen so far, I can't find it. And to be honest, it's driving me up the wall."

We chew in silence for a moment as the sounds of the restaurant seem to increase all around us. It's the middle of the lunch rush and given our only other lead is in the Bethesda forensics' garage right now, I figured we might as well get in a good meal.

"How is your other case coming?" Rodriguez asks. "The one you told me about."

"Oh," I say, shaking my head. "It's not an official case, though I haven't made much headway. Like I said, those people are hard to track down."

I sigh and put my sandwich down, my appetite having just disappeared. "It doesn't really matter anyway. If this case stalls out, and it looks like it will, I'll be shipped off to who-knows-where by the middle of next week."

"You can't keep investigating from wherever your new assignment is?" Rodriguez asks.

I shrug. "I suppose. But my husband died *here*. Everything we've found, we've found *here*. It feels like if I'm shuffled off somewhere else, I'll lose what little ground I've gained."

"Maybe a new place could be an opportunity to start over," she suggests.

"Yeah," I reply. "A hard restart. My life, if you can call it that, is in D.C. It wouldn't be so bad if my best friend and my boyfriend didn't also work out of the same office. I'll be starting brand new, without any of the support systems I've come to rely on. It's like ever since I lost my husband, I've been thrown into a tornado, and I just can't find my way out. I thought maybe I was making some progress, but…"

She squints in concern. "What?"

"I have a confession. I spent most of the weekend going over information about the Organization, information that I just found out, but hasn't brought me any closer to them. I didn't do a background check on my half of the list."

She sets her own food down. "Oh."

"I don't want you to get the wrong idea," I tell her. "I'm not that person, not usually. It's just lately…ever since the woman who had been hunting me died, and I found out my in-laws worked for this organization and were trying to kill me, I haven't felt like myself. Sometimes I'm okay, and I can pretend like everything is normal and I'm a normal person too. And other times I know I'm nothing but an imposter, that I have no place anywhere."

"Finding our true place in life is one of the hardest things we have to do," Rodriguez says. "But you shouldn't beat your-self up. You're a good Agent; I wouldn't have heard of you otherwise. And everyone feels like an imposter sometimes. In fact, I hear that true imposters don't get imposter syndrome. They're too cocky."

I smile. "I guess that's true." I never used to feel unsure of myself. But ever since Matt died, and ever since I learned that he'd managed to fool me for over four years, I haven't been able to shake the feeling that maybe I'm not as good at this job as I once thought I was. I don't care if I was off-duty or not, I should have seen it.

"I'm sorry I didn't tell you about the other half of the list sooner," I say. "I was…embarrassed."

Rodriguez wipes her hands. "That's okay. It's actually good news, because now we have more names to research. One of those people could be the killer we're looking for. So don't give up hope yet."

"I suppose that's true," I say. "But I should have done it by now."

Rodriguez smiles. "Then let's get some to-go containers and get on it."

I can't help but appreciate her positive attitude. Sometimes it's so easy to get lost in my own head. Having another voice around that has a bit more life experience is proving to be invaluable.

"Mary, thank you. Really," I say.

She gives me a wink. "Happy to do it."

Chapter Twenty-Four

AFTER RETRIEVING THE OTHER HALF OF THE LIST FROM ZARA again—who wasn't happy that she had to send me another copy—Rodriguez and I start narrowing the list of names, eliminating suspects either by the fact they couldn't have been at the scene during the time period Jaeden was captured, or by looking at their pattern of behavior over the past few years.

It's deep research, and before I know it, three hours have passed and we're barely through ten names. We still have another seven to go when Rodriguez's phone rings.

"Detective Rodriguez," she says. I look up from my station as she listens to the voice on the other end, nodding along. "Understood. We'll be right there." She hangs up and turns to me. "They found fingerprints on the car that don't belong to Peters or Haines."

"Really?"

"They're emailing me the information now," she replies. "Can we use the FBI's system to see if they belong to anyone with a record? It'll be quicker than trying to get back over to my office."

"Absolutely," I tell her. This might be the break we've been looking for. Maybe the killer thought all the rain would wash away any trace of fingerprints and decided not to wear gloves when they attacked Jaeden Peters in his car. "Did they say where they found the prints?"

"On the driver's side door," she replies. "As well as the hood."

"Wow," I say. "That's like hitting the jackpot. Anything inside the car?"

She shakes her head. "Not yet, but they're still looking, they wanted to get this over as soon as possible." She opens her phone back up. "I'm sending it over to you."

I open up my mail and download the attachment, reading through the preliminary report. Attached are copies of the prints found at the scene. There are two fulls and seven partials, and all of them came from the same person.

I upload the files into IAFIS, and run a basic search, looking for anyone who might be a match. If they don't already have a criminal record, the results will show zero, which means we'd need to have an actual suspect to compare them to before we could move forward.

Rodriguez comes over and looks over my shoulder as the computer runs through the options. "Even if it does return someone, it'll be circumstantial," she says.

"Right. But it will be a lead," I reply. The computer returns a result before I can even begin to ponder what our next step would be if it matched one of the names on my list. That would be at least enough to get a look inside the person's home.

"Albert Rosewater?" Rodriguez asks, looking at the file on my screen. "Name doesn't ring a bell to me, does it to you?"

I shake my head. His name wasn't one of the ones on either list, and I don't think I've ever heard it before. He has a mugshot from a few years ago. His eyes are sunken in, and at the time he had a black goatee that took up most of his small face. I can't see his entire body, but his height is listed at five-six and his weight at a hundred and forty-two pounds when he was incarcerated.

"Record shows two arrests, both for possession," Rodriguez reads off my screen. I scroll down a little farther to the more recent entries.

"Nope, one more here. He wasn't charged, but he was brought in when his mother passed away suddenly." I squint reading the report. "The detectives could find no evidence of foul play or any indication of guilt from Mr. Rosewater, but nonetheless concluded the case deserved a second look."

"Did it get it?" Rodriguez asks.

I check the log on the file and the case itself. "Doesn't look like it. This was three years ago, so once it was signed off, it was probably put into storage as a closed case. Processed by Montgomery County, 1st District. That's at least an hour outside of town."

"But it is within the area," she says. "He's local, see?" She points to his last known address on the screen. I open up the maps app on my phone and punch in the address. It looks like a farm, out on the Maryland side of the border. From what I can tell via the satellite photos, it doesn't look like the property is very well taken care of.

"Lemme see if he's still there," I say and run a quick search with the DMV. A minute later I get Mr. Rosewater's current address and all the vehicles registered in his name.

"This guy likes cars," Rodriguez says.

"Address is the same," I say, confirming they're a match. I turn in my chair to her.

She furrows her brow. "So what's the order here? Rosewater goes out on a rainy night, waits somewhere he knows won't have a lot of traffic, and takes the first victim he sees?"

"Or maybe Jaeden Peters drove up on something that he wasn't supposed to see. Maybe Rosewater didn't expect him to show up, but because the road had been flooded, he'd been forced down the side street," I say. "Peters could have surprised him or found Rosewater doing something nefarious. Rosewater opens the door, pulls Peters out and knocks him out. Rosewater then hides the car and takes Peters back with him and eventually decides to kill him."

"So why the prints on the hood?" Rodriguez asks.

"I'm not sure. I don't know why he'd need access to the engine if all he was doing was putting the car in neutral and steering it into the underbrush." I rub my temples for a moment. "Of course, this is all speculation."

"Fueled by the report surrounding his mother," she replies.

I nod. "I want to get the original file, see if there's something in there that explains why the detectives filed the file this way. What did they think really happened? That he killed her and covered it up?"

"That would be my guess." Rodriguez stands, giving her back a stretch. "Are we driving out to Montgomery County?"

"Without a doubt," I say.

The entire way out to the Montgomery County I try to ponder what this Albert Rosewater could have been thinking. If he's the man who killed Jaeden, then what is his connection to *The Arrow of Guiding Light*? Was he a previous member who became disillusioned with the cult and decided to leave? Or did he just read about them on the news? And if this really is his work, then what message was he trying to send by doing all of this? From what little information we have, the man lives alone on a farm and seems to collect old vehicles, parts of them anyway.

"You're trying to figure out why he did this, aren't you?" Rodriguez asks from the passenger seat. I opted to drive, seeing as she's been doing more than her fair share.

"Aren't you?"

She stares straight ahead. "I stopped trying to figure out

why sick people do what they do a long time ago. After a while, it'll make you go crazy if you think about it enough."

I shrug. "I guess I'm not there yet. If I can't get inside the killer's head, then I can't predict what they'll do next. I have to understand them. But in this case, we're still not sure Rosewater is even our suspect. All we have are some fingerprints. We need to make sure he doesn't have any other connection with Jaeden that could explain them."

Rodriguez nods. "You're right, I shouldn't be making assumptions. I just want to nab this guy to make sure he can't do it to someone else again."

"Me too," I tell her. "As long as it's the right person."

It's another twenty minutes before we reach the Montgomery County Sherriff's office. Inside, I take a minute to introduce us to the officer on duty before we're directed to a man named Hank Gentry, who is the official file clerk for the Sherriff. We're left to find our way down into the stacks under the building when we come upon a man who is probably in his seventies, sitting at a small desk with a singular light above his head while he examines the contents of a white box.

"Hank Gentry?"

The man looks up, blinking a few times. His glasses are honest-to-God coke bottles and for a moment I'm starting to feel less than optimistic about this man being able to help us.

"That's me," he says. He's not wearing a uniform, just civilian clothes, though his button-up shirt is pressed, and his slacks are as sharp as a marine's when he stands. He holds out a hand that we both shake. For a man of his age, he's got a good grip.

"I'm Special Agent Emily Slate with the FBI. This is Detective Rodriguez with Bethesda Police. We were told you could help us find an old case file down here."

He takes off his glasses and I can see his blue eyes are clear and bright. "Sure can. Been the file clerk for the County for over twenty years, ever since they made me retire from the military."

So that explains a few things.

"What can I help you find?" he asks.

"We're looking for the Rosewater case," I tell him. "Albert Rosewater. His mother died under mysterious circumstances, and he was investigated, but never charged. We think he might be our suspect in another case and just wanted some background on him."

"Rosewater…" he says looking off into the distance. "Do you have a case number?"

"I've got it," Rodriguez says, pulling a sticky note from her pocket. "MC-L42519-K-03."

"L Series, got it," he says, stepping around his desk and heading down one of the dark stacks. The lighting down here is so bad I'm afraid he'll trip and fall, but he moves with the swiftness of someone twenty years his junior and returns a moment later with a small white box. "Not much in this one, I'm afraid." He sets the box down on the desk and pops the top, making his initials and the date on the small sticker on the front.

Inside are a couple of folders which are probably the case files, along with a couple of pieces of evidence, clothes, and a glass candlestick, all bagged in evidence.

"If you want to leave with the files, I'll need you to fill out requisition forms for the county," he says.

I shake my head, handing one of the files to Rodriguez while I take the other one. "That won't be necessary. We're just taking a quick look."

Gentry chuckles. "I've heard that one before." He heads back around his desk and takes a seat, putting his glasses back on as he continues to examine his own project, making notes as he goes along.

"Anything in yours?" Rodriguez asks. "This is mostly just the reports on the condition of all the box's contents."

My eyes scan the reports filed by the detectives at the time. I note the date: 2009. Over a decade ago, but during the same time *The Arrow* was operating. "It says suspect was brought in for questioning relating to the recent death of his mother. While no foul play was obvious, the detectives investigating the case thought Rosewater seemed…strange during his interview. He didn't seem particularly disturbed that his mother had died, nor did he seem to care, even though they lived in the same house."

"So?" Rodriguez says. "He didn't like his mother. Lots of people in that situation."

"While the official cause of her death is listed as a stroke, the coroner did find a small bruise on the back of her head, which could have been from a fall, or impact. But the evidence was inconclusive." I reach in and take out the glass candlestick. "Is this in your report?"

She nods. "One glass candlestick, has suspect's fingerprints on the base. No blood detected, but there was a small chip present, as if it had fallen or been hit on something."

I shake my head. "Wow, that really is nothing. They were reaching." I turn to Gentry. "Do you know anything about this case?"

He shakes his head. "Just one of a hundred more like it. We've got cases going back to the early 1900's down here. It's impossible to keep them all straight."

I read over the file again. "What about this Detective Waters, is he still on the force?"

Gentry shakes his head. "He retired seven or eight years ago. I couldn't tell you where he is now."

Frustrated, I put the files back into the box. "Thank you for your help," I tell him, though this feels more like another dead end.

"Anytime," he says with a smile. "And just leave all that stuff there. I'll put it up before I'm done for the day."

Rodriguez and I head back out of the station, thanking the desk officer for his help as well.

"What do you want to do now?" Rodriguez asks. "That was hardly conclusive."

"No, it wasn't," I say. While the evidence on Rosewater is circumstantial at best, I feel like he's the best lead we're going to get. "I think we need to go pay Mr. Rosewater a visit."

Rodriguez opens her phone. "His place is another half hour away."

I nod. "Still. Maybe he'll be able to explain why his fingerprints were on Jaeden's car."

"And if he can't?" she asks.

"Then we'll bring him in." I'm tired of tiptoeing around this case. It's time we started making some real progress. I convince myself that it's not Wallace's deadline looming in the back of my mind that's telling me to get some results here, that I really want to get justice for Jaeden and find the killer so they can't ever do this again. But it would be nice to score some points too.

Maybe then Wallace won't be so quick to banish me.

Chapter Twenty-Five

"YOU REALLY THINK THIS IS A GOOD IDEA?" RODRIGUEZ ASKS as we head out to Rosewater's farm. "Just go up and ask him if he killed a teenager last week?"

I shoot her a look. "Maybe not that direct. He's just the same as any other suspect, and right now since all we have is circumstantial, all we *can* do is get a read on him."

"Which risks tipping him off," she says.

I shake my head. "Even if Rosewater did have something to do with his mother's death—and there's no solid evidence he did—it's a long way from slicing someone stem to stern and carving out their liver. His history doesn't fit the profile. Where did he learn how to do that? We've already established whoever killed Jaeden was skilled, especially with a knife. Rosewater doesn't strike me as someone who could have done that to Jaeden."

"You just want to eliminate him from the suspect pool," Rodriguez says, relaxing in her seat.

"I want to find out what his fingerprints were doing on Jaeden's car," I say. "We're a good hour outside the city. I don't see any solid reason why they should have crossed paths, but they obviously did. I want to know why. That will give me a better understanding of who might have done this."

"Are you thinking he might not have been working alone?" she asks.

"I'm trying to keep all my options open right now," I tell her. "Maybe we'll spook him, and he might lead us to the person who really did this. Then again, he might not have any idea what we're talking about. We know he likes to collect cars, maybe he just saw the car in passing one day and inadvertently touched it."

"You don't really believe that," she says.

"No. But ever since we've found Jaeden's body, nothing about this case has made sense. And I'm tired of trying to poke around until we stumble on something that happens to fit. Which is why I want to ask Rosewater directly."

"Fair enough. I can back that play."

"Thank you," I say. "Still think the FBI is for you?"

"Oh, definitely," she says, grinning. "It's even better than I imagined. But what's really impressed me is your ability to work as both a group and individuals. For the agents I've met, you all have a really good working relationship with each other, which means you don't have to put up with all the regular bullshit and egos that plague my department."

"Part of that is luck, part of it is design. We've had a few bad apples in the department, but thanks to Janice and their own incompetence, most of those got rid of themselves." I'm specifically thinking of Nick, my old partner on my first job back after Matt died. At the time I thought him to be a competent agent, only later did I realize what a weasel he was. I can't help but wonder though, if Wallace had been in charge back then, would Nick still be there? I shake the idea out of my head.

"You okay?" Rodriguez asks.

"Yeah, just bad memories. Anyway, when Zara got promoted to a field agent, we both decided we were going to make the FBI different, even if it was just in our own department. Even if it was just the two of us. At some point you get tired of all the dick-measuring, and you just want to focus on the job. Know what I mean?"

"Oh absolutely," she laughs. "I've seen more than my fair share of egos clash. And I've seen it interfere with more cases than I'd like to admit. But there would be no guarantee I'd be assigned to your unit, would there?"

"More than likely you'd be assigned to different office altogether. Unless we had a specific opening. I'd have to get another agent transferred out or fired, but I'm sure I could handle it." I give her a wink and it takes her a second to realize I'm joking before she laughs aloud.

"It really would be fun," she says. "Working on your team."

I furrow my brow. "I don't have a team," I say.

"Sure you do. Agent Foley, for one. And she slipped me some info about Agent Coll, who has been a big asset to you."

I grimace. "That's because she doesn't know when to shut up."

"She's just proud of you," Rodriguez says. "Did you ever consider the reason your boss might want you out is because he's threatened by you? Not because you don't know how to do your job?"

I sit there, stunned. I *hadn't* thought of that. "No, that couldn't be the reason...could it?"

"From what I know about you, you crush almost every case you work. How can someone say you don't know how to do your job if that's the case?"

I purse my lips. "Well, this last case was a little different. I did go...*off book*...more than I usually do. But it was a no-win situation. I had to make a choice, and in the end, I chose to save a little girl than capture a crucial member of the Organization. And I would do it again if I had to."

"Still, it might be worth considering. Someone could be

trying to undermine all the good work you've been doing by getting you out of the way."

Wallace didn't come across that way to me; he seemed genuinely perturbed by me. At first, I thought it was personal, that he just didn't like my attitude or the way I went about my work. But now that Rodriguez mentions it, I can't help but wonder if she's right.

"Then again, what do I know?" she asks. "I've only seen what's on the surface. It could be completely different."

But the gears in my mind are already turning. Wallace wants me out of D.C. because he says I'm a liability to the Bureau. That he can't trust someone on his team that doesn't follow orders to the letter. Knowing what I know about Wallace, this makes sense. He's a stickler for the letter of the law, not the spirit. Still, it does seem a little…extreme now that I think about it. People get transferred all the time, sure, and some people don't mesh very well with their teams.

Then again, when Wallace had the chance to pull me off this case, especially after the airline incident, he didn't, and I can't figure out why. I thought for sure I'd be on the next flight to Montana after that, but he barely gave me a warning. Maybe he's just counting down the days until I'm gone, but if that's the case, what is he waiting for? He could assign Zara or someone else to take my place in an instant.

Suddenly, I don't feel so good about any of this. I pull out my phone and dial Zara's number.

"Yo. What's the haps?" she says when she answers.

I ignore her use of the word "haps". We'll be having a discussion about that later. "Hey, are you at the office?"

"Yep."

"Is Wallace there?"

"Uh…yeah, he is, why?" she says.

"What's he doing?"

"Jeez, Em, I don't know. Do you want me to go ask him? What's going on?"

"I'm not sure," I say. "I've just got a funny feeling all of a sudden. Do you think Wallace is trying to get rid of me because he's threatened by me?"

There's a pause on the other end of the line. "I guess that's a possibility. But he doesn't strike me as the jealous type."

"Let me ask you, why do you think he's keeping me around for this case? Why not just assign it to someone else if he wants me gone so bad?"

"Maybe he wants to give you one last chance to prove you can do the job in his eyes?" she suggests. "I don't really know. Doesn't make a lot of sense, does it?"

"No," I say, "It doesn't. We're headed out to check on a suspect now, but when I get back, will you go in there with me and confront him? I need to know what his agenda is."

"Of course," she says. "If you think that's smart. You know I have your back."

I let out a breath of relief. "Thank you. I don't want you to risk your career, but I think there's something very wrong here. And we need to figure out what it is."

"No, you're absolutely right," Zara replies. "I'll do a little digging until you get back. Wanna exchange notes tonight over a pizza?"

"Sounds good to me. See you then," I tell her and hang up.

"I'm sorry," Rodriguez says. "I didn't mean to throw a wrench into things."

I shake my head. "No, you could be right. See, this is how I know you'll make a good agent. You're not afraid to ask some potentially tough questions."

"I just hope you get it figured out," she says. "Before it's too late."

"So do I," I say, checking the GPS. According to the map, we're less than a mile away. "Better get ready, just in case. It's almost showtime."

Chapter Twenty-Six

ROSEWATER'S PROPERTY IS OFF THE MAIN DRAG, DOWN A
gravel driveway that winds around a small hill before reaching
the actual house itself. I pull up to the beginning of the driveway, then take out my weapon and check to make sure it's
ready and the safety is on while Rodriguez does the same. I
have no idea how this is going to go. Rosewater strikes me as
one of those men who doesn't really like anyone on his property, so he may come out of his house brandishing a shotgun
before we can even get a word out. I hope that's not the case,
as I'd really like to get a read on him before he gets too
defensive.

"Ready?" I ask Rodriguez and she gives me a nod. The
nice thing about working with someone who has so much
experience, is she's not rattled at all. In fact, she looks ready
and willing. I just hope Rosewater can give us some solid
answers. I feel like I'm flailing here with the direction this case
has taken. I struck out with the remaining members of *The
Arrow*, the boys at Jaeden's school proved to be useless, and so
far the entire list of anyone who might have had a hand in this
has turned up no viable suspects. If Albert here can't help us,

we'll be completely out of options with nowhere to turn, at least until another body shows up.

And more than likely I'll be on my way to another state by then. Unless Zara finds something on Wallace. I would love to go to Deputy Director Cochran armed with information showing that Wallace has been running his own private game in our department. It might even be enough to get Janice back.

I drive my car up the driveway, doing my best not to kick up a lot of dirt. I'm also on the lookout for devices that might give Rosewater a warning that we're on our way. But so far, I haven't seen anything.

When we come around the bend, the entire property lays before us. It's larger than I expected and has changed a lot from the satellite photos I looked up earlier. There's a trailer home on the property now, and looks to have been deposited here within the past four or five years. It was probably white at one time but has faded to a dull yellow and is covered in rust spots. It sits off to the right side of the drive, back from the road about a hundred feet with weeds growing up all around its base. There's a power line post next to it, leaning at a slight angle, that attaches a line that comes from the main house down to the trailer. It could be some kind of auxiliary home, or even a home office for Rosewater.

The property is also littered with vehicles in various states and conditions. Some are completely rusted out, barely skeletons of the vehicles they used to be, while others are in better condition, though none of them are what I would call road worthy. The place resembles a makeshift junkyard. At least all the vehicles have been lined up and about ten of them sit between the trailer home and the driveway, while another dozen are on the left side, between us and the house at the end of the drive.

"Well, that explains his love of cars," Rodriguez says. "Do you think he restores them?"

"Probably sells the parts," I say. What little information we pulled on Rosewater showed that he was unemployed. Perhaps he works on the cars on the side to supplement his unemployment, or maybe he just likes to collect junky cars like other people like to collect coins or stamps. Regardless, parts are strewn all over the lawn, which will make navigation in this area hazardous.

At the center of the property stands an old farmhouse, probably built in the 1800s from the look of it. Paint peels from the old siding and the red brick chimney has seen better days as chunks are missing out of it. The entire house looks as though its shifted on its foundation, which may no longer make it livable. Perhaps this is why Rosewater has added the trailer home to his collection.

"We should try the trailer first. That house doesn't look structurally safe."

"Agreed," Rodriguez says. I pull the car to a stop right in the middle of the drive and we both get out. The smell of dust and oil hits my lungs. This is not a place that is used often.

As we approach the mobile home, Rodriguez and I keep about six feet between us. "Hello?" I call out. "Mr. Rosewater?"

There's no response. Looking around, I can't tell which of the vehicles here run and which ones don't. And given they're all registered to him; I have no idea which one he uses for his regular trips. It's possible he's not here.

"Mr. Rosewater," I call again as we approach the mobile home. "Answer if you are here, please."

Nothing but silence. We're so far away from the main drag that there's no sound of traffic. The only noise I hear is the occasional cicada off in the distance. A soft breeze blows through the air, ruffling our hair, though it also sends an involuntary chill down my spine. I don't like this place.

"Stay here," I tell Rodriguez. "I'm going to check the home." It's possible Rosewater is asleep inside and he just hasn't heard us. But it's also possible he's sitting on the other side of the door, gun in hand.

I stand to the side of the door and give Rodriguez a nod, who signals back that she's ready. I give it a heavy knock. "Mr. Rosewater? Are you home?"

There's no response. And no sound of any movement inside. I wait a moment longer, then walk along the porch to where I can see into one of the trailer's windows. It's covered in a dirty screen, so I can't see much inside. But it's dark; no lights or television on inside.

"I don't think he's in here," I say. My knock is notoriously loud, as Zara always likes to remind me. I feel like he would have heard it, even if he was passed out on his bed.

"What do we do?" Rodriguez asks.

I knock on the door one more time just to make sure, but there is still no answer. Against my better judgement I try the handle, finding the trailer is unlocked. "It's open," I tell her. "Hang back, I'm just going to make sure he's not in there dead."

"You've got no cause," she says.

"I'll tell them it was all my idea and you tried to stop me." If Rosewater did have something to do with Jaeden's death, then it's possible he could have fled the state. A quick look around should tell me one way or another, even though I don't technically have the authority to go inside.

I open the door and pull my weapon, just in case, keeping it pointed to the ground and my finger off the trigger. The interior of the trailer has the distinct smell of body odor. To my right is the kitchen, with a small table and a refrigerator. A hot plate sits on the counter, unplugged. There isn't any food on the counter or anything that would indicate he's been here lately or left in a hurry.

A ratty couch sits opposite the door to the trailer, and stains cover half of it. One of the cushions is ripped and a small piece of foam sticks out. I continue on to the back of the trailer, passing a small bathroom to my right, which isn't anything to speak of, unless you count the cockroach I see skitter across the floor as I pass.

When I reach the back bedroom, the bed itself is a mess and there are some clothes scattered around, but nothing that leads me to believe he took everything he owned and left. The single closet is open, allowing me to get a good look inside. It's full of his clothes, and I notice a rifle sitting up against the inside of the closet wall, near the back.

I return to Rodriguez outside. "No one here. Doesn't look like he left for good, though. He may be coming back soon." I elected to leave the rifle as I didn't have the authority to be in there in the first place. If he comes motoring over that hill, we'll be able to stop and question him before he could get to it. Otherwise, I would have removed it and placed it my car for the time being.

"While you were in there, I thought I heard something from the house over there," Rodriguez says, pointing to the old farmhouse. "Might have been nothing, just an animal or something."

I stare at the house a minute, trying to determine the like-lihood Rosewater is over there waiting for us instead. It's possible I missed an early-warning sensor near the front of the property. He could have had time to run from the trailer to wait us out and see if we'd leave.

I sigh. "I guess we better make sure. I don't want to be sitting here waiting for him to come down the driveway and have him sneak up behind us."

"My thoughts exactly," Rodriguez says.

I don't want to spook Rosewater, and I know if he sees two people with guns drawn coming toward him, he could do something rash. I stow my weapon again and will keep it there, at least until we've determined the scope of the situation.

"Careful," I tell Rodriguez. "That house already looks like it's on its last legs. Let's try to stay out here if possible."

"Don't have to tell me twice," she says. "I'll take point, since you got the last one."

I smile. I don't know if she's doing it because she wants me to think she's got initiative, or if she's just really eager to get this over with, but I'm not about to argue with her. If Rosewater is our killer and has suspected a police presence ever since he killed Jaeden, he could have this entire place wired. I'm not convinced that's the case, but I'm not going to let my guard down either.

We approach the farmhouse with Rodriguez in front and me off to her left, continuing to watch the abandoned cars and anywhere else Rosewater might be hiding. When Rodriguez reaches the farmhouse she stops. "Mr. Rosewater? Are you in there?"

Still no reply.

There's a rustle to my left and in less than a second my gun is out and pointed at a crow flying away from one of the cars. My heart is hammering in my chest as the adrenaline floods my body. I keep my weapon trained on the vehicle as there is always the chance something spooked that crow. I make a slow circle around the abandoned vehicle, seeing no one. It must have just picked a very bad time to fly off on its own.

"Nothing," I tell Rodriguez. I notice her weapon is out too.

"Sure?" she asks.

I recall my encounter with Chris a few months ago. And how I hid under the car to avoid him. I bend down, my weapon pointed right under the vehicle, but when my eyes reach the underside, there's no one there.

"Yeah, I'm sure," I say, standing again.

Rodriguez nods and waits until I've joined her again before stepping on to the rickety porch. She knocks a few times at the farmhouse door. "Mr. Rosewater?" She looks back to me. "Should we go in?"

I stand on my tiptoes and peer in through one of the windows, seeing a few abandoned pieces of furniture in what looks like a formal sitting room. There's a rug inside as well, but it's hard to make out through the dirt. As I squint, it looks to me like there's something large on the rug.

Something like a body.

I put my finger to my lips and motion for her to open that door. Immediately her body posture changes from tense to guarded. She carefully tries the handle as I join her on the porch.

"Possible body in the room to the left," I whisper.

She nods as the door gives, swinging inward. The old hinges cause it to creak louder and longer than I would like.

We wait another second before Rodriguez takes a step inside and I give her cover. The house seems to bend under the pressure of a person being inside it and I follow her in. She makes an immediate turn to the left as I start checking all the of the corners I can, staying close to her back. The house has obviously been abandoned for a while; a solid layer of dust covers everything.

"Slate," Rodriguez whispers as she moves into the formal living room closer to the body.

And that's when I see them. The soft tracks in the dust off to the left. I'm about to call out to Rodriguez to stop when an earthshattering boom explodes in my ear.

Immediately I'm covered in hot, sticky liquid. I blink a few times, but when my vision clears, I see the eyes of Detective Rodriguez staring at me in shock. Only then do I notice the giant hole in the side of her head, and she falls to the ground, dead. I barely have time to register the fact I'm covered in her blood and brains before something strikes me on the back of the skull.

I watch the floor rush up to me before I black out.

Chapter Twenty-Seven

I WAKE WITH A START, MY HEAD POUNDING. DARKNESS surrounds me and it takes me a full two seconds to remember what happened.

I sit up as fast as I can, only for a headache to rush to the forefront, beating on the inside of my skull so hard that I cry out, and have to lay back down. My mind is a mess of images and sounds; it's like a symphony is playing over and over in my head but there's no rhythm or tempo. It's just a bunch of noise. When I try to stand, my stomach pitches and I wretch all over the ground. I take a few deep breaths, the acrid taste on my lips only intensifying. Nothing about any of this is good. Things have gone very wrong. Based on my response to trying to get up, I have to assume I have a concussion. Which means it's a miracle I woke up at all. And I can't let myself fall back asleep, no matter what. The ground beneath me is anything but soft. It feels like hardened concrete, though not one bit of it is even or smooth. It's like laying on top of a rock.

I close my eyes again to stop my head from spinning and to try to gather enough strength to stand, but all I see are Rodriguez's eyes staring back at me. Accusing me. Blaming me.

I don't even know what happened. One minute we were investigating the house, then I saw the footprints leading away. Now I realize there was a large cabinet or armoire in that room, and the prints led to it. He must have been hiding in there, waiting for us. I completely misjudged the situation, and now a good cop is dead and I'm...I have no idea where I am. Or what is about to happen.

A sliver of light cuts through the darkness above me, streaming through what look like old wooden boards. But they're at least ten feet above my head and the light coming through is barely enough so that I can see my own hands, much less the space that I'm in.

Reaching back and feeling my head, there's a lump and what feels like dried blood where I was struck. It's impossible to tell what hit me, all I know is it was hard and metal, and it was enough to take me out. It could have killed me, but fortunately it hasn't yet. Finally, I manage to sit up again and check the rest of myself. No other wounds as far as I can tell, but from the coppery smell close to my nose, I have to assume I'm still covered in Rodriguez's blood.

How could I have been so blind? I didn't even see him until it was too late. No, scratch that, I didn't see him at all. I *heard* the gunshot and I saw the blood spray, but I never saw him. I really need to give Rosewater some credit, he's a much more ruthless individual than I'd anticipated. Perhaps he killed Jaeden after all—it would at least explain this brutality.

What it doesn't explain is why I am still alive.

He obviously had no problem or hesitation in killing Rodriguez, but why not kill me too? Why not just shoot us both? And if Rosewater was the one who attacked us, who was that I saw in the living room? Another victim he hadn't finished with yet?

The whole space spins again as vertigo takes over and I flop over on my side, my shoulder hitting the hard ground. It takes every bit of my willpower not to cry out again, but the pain in my head is intense and all I want to do is close my eyes and try to sleep it off. But I force them open, force myself to stay awake, to keep my mind active.

Everything I had on me is gone. My gun, badge, holster, phone, keys, wallet, everything. Even my blazer is missing, which would have been required to remove to get my holster off. Rosewater is clever. He's not about to leave me leather straps that I might be able to fashion a tool with. This man has done this before. Perhaps many times before. He's experienced, and he knows how to keep someone in captivity.

Maybe I'm looking at this the wrong way. He could have done the same thing to Jaeden he's doing with me. He could have held him for a time before deciding to finally kill him. In fact, he may have even held him in here.

I crane my head as far as I can, trying to get my eyes to adjust, only to find that I'm in what seems like a well of some sort. The dark edges of the walls are curved and the walls look to be made out of the same material as the floor, like the concrete has been worn away over years of use.

The walls of the room curve all the way around so that I can at least determine I'm in a large cylinder. The only interruption I see in the walls is either a feed or a drainage pipe at the base of the wall near my feet. I take a deep breath and sit up again, the entire room spinning for a good minute before it calms down. Once I'm sure I won't throw up again, I reach over to the pipe. It's barely large enough for my hand. Other than that, there's nothing else here. It's an empty room. I look up again, only to see the wooden slats that look like a cover. It really does feel like a well. If I had to make a guess, I'd say I'm still on the farm somewhere. Rosewater must have put me here for safekeeping until he's ready for the next stage of his plan.

Either that, or he's waiting for me to die. Without water down here I'll last two days, maybe three at best. But honestly, if I don't get medical attention for this wound, I'll probably succumb to a brain hemorrhage before that.

It takes me a good fifteen minutes to get on my feet without feeling like I'm going to fall over. I take it slow at first, and the pounding in my head increases, but this is my best option for staying awake. If I keep lying on the ground, I'll lose consciousness eventually. I need to find some way out of here, contact Zara and the Bureau. We're way out here though, which means I'm going to have a hard time finding help without my phone. When Rodriguez and I drove up, I think the last house I saw was at least a mile or two down the road. There's no way I can walk a mile in my condition. I'll be good to make it from the farmhouse back to the trailer. I remember seeing a landline in the trailer, but there's a good chance that's where Rosewater is holed up. Somehow he managed to lure us into his trap. Maybe he does that with all his victims. I shut my eyes for a second and think back to the profile. He's a solitary killer—he takes one victim at a time. Is that why he killed Rodriguez immediately and spared me? Am I only alive because I happened to be the second person in the house?

I can't think about that now. I need to focus on getting out of here and finding help. Everything else is secondary. I manage to feel the walls, looking for handholds, old pipes or rocks that might have fallen away, anything that might allow me to grab hold and hoist myself out of here. But there's nothing. Somehow Rosewater got me down in this hole; he didn't just toss me in. If he had, I'd be sporting broken bones, or I'd already be dead. He must have a ladder outside the well. But given we're all alone out here, I'm not about to start calling for help. He lives alone, miles away from the nearest neighbor. No one else is going to be out here to help me, and I don't necessarily want him to know I'm awake. That might inadvertently push things into motion.

Right now, I see two options. Either he leaves me down

201 The Secret Seven

here until I expire from dehydration or this damn concussion, or he's coming to get me at some point. My guess is on the latter, given what I know about Jaeden Peters. There was no indication he was starved of food or water before he was killed, not to mention there wasn't enough time. He was last seen Tuesday night and his body was found the following morning. If Rosewater sticks to his M.O., then he'll come for me soon. Which means my only hope of getting out of here is to continue to pretend like I'm unconscious, then when he lowers himself down here to get me, I can fend him off, use the ladder to get out, and then get to the phone in the trailer.

It's not a great plan, as it requires me to lie back down. But it's all I've got. Otherwise, this well will be the last thing I ever see.

Zara's going to kill me either way. We've had discussions about me going out into the field on my own before. I just hadn't expected Rosewater to be our killer; he didn't seem like he fit. But I have to remember that not everyone fits into a pre-defined box and sometimes you never really know what a person is capable of. That mis-estimation cost Rodriguez her life. I only hope it doesn't cost me mine as well. I need to make this right, for her and her kids, at least.

Inching myself back down slowly, I lay back on the hard concrete. Immediately the tension in my head relaxes and it's like I can breathe again. But a second later I have to snap my eyes open as I could feel myself falling back into unconsciousness.

I only hope I can hold on, a while longer.

Chapter Twenty-Eight

MY EYES FLUTTER AS AN INTENSE PRESSURE FILLS THE BACK OF my head. It isn't painful, but it is jarring, and I try to get up, only to realize I've been restrained. I'm also no longer in the well, as this room is bright and well-lit. Dammit, I lost consciousness again and didn't even realize it. And now I've missed my only chance to get out of here, but I don't even know where here is. The entire room smells of antiseptic and I realize I'm lying on a gurney of sorts. For a moment I feel a flood of relief as I think maybe someone found me after all and transported me to a hospital.

But then I remember the restraints and as I try to pull on them again, I can tell both my legs and arms have been strapped down, but I'm upside down, looking at a tile floor through a cut-out in the gurney. "That's going to be a problem," a male voice says. I don't recognize it.

"Wha—" I say, but my voice is foreign to me. It's rough and dry and I realize just how thirsty I am.

"She's awake," the voice says. "Call them in, this will have to wait."

"How is it supposed to work with a massive gash on the

back of her head? Can he incorporate that?" another voice asks, also male. It's another voice I've never heard before.

"That's not our problem, at least not yet. We've done all we can for now, we'll let him figure it out. I still don't think this is the best course of action."

What are they talking about? What's going on here? And where is Rosewater? I don't understand any of this.

"What if she falls back asleep?" the second voice asks.

"She'll be okay for a few hours. I gave her a stimulant. It should keep her awake long enough, even with the swelling."

They're talking about my injury. Someone gave me a stimulant? To wake me back up?

I feel hands yanking on the restraints around my legs, freeing them, and then around my arms as well. I want to jump off this gurney and start showing these two they've messed with the wrong FBI agent, but I feel like I can barely move. It's like my entire body is stuck in molasses and it takes everything I have just to try and push myself up. Two pairs of arms grab me and help me off the gurney. I end up collapsing on the tile floor.

"Goddammit," the first voice says. "Keep her standing, we have to get her cleaned up."

"Sorry, I didn't expect her to be so heavy."

My nostrils flare and I try to respond but I'm finding it hard to form any words. It's like I've become trapped in my own body. Hands wrap around both of my arms and hoist me up. I'm in what looks like a surgical bay, though there are no windows. Bright fluorescents above me cause me to squint and I try to raise my hand to block out the light, but it's no good. I'm being propelled forward, with my legs only doing the bare minimum. The two men are keeping me upright and ushering me through a pair of double doors, away from the gurney room.

The hallway is dark and empty, though every other light above us is on. We turn down another hallway and as we do I get a partial look at one of the men carrying me. He's on the younger side, probably no older than thirty, with a beard and glasses. He's wearing a workman's coveralls over his clothes, and he has on gloves. I manage to turn my head to the other side to see the other man, the "boss". He's probably in his forties, his hair beginning to gray, though his face is lined, and he sports more of a paunch than his compatriot. Like his associate, though, he's also wearing coveralls and gloves.

As they carry me through the halls, I feel some strength begin to come back to my legs and I manage to get them to move in tandem with the two men. I don't have nearly the strength to fight them off, but at least I can help support myself.

"See, she'll be okay in a few minutes," the first man tells the second. "It just takes a minute to get through her system."

"What's…going on?" I finally manage to ask.

"You'll find out," he says as we head through another swinging door into another room with a tile floor. There's a grate in the middle of the floor and I notice the hoses that are hung on the wall, attached to large sprayers.

They bring me to the middle of the room and let go of me. For a second I think I'll fall, but I manage to remain standing under my own power, though it's taking a lot of effort. The first man goes to the swinging door and throws a deadbolt on it. "Strip," he says.

I glare at him like he's lost his mind.

He pulls a Glock from his waistband that I'd missed before and points it at the ground. "Are you going to make this difficult?"

A glance to the second man tells me he's armed as well, but he hasn't pulled his weapon. If I felt like myself, I have no doubt I could take them. But they've given me something. It's taking everything I have to remain standing right now.

"Listen, girlie," the first man says. "We got a job to do.

Now I don't give two shits about your modesty. Either strip, or we do it for you. One way or another, it's happening."

"I'd rather die," I growl through my teeth.

He rolls his eyes. "Oh for…fine, we'll do this the hard way." He places his weapon back in his waistband and grabs one of the hoses from the wall, where it's attached to what looks like a power sprayer. The whole unit is attached to a control panel on the wall, which he switches on. It hums and one of the lights on it turns green. "I tried to warn you," he says.

He lifts the sprayer and pulls the trigger.

I'm hit with a blast of water so strong that it knocks me over, completely drenching me. The water is freezing cold, which does something to my muscles, invigorating them with enough energy that I manage to actually put my hands up for all the good it does me. But he keeps spraying and just as I feel like I'm going to drown, he turns off the water.

I'm completely soaked, sitting up against the far wall which I didn't even realize I'd hit due to the force of the power sprayer. Dark brown and crimson water travels from me to the drain in the middle of the room. I reach up and wipe my face, only to realize I'm still covered in what's left of Rodriguez's dried blood.

"Now get out of those clothes so we can get you cleaned off, or I'll just keep spraying you on the highest setting," the man says.

Seeing as the sprayer is like a firehose, strong enough to knock me over, I don't see that I have much choice, especially if I want to see what this is all about. I lock my gaze on him and remove my soaked blouse, then my shoes and suit pants.

"All of it," he says, indicating my underwear. He's got a sneer on his face but I see the glint in his eye. When I look over to his partner, he's averting his eyes, but not doing a very good job of it.

The first man points the sprayer at me again and I

grimace. I remove my bra and panties, and manage to stand back up, not bothering to cover myself.

"Finally," he says and returns to the control unit, turning the pressure on the sprayer down. "Now hold still."

I shut my eyes while he sprays me all over and I feel the second jet of water from the other man. I'm humiliated, but I'm not going to let them see it. "Turn around." I do, opening my eyes. I look down and see the dark blood stains running down my legs and to the drain. How much of her blood did I have on me? When the water hits the back of my head I wince.

"Careful, you idiot!" the first man says. "You want that to split back open?"

"Sorry Vince," he says.

"Don't use my name," Vince barks.

They finish spraying, though I keep my back to them. I hear the bolt to the door being thrown again and look over my shoulder to see the second man leave then return with two towels. He tosses them to me, which I take and wrap one around myself. Vince grabs something from outside the room then returns as well with a metal stool and a stack of clean clothes on it, along with a pair of shoes. Strangely, they look exactly like the clothes I was wearing just a moment ago.

"Dry off, get dressed," Vince says. "And don't try anything." He steps back from the stool and pulls his weapon from his waist again, keeping his eyes on me.

I don't understand anything of what's going on here. Why are they cleaning me up and giving me fresh clothes? Who are these men and what do they have to do with Rosewater?

I take a moment to dry off, then pull on the new clothes. They fit so well they could have been from my own closet. In fact, when I look closely, they are the same brand and size as items in my closet. There's one item in the pile that I didn't have before: my blazer. I pull it back on and slip on my shoes, glad to be clean and dry. Though my hair is still damp. There's only so much I can do with a towel.

"C'mon, you look perfect," Vince says, sarcasm seeping from his words.

"What's going on?" I ask. After being blasted with ice-cold water, I feel more awake and alert than I have since before I woke up in that hole. "Where am I? What happened to Rosewater?"

Vince motions with the gun, indicating I should head back out into the hallway, which I do. He and the other man follow me out. "That way," he says, pointing down the dark hallway. "All the way to the elevators."

I turn to him. "No, tell me what's going on here. Who are you?"

"Lady," he says, his impatience getting the better of him. "I just spent the last half hour cleaning your wounds and getting you ready. Now I will shoot you if I have to, but that means we have to start all over and I really don't want to waste my time. Now, do the smart thing and walk down there to the elevators and don't ask any more questions."

I can tell that Vince doesn't have a stake in this game. This is just a job to him, one that he will do no matter what happens. He's not the person I need to be asking. And I have to assume they wouldn't have gone to all this trouble to clean me up if they were just going to kill me anyway. Something more is going on here, and I need to find out what it is.

I glance between him and his partner, then I turn and head down the hallway to the elevators. When we reach them, there is only one button, which tells me we're either on the top or the bottom floor of whatever building this is, though my bet is on the bottom, hence the lack of windows.

"Go ahead, press it," Vince says and I do. A second later the doors ding and open and the three of us step inside."

"Top floor," Vince says as the doors close. Whatever building we're in has twenty floors total, including a basement level, which is where I assume we are. The ground level is marked with a big "L". But there's no way I could incapacitate both these guys and get out of here unscathed. The ringing in my head is beginning to return now that my adrenaline has peaked.

I reach over and press the button for the top floor. We stand in silence as the elevator takes us up, though I catch myself swaying a bit. I'm still not back to even twenty-five percent yet, but at least I'm standing under my own power.

When the doors open, I'm ushered out into the plush foyer which is done up in dark woods. There's a large plant opposite the wall with the elevator banks and a pair of plate glass windows finally gives me the sense of where I am and what time of day it is.

Before us, the lights of a city glisten in the night. In the distance I can see the Washington Monument lit up. A white, stone obelisk in the middle of the lawn. I'm back in D.C. More accurately, I'm just across the Potomac in one of the high rises that are part of Crystal City, Virginia.

"This way," Vince says, pointing down the hallway to large, wooden double doors.

I do as I'm told, trying to work out how long I've been out. If it's nighttime, then it's been at least eight hours already, maybe longer. As we reach the double doors, they open from the inside, two men in dark suits and dark sunglasses opening them as we arrive.

Before me sits a reception desk for a law firm, one I've never heard of, but there's no one at the station. However all the lights in the office are on. I'm led down one of the corridors all the way to the end where I'm presented with another set of double doors. Whatever this is, I doubt I'm getting out of it. There are too many passages, too many bodies in my way.

Behind this set of doors is a large, impressive, two-story office. Large windows frame out the back wall, giving me a gorgeous view of the city beyond, and the room itself is lush with plush furniture and rich woods that accentuate the room. A large desk sits in the middle, behind which sits a large, green high-back chair, though it's empty.

I look around, but there's no one in here. I turn back to look at the two men who brought me here and the two other men in dark sunglasses who seem to be guarding the place.

"Now what?" I ask. "Are you guys part of the Organization or what?"

"I would have thought that was obvious," a familiar voice says. I turn and see a false part of the wall has opened up, revealing a second room off to the side. And standing there, wiping out a rocks glass is my boss's boss, Deputy Director Cochran.

Chapter Twenty-Nine

"I WISH I COULD SAY I'M SURPRISED," I SAY UPON SEEING Cochran's face. The truth is, I *am* surprised, I just don't want him to know it. My mind is lit up like a Christmas Tree trying to figure out what this means,. What damage has Cochran done, seeing as he's obviously been a member of the Organization this entire time.

Cochran smiles, and finishes wiping out the glass. I can see now that the room he was in is a bar of sorts, stocked to the brim with old and rare liquors. "Can I get you something?" He points at me with the glass. "You like...single malts? Am I right?"

"Are we good here?" Vince asks from behind me.

Cochran makes a motion with his hand, and they retreat from the room while the two bodyguards stay. "Take a seat, Emily. Let's have a chat."

"I'd rather stand," I say.

"I'm sure you would. You're stubborn like that," he replies as he pulls out a bottle of scotch older than me. "But you're weak and will probably fall over in about three minutes from that blow to your head if you don't take a load off."

I eye one of the plush chairs that sits opposite his desk and grumble as I take a seat, sinking into it. I do feel a little better sitting, but I have so many questions that my brain feels like it's going to explode.

He finishes pouring our drinks then walks over and places mine on the desk in front of me. "Your file says you have experience in hand-to-hand combat. I've never seen it myself, but I'm willing to bet if you could get a hold of me right now, you'd take me down in a second."

"You can count on it," I reply.

He chuckles and takes a seat in the high back, holding his drink between his hands. "Thankfully, you're in no shape to attack anyone. Which is good for both of us, it gives us a chance to talk."

"I don't want to talk," I say. "I want to arrest you."

"That's not true," he says. "You do want to talk. You want to know what this is all about. You want to know how you got here from that farm out in Maryland. You want to know who killed Jaeden Peters and Mariel Rodriguez. And most of all, you want to know why you're here right now."

He's right. He obviously already knows everything, which means none of this was a coincidence. Was I always *supposed* to end up here?

"That's what it always comes down to, doesn't it?" he asks. "Finding the truth. Seeking out justice for those who've been wronged. Solving a case and bringing those responsible in to bear the weight of their misdeeds. It's all very noble."

I don't reply. It's obvious he wants an audience, otherwise I wouldn't be here. So I'm content to just let him spill his guts until I have enough energy to take him and his cronies on. There has to be a phone somewhere in this office.

"Not even a rebuttal?" he asks, smiling. "And here I was, thinking you were a trained investigator." He leans forward, placing his drink on the desk. "Don't you want to get to the heart of the matter? Solve the mystery?"

"I'd rather see you behind bars," I tell him. "You're a traitor. You've betrayed everything you gave an oath to protect. And for what? Money? Power? I think what's most disappointing is it's all so cliché. I would have expected better from the Deputy Director of the FBI."

"There's that biting wit I've heard so much about," he says, sitting back and taking a sip. He relishes it for a moment. "You really should try it. It only gets better with age."

"I'll pass."

"As you wish." He stands, walking around to the back of his chair and placing his hands on either side, staring at me. "Let's get down to it, shall we. Why are you sitting here, in front of me, instead of lying at the bottom of that well? Or worse, with a hole in your head, like poor Detective Rodriguez."

"You seem to have all the answers," I say. "You tell me."

"Spitball for me a minute. Let's see how good your powers of deduction are. I keep hearing about how you manage to solve all these miracle cases, sometimes one after another. But you've been quiet the past few weeks. No big breaks?"

I can't believe I'm sitting here, being subjected to this. I almost wish he'd just do whatever it is he plans on doing and gets on with it. But this could be my only opportunity. I still don't know what he wants from me, but maybe stalling will give me enough time to figure a way out of this place.

"You're in league with Rosewater somehow," I say. "That's my initial thought, though it doesn't make sense. If you're part of the Organization, why would you align yourself with a copycat killer?"

"You're right, that doesn't make much sense at all," he says, and picks his drink back up, taking another sip. "Keep going."

"So if you're not working with him, then you must have been tracking him," I say. "And you obviously still have eyes on me, despite Camille's death. Wallace thought you'd gone underground, that there had been too much heat lately, and we were unlikely to find you again. Obviously, that was wrong. But you're the one who brought Wallace in…" I trail off, my train of thought completely jumping the tracks. Is Wallace part of the Organization too? I'd potentially considered that at one point, when Rodriguez pointed out his motivations, and now it seems like it's even more certain. How many people in this Organization have infiltrated the FBI? "DuBois wasn't the only one, was he?"

Cochran purses his lips, disappointment clouding his face. "Ah, Emily. I was really hoping you'd be able to work it out. But then again, you never had all the cards, did you?"

"Enough with these games," I tell him, getting frustrated. "Just tell me what this is all about."

He gives me a rueful smile. "The heat. The passion. The anger. You are one of the most promising young agents in the Bureau, did you know that? And would you like to know why? It's because you put the job first. You put it above your family, your friendships, your personal health…everything. You're exactly the kind of person we look for. The one who will give the Bureau her all and leave nothing on the table."

I want to refute him. I want to tell him he's wrong, that I don't put my job first. But he's right. Tears sting my eyes, but I manage to keep them from cascading over and on to my cheeks. I have sacrificed everything for this job. I did it because being an FBI agent was the first thing in my life I was good at. And I couldn't lose that. I couldn't stop being the best I could be. Which meant I had to sacrifice a lot.

"Now you take someone like Agent Sutton. Married, kids, a life outside the Bureau. He's a good Agent, don't get me wrong. But he's no Emily Slate. When the workday is done, he'll put the cases away and go home to his loving family. He'll waste precious time with his loved ones, time that could be used hunting down a kidnapper, or a killer. People will suffer because he decided his family time was more important than their lives. But not you."

I look away as the tears finally do break. And I have to wipe them away. "Just get on with it already," I say, my voice shaky. "You didn't bring me here to sing my praises."

"No, I didn't," Cochran says. "I just want you to know that we understand each other, Emily. You and I are the same. We put the job first, everything else comes second."

"If you put the job first, you wouldn't have failed in your duty," I say.

"You misunderstand. *My* job is not with the Bureau. That's just a tool I use. My primary job is to ensure the safety and survival of the members of my organization. *That* is the true oath I have taken."

"Great for you," I say.

He sighs. "Emily, we don't have a lot of time. And I want to try and get through as much of this as I can."

"Why?" I spit. "Need to go back and throw up a smoke-screen to explain my disappearance? Or even better, are you going to offer me a job?"

His face falls a little, but he manages to recover. "I'm afraid not, no. I'd love to spar with you all evening, but seeing as we're limited in how much time we have together, I'm afraid I must get on with it." He walks around the chair and takes a seat again. "The reason for all of this...Jaeden's death, Rodriguez, the farm, Rosewater...all of it was for you."

"For me?" I ask.

He nods. "To draw you in. So that you and I might have this sacred time together."

"You mean...you engineered all of this, just to get me here?" He nods and I find the strength to shoot up out of my chair. "Why?" I demand. I feel the two men close in from behind me. Cochran raises a hand that stops them. "Why all the unnecessary killing? Why such an elaborate—oh my God, Rosewater, he wasn't even part of this, was he? You killed him too? He was the body I saw in the house."

Cochran nods.

"You are my *boss*. If you wanted to talk to me all you had to do was call me into your office. Or invite me out for a drink. This is…this is insane."

He shakes his head. "You still don't understand, Emily. I did all of this because this is the last time we will ever meet."

My eyes widen. I should have known. They *are* going to kill me, after all. Camille was right, they were never going to stop. "Then why not just shoot me in the head like Rodriguez? Why all this…theater?"

He takes a deep breath. "Because you loved my son very deeply. And I thought you deserved an explanation." I stumble back and fall back into the chair when his words hit me. He sees the recognition on my face. "That's right. Your husband was my son. My given name is James Hunter. It's a pleasure to finally meet you."

Chapter Thirty

AT FIRST MY MIND CAN'T PROCESS IT. HE HAS TO BE LYING IN
order to get under my skin. Or for some other reason that I
can't see right now. There's no way he can be Matt's father.
Matt's father died before we ever met. But as I study his face, I
see some resemblance. Is my mind trying to make sense of the
situation? I don't know. What I do know is I'm not getting out
of this. The Organization has had its sights on me ever since I
found out they killed Gerald Wright. It seems like their elaborate trap has worked.

"I...don't understand," I manage to say.

He gives me a solemn nod. "I wouldn't expect you to.
Matt told you I was dead. My son had a natural talent for
telling lies. Ever since he was little, he could tell a lie like it was
the truth and unless you *knew* different, you'd believe it. It's
what made him such a good member of our organization.
Chris, on the other hand...I had to teach Chris how to hide
his lies in his anger. It was the only way he could do it and not
be found out, which unfortunately meant he was angry a lot
of the time. As I'm sure you know, anger produces a lot of the
same physiological effects that lying does, which is why when
our suspects take lie detector tests, we require them to be calm

as their agitation will skew the test. That's what Chris did." He leans back in his chair. "But not Matt. He could lie with a straight face and a smile, and his blood pressure wouldn't even move. Most of us are afraid of getting caught. But not him. It was a true gift."

"Matt," I say, my eyes tearing up again. The bastard never told me a single truth the entire time we were married.

Cochran—or Hunter smiles. "Try not to be too hard on him. He was only doing his job. I tried to warn him not to get involved with an FBI agent, that it was too dangerous. But he was head over heels in love with you. He'd talk about you all the time, and he was confident he could live with a foot in both worlds. With an expertly crafted story, he said he could still do his job, and be a good husband to you."

"How was he a good husband if all he did was lie to me all the time?" I ask.

Hunter gives me a sad smile. "Do you think *I* could talk him out of it? Believe me, I tried. I told him it would only lead to trouble. I knew one day he'd slip up and you'd find out. Then we'd either be forced to bring you into the Organization or kill you."

"He never slipped up," I say. "Never said a word about it. Every day he came home like he'd been counseling students all day. He even told me some of their stories. I never suspected." I pause. "Is that what happened with Dani and Chris? Did he let it slip to her?"

"Dani was...unique. She already had a lot of the qualifications we were looking for in new candidates, due to her troubled past. Chris just came right out and told her and gave her the offer right there. Brought her in the next day and we began her training." He pauses. "Dani was smart enough to know that as soon as Chris told her, she was either with us, or a corpse. But I was always worried about you. I made sure we had someone keeping an eye on you in the Bureau, just in case you got wind of anything."

"You," I say.

He nods. "And a few key others. DuBois, for instance. I had to make sure you never suspected who Matt really was, otherwise, you could have blindsided us. You almost did with that whole fiasco at the barn."

"I stopped a young girl from being raped," I say. "What you call a fiasco I call a sick and twisted individual trying to irreparably damage a young girl."

He nods. "I agree. Hirst always did have his...proclivities. As do a few of our other members. Unfortunately, we must look the other way if we want to survive. The greater good and all that."

"You make me want to puke," I tell him. "Was Matt involved in those *proclivities* as well? Or did he just like to watch?"

Hunter grimaces. "Matt never approved and lobbied the group on multiple occasions to banish those members but was struck down. You know what he did for us, don't you?" I shake my head; not like I care. "He provided counseling services for all our members and associates. That was his primary function."

"I'm glad to know not all of it was a lie, then," I say, sarcasm dripping from my words. When I first met Matt, he said he was working as a counselor at a local college. Only come to find out the college had never heard of him. Zara managed to fish that one out.

"No, it wasn't," Hunter continues. "In fact, as time went on, Matt began to express more and more dissatisfaction with the Organization as a whole. Here he was, an integral part of this organization that he'd been a part of his entire life, and all of a sudden he no longer thought what he was doing was moral."

"I don't see how he ever thought that," I spit. "What changed his mind?"

Hunter points at me with his glass in hand. "You did."

"Me?" I give him a blank stare.

He nods. "I didn't anticipate it at the time, but apparently, being married to you and seeing all the good you were doing had quite the effect on my son. As the days and months went on, he continued to call for radical change to the organization. And when he was met with nothing but rebuttal from all seven of our primary members, including myself, he decided to take matters in his own hands."

I furrow my brow. "What does that mean?"

"It means he was going to expose us, to you, Emily," Hunter says. "I only found out through Chris. And I knew we didn't have much time. Matt was becoming more combative by the day, but he was smart enough to keep his plans from me. Regardless, I couldn't let him move forward."

My heart is hammering in my chest as it hits me. "*You*. You ordered Camille to kill him."

Hunter's eyes begin to well with his own tears. "He was my own flesh and blood, the heir to an empire passed down from his grandfather. But I couldn't let him disrupt everything we'd built. I did what I did, for the good of the Organization. So now you know why I say that we two are alike—we're willing to do anything for our jobs. Even if it comes at great personal cost."

"You *bastard!*" I yell. A burst of energy surges through me and I scramble over the desk, trying to get at him, knocking my glass away as I do. I hear it hit something hard and shatter. I don't care about anything in the moment except wrapping my hands around his neck and squeezing the life out of him. But before I'm halfway across the desk, two pairs of strong hands pull me back and force me back into the seat again, holding me down. The two guards have me in what is essentially a death lock.

"I'm sorry, Emily, I thought you'd understand," Hunter says, standing and crossing in front of the desk. I hear the door open behind me, but I can't turn my head to look and see who it is.

"How could you?" I say. "He was your *son*. My *husband*. And you killed him because he wanted to do the right thing!"

Hunter shakes his head. "I thought you were smarter than this, that you understood the sacrifice I made. I've lost both of my sons, one by my own actions, and one by yours. It was my hope that with this meeting we could come to an understanding. I thought I owed you that much, at least, for taking such good care of him for those four years. If it's any consolation, he never stopped loving you." Tears stream down my face at his words.

Another man appears beside Hunter, causing me to squirm even more. I recognize him immediately. It's Rossovich, the same man I had in custody when I was trying to track down Avery Huxley. I ended up letting him go in exchange for her location.

He's gaunter than when I last saw him; the cancer must be getting more aggressive. But his face is as impassionate as ever.

"James," he says, staring at me through his spectacles.

"Hello Maurice," Hunter says. "You're right on time. We're just about done here. Unfortunately, I wasn't able to get through to her."

"I told you this was a waste of time and resources," Rossovich says. "The capture, fixing her wound, the cleanup. It's all taken valuable time. What do you think the coroner is going to say when they discover she has a concussion?"

"That she got it in the shootout with Rosewater," Hunter says, walking back around the desk. "It doesn't need to be perfect, just believable enough."

"What are you going to do?" I growl.

"Now, Emily. We can't have you die the same way as your husband, can we? I think two heart attacks would look a little too suspicious," Hunter says. "We'll be returning you to the farm, where everything else is already staged and ready." He looks at Rossovich who nods. "The evidence will show you went to confront Rosewater upon the suspicion he had something to do with Jaeden's murder, he surprised you and shot both you and Rodriguez, but not before you got off a fatal shot yourself. Your bullet is already lodged inside his body and my associates have spent the past few hours setting the detective and all the additional evidence. All we need is to finish the scene is you."

Rossovich reaches down and pulls my blazer over my bare shoulder, then rubs the area with an alcoholic pad. He then sticks a needle in my arm and pushes the plunger. "What is that?" I say, trying to struggle away from him, but the two men have me pinned hard. Even at full strength I'd have a hard time getting them off me.

"The same thing that killed your husband," he says. "Succinylcholine. It's hard to detect and simulates a heart attack in the victim. It's what Camille used on Gerald Wright, if you're curious." He retrieves the needle from my skin and puts a cap back on it, placing it back in his jacket pocket.

I'm horrified that stuff is already in my bloodstream and there's nothing I can do about it. "I thought you said it would look too obvious if I had a heart attack."

"It will render your body inert without leaving any evidence," Hunter says. "Then we'll be able to stage it as we see fit, including putting as many bullets in you as necessary, but not until you're in the right place to make sure the blood splatter patterns match up. We've already had to re-stage the scene with Rodriguez's blood."

"That's why you wanted me clean," I say. "So you could set the scene differently."

He points at me again. "Clever girl." He addresses Rossovich again. "You better get going, while she can still walk."

This is it. I'm about to be taken to my death, and there's nothing I can do about it. Hunter will continue working for the Bureau, perhaps even becoming director one day. I can't imagine the level of damage he'll do once he's in place.

"I'll call you once it's done," Rossovich replies, and the two men yank me up on my feet. The sensation is jarring, especially after I almost launched myself over the table and my knees give out. I hit the ground, my face landing on the plush carpet right beside what's left of my overturned glass. I can still smell the scotch soaking into the fibers.

"Get her up," Hunter says. Once the men pull me to my feet again, I face him one last time. "It was a pleasure meeting you, Emily. I'm sorry it couldn't have been under better circumstances. I wish you a swift and painless death."

I want to tell him to go fuck himself, but I just give him the hardest glare I can before I'm dragged from the room to my fate.

Chapter Thirty-One

"STEP ON IT, I WANT TO GET BACK OUT THERE AS SOON AS possible," Rossovich says, sliding into the car beside me. My hands were bound before I was led into the back of the SUV. Once I'm inside, one of the guards binds my feet as well before closing the door. He gets in the driver's side while the other guard gets in the passenger seat.

I look over at Rossovich, sitting beside me and he only gives me a creepy smile as the SUV pulls away from the building and onto the main road. "Quite the turn of events, wouldn't you say?"

I don't reply. I'm not about to give this man the satisfaction of hearing my voice again.

"I bet you're thinking now you probably should have arrested me after all," he continues, turning to look out his window. "Perhaps little Avery Huxley would have suffered, but you would have made the biggest case of your career, and potentially taken down our entire organization. You didn't know this at the time, but all of the Organization's records were right inside my house that night. Less than a hundred feet away. All you would have had to do was walk through the front door."

I wince at the missed opportunity. I knew letting Rossovich go was a risk, but it was one I had to take, for Avery's sake. I'd still make the same decision, even knowing that the entire organization only lay a few feet away from me.

My eyelids begin to feel heavy, and I can't help but wonder if this is the drug taking effect. Is that what will happen? I'll just fall into a painless sleep and pass away? Just like Matt.

God. Matt. I don't know whether I can trust what Hunter told me or not, but at least now I have something of an explanation. To know that he was going to turn on them...because of my influence. It makes me want to forgive him. But everything else he did...even if he lobbied for change within the Organization, he was still part of it. It took him four years to come to his senses, and *that* I may not be able to ever forgive.

Not like it matters much now. Seeing as I probably have less than twenty minutes to live.

"You proved quite the adversary, Ms. Slate," Rossovich says out of the blue. "I have to commend you on that much. Not only did you manage to turn one of our own assassins against us, but you were treated to something none of our other victims has ever experienced before: a meeting with one of the seven."

He leans closer, and I catch a whiff of something putrid, like an open wound, causing me to wrinkle my nose. "Did you know that once your sister-in-law was killed, I managed to lobby myself a position as a full chamber member? Seeing as you conveniently removed one from the ranks, I managed to take Jack Hirst's place."

He seems content to keep talking, so I let him. It's not like I'm going anywhere.

"You see, there are always seven members and fourteen associates. Only an associate can become a full chamber member, and the only way to do that is to wait for one of them to die. It's a lifelong oath we take when we join the organization. Your husband was an associate, due to take the place of his father when he finally passed. Of course, now that can't happen. The Hunter line will die with James when he passes, which means his spot will be up for grabs from any of the other associates." He leans a little closer, causing me to recoil. "You know, your actions inadvertently removed not one, but two full members from the council. Gerald Wright had been a longtime member, but we always knew if he was ever caught, he'd never be able to keep his mouth shut. Which is where Camille came in, of course."

This whole thing started with Gerald Wright. He had been a member of this organization and had been willing to spill his guts about them in exchange for leniency. I always thought he was full of shit. But when he told me he could tell me about my husband, he was actually telling the truth.

"You know, Emily," Rossovich says, inching even closer to me. I feel his hand on my thigh and look up to see a smarmy sneer on his face. "I don't have long for this world. And I've always been impressed by you. Once the succinylcholine takes hold and you…pass, I think I'll take my opportunity, seeing as I know you won't be able to do anything about it then. You've been a thorn in my side for far too long, it will feel good to get some of that frustration out."

My eyes widen at what he's suggesting.

He removes his glasses, his face coming even closer. The smell of death permeates my pores. "Don't worry about the mess. By then, we'll be able to clean you up with no problem. You'll have no fight left in you, if you get my meaning."

His grin is stomach-churning. I see my opening.

I suck in a deep breath through my nose and spit the shards of glass I managed to gather in my mouth from the carpet in his face. I can already taste my own blood in my mouth, but with the amount of adrenaline running through my system, I don't care.

Rossovich screams as pieces of glass strike his eyes and

face. He pulls back and I pitch forward, slamming my head into his, driving the glass even deeper.

"What the..." One of the guards turns and I sit back, raising my feet up and kick both of them out at the same time, striking him in the head. He jerks back and the back of his head hits the windshield with a crunch. The driver turns to try and grab me, but we're on the interstate by now and he begins swerving, causing another car to blare its horn.

"You bitch!" Rossovich yells, his hands flailing in front of him. I'm pretty sure I've blinded him as blood is running down his cheeks from his eyes. I hold my bound hands up as he flails around and manage to catch one of his arms between the two of mine. With a twist and a snap, his arm is broken and he's crying out in pain. The driver keeps trying to turn around but every time he does, the car veers out of the lane and cars all around us honk and sound their horns. If I can cause enough of a scene, I can get the local cops on our tail, but I don't know how long I have. This stuff is already in my bloodstream and despite my heart racing, I can feel myself growing more and more tired.

I won't last long at this pace.

Both Rossovich and the other guard are incapacitated, so I have to hedge my bets. I lift both arms up and over the head-rest of the driver's seat and get my bound hands around the neck of the driver. With all my strength I pull as hard as I can as he scratches and claws at my arms, doing everything he can to stop himself from being choked out.

From somewhere he produces a gun which he tries to fire behind him, but is flailing so hard the shot just goes into the vehicle's roof, though the sounds deafening. He fires seven more times, but each one misses, and I put my knees up against the back of the seat, pulling as hard as I possibly can. A few seconds later I hear a snap and he goes limp. The car lurches forward as the dead weight of his foot presses on the accelerator and the SUV begins to veer wildly. I pitch forward to grab the steering wheel, but my face is pressed up against the seat and all I can see is the interstate passing along beside us. I can't endanger the public any further than I already have, but I also have no way of controlling this vehicle.

The SUV continues to speed up and I know we have to be closing in on a hundred miles per hour. It's a miracle we haven't hit anyone else yet. I try to veer the wheel to the right, hoping we'll connect with one of the concrete barriers and the friction will slow us down when I feel a hand on my arm, jerking it away.

I turn my head to see the other guard has regained consciousness and is trying to get control of the vehicle too. If he somehow manages it, I'm definitely dead.

I'm sorry.

I yank the wheel as hard as I can to the left and immediately feel weightlessness take over as the SUV flips. My back hits the ceiling before I'm weightless again and thrown into the floorboard. I brace myself as best I can, and I see Rossovich above me, flailing about as the SUV continues to roll. At some point, his head breaks through the glass of one of the back windows, and then disappears completely when it's severed from his body, sending a spray of blood all over the inside of the SUV. My entire world is nothing but the sound of bending metal and breaking glass.

When the vehicle finally comes to a stop, I'm still in the floorboard, braced between the back of the front seats and the well of the back ones. What's left of Rossovich's body lays on the back seat itself, and in the front seats, both airbags have deployed, and I can't see the bodies of the guards.

My ears are ringing, and my entire world is still spinning. I feel the warmth of blood but don't know where it's coming from or if it's even mine. I can't forget I still have this shit inside me and I need to get to a hospital. Maybe it's not too late.

I kick as hard as I can against the bent back door closest to my feet. It's warped and bent, but moves when I keep kicking it, finally swinging open.

As soon as I move, I feel a sharp pain from somewhere in my side, though I don't know where, and at the moment it doesn't matter. Seeing as my hands and feet are still bound, I have to wiggle my way out of the car until I fall onto the hard pavement. All around me I see other vehicles that have stopped because of the crash. But there's no telling how far away emergency services are.

"Holy shit, someone is alive," I hear a voice say. A man rushes up to me his face coming into my vision. He's got a kind face, not unlike Matt's. "Hey, are you okay?"

I shake my head and he notices the bindings. "I…was… kidnapped," I croak. It doesn't sound like me.

He goes to work getting the ropes off my arms while another woman rushes over and starts working on my legs. "Call 911," I say.

"Someone already has," he tells me. "They're six minutes away."

I'm not sure I have six minutes. My vision is beginning to blur at the edges and my mind is getting fuzzy. I think the stuff is taking effect. I'll be dead soon, and the coroner will probably assume it's from the car wreck.

I feel my hands and legs go free and I try to sit up.

"Whoa there," the man says. "They're on their way."

"I can't wait," I manage to say. "I need to get to the clos-est…hospital."

He looks me over and seems to agree. "Here," he says, trying to help me up. "I can't take you; I ran into the back of another car when the accident happened."

"I can," the woman who removed the binds from my legs says. "My car just has a dent. My insurance won't cover it anyway."

The man passes me off to her and she puts my arm around her neck as she leads me to her car. "Are you sure this is a good idea? I've heard you're not supposed to move car crash victims."

I shake my head and it had the effect of sending me into vertigo, which almost causes me to collapse. "Urgent," I say.

She helps me over to her car, which I think is a Prius and a moment later I'm in the passenger seat. She gets in the driver's side. "The police are going to give me hell for leaving," she says.

I wave her off. "I'm...FBI. Don't worry about it."

"Jeez," she says, starting the car. "This *must* be serious." She guns it and I feel us take off down the highway. "The closest hospital is VHC, about three minutes from here. It's just the next exit."

I nod and feel the darkness begging to take over. I know if I fall asleep it's all over. If I don't tell the doctors what Hunter gave me, they'll never find it in time, and I'll die while they weigh their options. But I'm not sure I can make it in time.

"Do you...have a pen?" I croak.

"A pen?" she says, looking over at me like I'm crazy. She reaches down for her purse and digs in it while she keeps her eyes on the road. "Here, this is all I have." She hands me a sharpie.

"Perfect." With great effort I remove my blazer, which is ripped, torn and covered in blood. Some of which may be my own. I don't even know at this point.

I take my time to write each letter along my arm, though I'm sure I'm misspelling it. When I'm done, I draw a line to where I was injected with no idea if that will help or not.

"What are you doing?" the woman asks.

"They...injected me," I manage to say as I watch the pen fall from my hand, seemingly uncontrollably. I feel myself fall back against the seat.

"Ma'am? Ma'am! Hang on, we're almost there!" We zip down the exit ramp and blow through a red stoplight as the woman honks the whole way. I see the lights of the hospital sign pointing to the emergency room exit.

I'm here. I've made it.

But before we arrive everything goes dark. The last thing I see is a giant "E", glowing in the night.

E for Emily.

Chapter Thirty-Two

MY EYES SNAP OPEN. THE ROOM IS DARK, BUT I'M LYING ON something soft. A machine to my right makes a soft buzzing noise. The lights on the ceiling are off, but warm light is coming from somewhere behind me. I'm in a hospital room. I made it.

Reaching up, I feel my head, which has a bandage over part of it. The back of my head where I'd been hit has also been bandaged. I lift the covers to find I'm in a hospital gown, and I have another bandage across my midsection. I don't remember what that one is for. The word succinylcholine is still written on my left arm, though it looks as though it's a little faded. I also realize I completely spelled it wrong, but it looks like I got the message across.

A moment later a young woman in a lime green uniform pokes her head in. "You're awake," she says, approaching and checking my vitals. "How are you feeling?"

I blink a few times. "Sore." The word comes out a little muffled.

"Here," she says, reaching for my mouth. I open up and she removes some gauze that I didn't even know was in there. There's dried blood all over it.

"You're lucky to be alive," she says, looking at all the machines I realize I'm hooked up to. "Give me just a minute, I'll get the doctor."

"Wait," I say. "What day is it?"

"It's Wednesday morning," she says. "Still early."

Wednesday morning. Rodriguez and I got to the farm on Tuesday afternoon. That means everything that's happened has been in less than a day. "Am I…going to be okay?" I ask.

"Let me get the doctor," she says and heads out.

I hate hospitals. But at least my mind doesn't feel as woozy as I did before, though I'm worried about my heart. Not to mention I was just in a violent car wreck.

A few minutes later, an older woman with silver hair steps into the room. She's got on a while coat and a stethoscope hangs around her neck. While her face is lined, it's also soft, and she has kind eyes. "Good morning, Emily," she says.

"You know who I am?" I ask.

"Of course, the FBI was adamant we give you the best treatment we could. We've also had to shoo away some of your more…fervent associates."

I smile. Zara, I'm sure. Good, they know I'm here.

"Let's take a look," she says, making the same checks the nurse did, before shining a light in both my eyes. "How do you feel?"

"Better than I did, but still like I've been hit by a truck."

She nods. "I'm not sure how you got out of that vehicle under your own power. The other three occupants were dead on arrival. You're very lucky, though it did leave you with a nasty puncture wound in your spleen, which we've managed to stabilize."

"I didn't even realize," I say, looking down at the bandage around my midsection again.

"Probably because you were focused on this," she says, tapping my arm. "Had you not given us this information, you would have died within fifteen minutes of arriving. Thankfully, we were able to give you a healthy dose of dantrolene which counteracted the effects. But your body has been through a lot of trauma, including a head injury. And you had a lot of minor cuts inside your mouth, which I don't know how to explain. Fortunately, those look like they've healed up. Still, I want you staying here for the next couple of days for observation."

"Can I at least get up?"

She shakes her head. "Not until we're sure you're stabilized. I don't want to risk something because we were impatient." She gives me a smile. "Give your body time to heal, and you'll be back to your old self in a few weeks."

"*Weeks?*" The way I phrase it makes her laugh.

"Always with the FBI, you don't do well with down time, do you?"

I flick my gaze to the side. "I've been told that on more than one occasion."

"The good news is you don't have any dietary restrictions. And while we don't have the best food around, I'm sure your friends will be more than happy to bring you whatever you want."

I manage to relax back into the bed, nodding.

"I'll send Sarah back in here so she can start getting you used to your medication routine," the doctor says. "Just things to help you heal, and to keep your blood pressure low while we make sure all the succinylcholine is out of your system. If necessary, we can do a transfusion, but I don't think we'll need to go that far."

"Thanks," I say. "Do you have a phone I could use?"

"When the hospital renovated, they removed phones from the rooms because no one used them anymore. A cost cutting measure, I'm sure. But we have one at the nurse's station. I'll have someone bring it to you." She pats my shoulder. "Sit tight. Sarah will be back in a little while."

I give her a reassuring nod and she leaves, keeping the door cracked open.

As soon as she's gone, I push myself up out of the bed, and wheel the IV unit that I'm still attached to over to the small closet in the corner of the room. Inside are my dirty and bloody clothes, sealed in a bag. They may not be clean, but they're all I have. I manage to get the gown off and get dressed, despite the state of them.

I can't let Hunter—Cochran stay in his position a minute longer. He needs to be exposed as the traitor he is, though I'm not sure I have any physical evidence against him. I need to get in touch with...I don't know who. I can't trust Wallace, Cochran appointed him. There are only three people I know I *can* trust, so those need to be the people who I call.

Wincing, I pull out the IV last, and the machine beeps once, but seeing as I'm already dressed, nothing is stopping me from just leaving. Though as I take a few steps for the door, I realize that maybe I'm not in as good shape as I thought as my whole body is sore and doesn't want to cooperate. Still, I force the issue. Seeing as I don't have my ID, phone or vehicle, I'll need to call Liam to come and get me.

I make it out into the hallway, though I have to brace myself up against the wall.

"What in the hell do you think you're doing?" I look up, expecting to see Sarah the nurse, only to see Zara walking down the hallway toward me, a bouquet of flowers in one hand and a bag of fast-food breakfast in the other.

I smile. "Right on time. You just saved me a phone call."

"Emily," she chides. "You can't be out of bed. You have *trauma*. IA is sending two agents over here in a couple of hours to debrief you."

I shake my head. "It's not enough time. Cochran...he's a member of the organization. And Matt's father."

"*What?*" she says, nearly dropping the bag of food.

I nod. "He was the one behind Rodriguez's death. And Jaeden Peters. He was going to kill me too."

"Jesus, Em," Zara says. "Let's get you back in bed and I'll make a few calls. We have to keep a lid on this." She puts her arm around me, trying to guide me back to my room.

"Call Janice," I tell her. "She'll know who to trust. We have to go to the director himself. I don't know what Cochran will do when he finds out I'm alive. If he hasn't already."

"Okay, just…get back in bed before you start bleeding out all over the floor. I leave for one hour and all of a sudden you're running around like nothing happened?"

"You were here?" I ask.

"Came as soon as I heard about the wreck, since they said a woman with long dark hair who said she was with the FBI climbed out of that vehicle. I'm the one who ID'd you. I'm just glad I didn't have to ID a corpse."

"You almost did," I say. "Where's Liam?"

"He's at your apartment, taking care of Timber." She checks her watch. "He should be here by nine. You scared the shit out of both of us."

"I'm sorry," I say, turning around and heading back to my room. Maybe I'm not in good enough shape to face Cochran right now. But when I turn, I see a tall man striding toward us down the hall. He's wearing a dark trench coat with the top three buttons undone. Underneath I spot a nurse's uniform.

It's the exact same thing Camille had on when she came to kill Gerald Wright.

"Z," I say, staring at the man who has just spotted both of us. His eyes go wide. "He's with them. He's here to kill me."

Zara drops the flowers and the bag of food and pulls her weapon on the man. "Freeze! FBI!"

He produces a handgun from the overcoat and Zara squeezes off three rounds, which slam into his chest, and he falls back. Someone behind us screams and an alarm code goes off all around us.

Zara runs up to the man and kicks the gun away from his hand while keeping hers trained on him. Nurses and doctors come swarming up on her, while someone grabs hold of me from behind. I turn to see it's the same nurse from before—Sarah. "What are you doing out of bed? What's going on here? Did she just *shoot* that man?" she asks.

"It was an assassination attempt," I tell her as Zara calls it in and doctors begin working on the man to save his life.

"If you don't get back in bed you won't need an assassin to kill you," she chides, seemingly unaffected by the whole event. "Now come with me. We're getting you back in bed."

I'm in no condition to argue.

"I'm not going in there like this," I tell Zara, looking up at her face above me.

Liam leans down beside me, his cologne filling my nostrils. "Listen, hardhead. You're going in there like this, or you're not going at all."

I give him a glare that could melt steel.

"Or we could try it your way," he amends.

"No," Zara replies. "Don't let her get to you. She's been in a wreck, had a near-concussion, been held against her will, apparently hosed down with firehoses, and almost drugged to death. Oh yeah, and she spit glass at someone, which explains a lot about the head we found. She *is not* going into the office in anything other than a wheelchair." She places her hands on the handles behind me, pushing me forward.

"I'd listen to both of them," Janice says, having taken up a position on my right, while Liam is on my left. In the time since the assassination attempt, Zara has done an amazing job coordinating everything. She managed to get in contact with Janice and Liam and keep a wraps on the attempt at the hospital at least until we confronted Cochran. The only drawback was that because of my weakened state, she wouldn't let me come along unless I was in this damn chair.

Despite how tired I am, I feel energized and invigorated like I haven't in a long time.

"Ready?" Zara asks.

"Let's make it happen," I tell her. She nods and wheels me up to the elevator banks. The agent near the door eyes my chair for a second then nods, though his eyebrow goes up when he sees Janice. After everything that's happened, she was more than happy to come along and help. And seeing as how the Organization has infiltrated even higher than we thought, I'm not sure the FBI is going to be able to pass the buck on to her any longer.

The elevator doors open on the executive floor of the J. Edgar Hoover Building and Zara wheels me forward, with Liam and Janice walking beside us. She turns at the second to last door and we enter into a large secretary's office.

The woman at the desk looks up, confusion on her face. "Yes? How can I help you, agents?"

"We need to see the director," I say.

"I'm sorry, he's in a meeting right now," she replies. "His schedule is quite busy, but I'm sure I can find the time to pencil you in sometime next week."

"No thanks," Zara says. "We'll just take a minute." She wheels me to the closed door that leads to the FBI director's office and Janice opens it for us.

"Wait, you can't go in there," the secretary says. "I'm calling security."

"Go right ahead," Liam says. "We'll need them."

Zara wheels me into the office where Deputy Director Cochran sits on a sofa across from the Director David North. Both men stand as we barge into the room.

"Agents," Director North says. "What's going on?"

I glare at Cochran and for a moment his face is twisted in fury, but then it evens out and he actually smiles.

"Director North, we have some disturbing news," I tell him. "Deputy Director Cochran is not who he says he is. His real name is James Hunter, and he's a member of the organization that killed my husband, Gerald Wright, Galina Kiefer, Dani Hunter, and Jaeden Peters. His members have also been involved in child prostitution, racketeering, and conspiracy. While I have no doubt he will deny these charges, I can assure you I have evidence."

Director North looks over at Cochran. "Tom, what's going on here? Aren't these people under your supervision?"

"They seem to have been on the job too long," Cochran says. "In fact, I believe I've already relieved Agent Simmons of duty. She shouldn't even be here."

I pull a vacuum-sealed packet of clothes out from under my blazer and toss it on the table in front of Director North.

"What is this?" he asks.

"Those are the clothes they gave me when they kidnapped me," I say. "Their plan was to stage the scene, so it looked like Detective Rodriguez and I were killed by the man we suspected was responsible for Peters' death. In fact, it was all a setup, in order to make my death look believable and acceptable in the eyes of the Bureau. There never was a cult, it was all a ploy by Hunter's Organization. Those clothes have the fingerprints of Maurice Rossovich, one of the men killed in the wreck. But they also are covered in prints by another man named Vince Webb, who is prepared to testify against Mr. Hunter in exchange for leniency."

Cochran's face falls.

"In addition," Zara says. "Another man is at VHC in stable condition after coming to try and assassinate Emily a second time. We found this in his jacket pocket." She pulls out a syringe full of amber liquid. "When the Medical Examiner tests it, they will no doubt find it is succinylcholine, the same drug Gerald Wright and Matt Hunter were given to make it look like they had natural heart attacks."

"David," Cochran says. "Let me sort this out with my people. I'm sure there is a reasonable explanation for all of this."

"There is," Janice says. "I've spoken with SAC Wallace. He told me explicitly that you were the one who insisted that Emily take the Peters case. In fact he found it odd, because he was ready to give Emily a new assignment away from D.C. Coincidentally, or not, Jaeden Peters was killed the day after you discovered Emily's transfer was pending. Wallace also told me that you unequivocally to him not to hinder Emily's investigation in any way, even when she accidentally booked a private jet for transportation. Something that should have at least come with a formal reprimand." She gives me a wink. "At least, it would have when I was her boss."

I glare at Cochran. "You knew that if you didn't take care of me before I was transferred, you'd have a much more difficult time of it. You needed to find a way to make it look like I'd died in the line of duty, so the Organization could continue unhindered. That was the one thing Wallace was right about, wasn't it? You were afraid if you continued your operations with me around, I'd get wind of it and expose you. So you set this elaborate trap and killed innocent people so no one would question it when I was found dead."

I hear the shuffling of feet behind us, and four agents appear, though Director North makes a motion with one hand for them to stand down, much in the same way Cochran—or Hunter did when we last saw each other.

"This is all very serious," North says, turning to Cochran. "You need to explain yourself, right now."

Cochran's eyes find mine, but I can't decipher what's going on behind them. Finally, he breaks into a smile. "I should be upset, but I can't be. You have exceeded all my expectations of you, Emily. Well done."

"Then you admit to the charges," I say.

He stands, buttoning his suit. "In those matters, I think it's best if you speak with my lawyer." North grimaces, then looks at the agents that just came in. "Take him into custody. We'll sort this out downstairs."

Two of the men walk around to the couch and take Cochran by the arms. He gives me one more smile before leaving. "You were a worthy opponent. I can see what my son saw in you."

Using all my strength, I push myself up and stand to face him, not allowing him the pleasure of seeing me squirm. I can't wait to get him into an interrogation room. "You're going to pay for every person you ever wronged. I'll see to it personally."

Director North motions for the other two agents to wait outside then walks over to his desk and presses a button on his phone.

"Arlene. Clear my afternoon."

"Yes, sir," she replies.

"And call the Medical Examiner. We have some evidence here that needs examining."

North takes a seat behind his desk, motioning for us to join him. Zara helps me back down into the chair and wheels me over.

"God, what a mess," North says. "Seeing as Cochran, or whatever his name, was the one giving me the reports on your division, I'm going to need you to start all over, from the beginning. And don't leave anything out."

I look at my three compatriots. "That may take a while, sir."

He nods. "Take all the time you need, Agent Slate. I'm not going anywhere."

Chapter Thirty-Three

STEAM FROM THE WARM MUG WAFTS UP AND I INHALE THE scent through my nose. It's creamy and savory, just how I like my soup. I'm bundled up in a blanket on my couch with Timber at my feet, snoring away while I watch the leaves outside my large picture window fall. It's overcast today, perfect fall weather and for the first time in what feels like nine months, I feel like I can relax.

"Here you go," Liam says, setting a grilled cheese sandwich down on the table beside me while he takes a seat on the chair next to the couch, his own mug in his hand. Timber's eyes immediately pop open and he stares at the grilled cheese, drool beginning to escape his lips.

I laugh, though it still hurts a little. "Sorry, bud, not for you," I say, taking the plate into my lap. Fortunately, my injuries are healing well.

"How are you feeling?" Liam asks.

"Better now that Cochran has been officially charged," I say. I was in the courtroom today when the Federal Government brought charges against him in front of the judge, though it was a closed session. Before it began, Janice required me, Zara and Liam to be part of the team standing behind her on the steps to the courthouse as she addressed the charges and the future of the FBI. The amount of blowback the Bureau is going to have to deal with on this will be immense, ten times what we went through with DuBois. The good news is Janice was reinstated and even given a promotion, becoming the new Deputy Director of our division. After the news conference she pulled me aside and insinuated she could transfer Wallace if I wanted her to, but I didn't think that was fair, seeing as he was only doing his job. Though he's backed off ever since she became *his* boss.

All of us sat in the courtroom today as the official list of crimes were read. Cochran—as he's being charged, given that is his legal name—just stood there like a statue. Given everything that's happened—the kidnapping, the wreck, and everything at the building where I was being held, there's been a lot to sort through. Once IA was done debriefing us, Director North set our entire division on it, building a timeline of everything that happened, given the evidence and witnesses we now have.

"I'm just glad this is all finally coming to an end," Liam says, taking a sip from his mug. "You weren't kidding when you said this was an intense job."

I try not to laugh again. Poor Liam has really been through the wringer. He's seen more in his first four months on the job than half of what most agents see in their entire careers. "You've been a pretty good sport about it. I know plenty of people who would have gone running for the hills by now."

He grins, then gets up and comes over, planting a kiss right on my lips. "I'm not the kind of guy who gives up."

"Yeah. I kinda figured that," I reply. I sit up a little and he takes a seat beside me, so I can lean back against him. Now all three of us are on the same couch and Timber is practically shaking, hoping I'll share my sandwich with him.

"You sure you're feeling up to game night?" he asks. "Zara won't mind if we cancel."

I shake my head as I chew a bite from my sandwich. "No way. Plus I want to meet this new squeeze of hers. It'll be nice to watch her embarrass someone else for once."

"Did you decide about tomorrow?" he asks.

"I did," I say. "I'm going. I owe Rodriguez's kids that much, at least." After everything that happened, we determined that the man who came to kill me in the hospital was the one who ambushed us in Rosewater's farmhouse, and killed him as well. We also now know he was the one to kill Jaeden Peters too and I suspect he also murdered my sister-in-law. His name is Augustus Krause, and like Camille, he's a hired assassin who is wanted for questioning in three countries. We've had to partner with the CIA to make sure everyone gets their slice of him, but thanks to Zara's expert marksmanship, none of the bullets that hit him were fatal. He'll take the stand during Cochran's trial, as will Vince Webb, who we managed to nab shortly after making the case to Director North.

But none of that will bring Detective Rodriguez back. And I feel partially responsible. Even though we had no reason to expect an ambush like that, I should have been more cautious when going to confront Rosewater. Despite the fact my read on him had been right—he'd been working as a for-hire mechanic, which was why his prints were on Jaeden Peters' car. He'd never shown any killer-like tendencies, and had probably just been as surprised to find Krause in his home as we were.

As for Jaeden Peters, I delivered our findings to his parents myself. It was heartbreaking to tell them he was little more than a pawn in a much bigger conspiracy, but I was at least able to assuage their fears that their son had done something to "deserve" what happened to him. He didn't, not that anyone ever deserves that. But Jaeden was just an unlucky kid, who happened to be the perfect target.

"Given any more thought to Janice's offer?" Liam asks.

I'm so lost in thought it takes me a minute to respond. "About the transfer? Not really. Where would we go?"

He shrugs. "I dunno. Anywhere. I wouldn't mind the southern coast. Believe it or not, I actually like the warm weather."

"Ugh, not me," I say. "Give me more days like this." After everything settled down and Janice took up her new role as Deputy Director, she offered Zara, Liam, and me a transfer to any department in the country if we wanted. She said we'd more than deserved it. I know she was thinking that maybe I wouldn't want to be here any longer, after what happened with Matt and now his father. I'm still torn about that. On the one hand, Matt was involved in this terrible organization that hurt and killed people, and he lied to me about it. And on the other hand, he was ready to give them all up, to destroy his legacy, because of me. And he died because of it.

It's a complex situation, and I'm not sure I'll ever completely be okay with it. But for now, I can at least rest easy knowing the person behind his death will face justice, and we've dealt a crucial blow to the Organization.

Thankfully, after a raid of Cochran's office, the FBI managed to uncover documents identifying the other members of the Organization, who were promptly arrested and charged. Except for those that took their own lives, of course, saving us the trouble. It's been a massive operation, but thankfully it seems like we may have finally driven the death nell into this group once and for all.

I know I'll be glad to be done with them.

The doorbell rings and Liam gets up, setting his mug of soup on the table in front of us. "She can't be three hours early," he mutters.

I lean back, thinking how wrong he can be. Zara is the

most unpredictable person I know. And I'm lucky to have her in my life. I'm lucky to have them both. I don't want to become like Cochran, so determined and single-minded about my job or my beliefs, that I hurt those around me. And the fact that I work myself to the bone doesn't automatically make me worthy of being loved. I need to start taking a step back, start living life again, and stop ignoring the people I love. I think that was part of my mistake with Matt. I was too focused on my work to see what was really going on.

But from here on out it will be different.

"Emily Slate?" I hear a voice say from the door. I frown and set what's left of my grilled cheese on the table and get up, noticing the soreness and aches radiating through my body. Timber sees his chance and snatches the sandwich from the plate, finishing it in one bite.

There goes that, I guess. I give him a pat on the head anyway and head to the front door where Liam is standing, holding the door open for a man in a delivery person's uniform.

"Are you Emily Slate?" he asks.

"I am," I say. "What's wrong?"

"Sign for this, please." He holds out an old envelope that is tied with a string on one side. I haven't seen one of those in years. He hands me a clipboard and I sign for the package. "Have a good day," he says and heads off.

I look at the brown envelope, flipping it over and back again. All that's written on it is my name and address. But the script is familiar.

"Who is it from?" Liam asks, closing the door.

"I have no idea." I unwrap the string and tear the top of the envelope. Inside is a single letter, wrapped carefully.

I remove the letter and begin reading. As I do, I can't seem to stop my hand from trembling. Liam must see something because he tries to catch my eye. "Em, what is it? You've gone white. What's wrong?"

I finish reading and start over again, not believing my eyes. "It's…from my mother."

"But I thought your mother was dead," he says.

"She is," I reply. "She died when I was twelve."

"Then I don't understand," he says. "What does it say?"

I hesitate, my heart hammering in my chest. "It says: You look so pretty on TV. See you soon."

The End?

To Be Continued…

Want to read more about Emily?

The Past Never Stays Buried.

Fresh off exposing the biggest security breach in the history of the FBI, Special Agent Emily Slate has come to terms with her husband's death. But before she can enjoy some peace of mind for once, a mysterious letter arrives in her dead mother's handwriting. Unwilling to entertain it as anything but a bad joke, she dismisses it in favor of a new case.

But no sooner have Emily and Zara arrived in a quaint skiing town in New Hampshire before they realize they're dealing with a twisted mind. A killer takes a new victim every Saturday night, staging them in a gruesome manner only for the bodies to be found days later. Each victim is from a different nearby town and the killer shows no hint of who could be next.

Emily and Zara will have to face a near-insurmountable number of obstacles if they want to get to the truth behind these murders. And when they discover the truth, Emily will find herself at a crossroads she's never faced before.

Will she stop the killer at any cost, or allow them to finish what they started, even though it's against everything she's sworn to uphold?

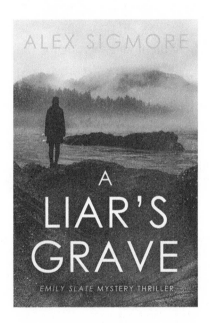

To get your copy of A LIAR'S GRAVE, CLICK HERE or scan the code below!

FREE book offer!
Where did it all go wrong for Emily?

I hope you enjoyed *The Secret Seven*. If you'd like to learn more about Emily's backstory and what happened in the days following her husband's unfortunate death, including what almost got her kicked out of the FBI, then you're in luck! *Her Last Shot* introduces Emily and tells the story of the case that almost ended her career. Interested? CLICK HERE to get your free copy now!

Not Available Anywhere Else!

You'll also be the first to know when each book in the Emily Slate series is available!

Download for FREE HERE or scan the code below!

The Emily Slate FBI Mystery Series

Free Prequel - Her Last Shot (Emily Slate Bonus Story)

His Perfect Crime - (Emily Slate Series Book One)

The Collection Girls - (Emily Slate Series Book Two)

Smoke and Ashes - (Emily Slate Series Book Three)

Her Final Words - (Emily Slate Series Book Four)

Can't Miss Her - (Emily Slate Series Book Five)

The Lost Daughter - (Emily Slate Series Book Six)

The Secret Seven - (Emily Slate Series Book Seven)

A Liar's Grave - (Emily Slate Series Book Eight)

The Girl in the Wall - (Emily Slate Series Book Nine)

His Final Act - (Emily Slate Series Book Ten)

The Vanishing Eyes - (Emily Slate Series Book Eleven)

Coming Soon!

Edge of the Woods - (Emily Slate Series Book Twelve)

The Missing Bones - (Emily Slate Series Book Thirteen)

A Note from Alex

Hi there! You've officially reached the end of season 1 in the Emily Slate Mystery Thriller series! I hope you've enjoyed this story arc as much as I enjoyed writing it!

But don't worry, there are plenty more books to come. Book eight is titled *A Liar's Grave* and begins a brand new chapter of Emily's life. While Matt's death will always be a significant event, Emily has decided it won't define her life forever. As you've already read, she's already facing a new mystery, one that ties into her very own past. I hope you'll stick around and continue reading as I love writing these books and exploring this world.

As I've always said, you are the reason I write!

Because I am still relatively new, all I ask that you please take the time to leave a review or recommend this series to a fellow book lover. This will ensure I'll be able to write many more books in the *Emily Slate Series* in the future.

Thank you for being a loyal reader,

Alex

Made in the USA
Las Vegas, NV
10 August 2024

93612122R00152